"Don't feel like you have to waste your time on my account, Win," she said then, her tone coming across as easy, as though she truly didn't care.

And maybe she didn't. He was just part of her new job.

"I'm going to look into it because I can't find another explanation for those initials. And, as you say, every single one fits."

"They do? I was only remembering a few of them offhand, but..."

Because she was right... While there was most likely a perfectly legitimate reason for those accounts and deposits—since they were just sitting out there, unclaimed—there were likely more of them. And finding them was his job.

"I'm on it," he told her, already calling up Connolly's number in his contacts. "Thank you, Sarah. This could be just what we needed, and even if it's not...this is great work."

He was impressed all over again—which probably wasn't good on a personal level. He'd deal with that later.

"Good. I'm glad I could help."

Telling her to be safe—wanting but refraining from asking her to text him when she was across the desert—he hung up, filled with anticipation.

For the work ahead only, he told himself.

But he didn't believe it.

Dear Reader,

My heart has never left this book. It started with questions. What would you do for the baby sister you raised from birth and lost two years later? If you heard she might be in trouble? We think we know ourselves, that we know how we'd react in a situation. But when faced with a young, vulnerable loved one in trouble, would you stretch the law to ensure she was safe? Even if it meant losing the love of your life?

And what if you hired a new employee, trusted her with your most high-security files, fell in love with her and found out that she'd been living a lie to get company information?

I started the book thinking I had the answers. I didn't. It got messy. And real. And larger-than-life, too. I can't wait for you to live this one. And I hope that Sarah and Winchester stay with you afterward, as they have with me.

Tara Taylor Quinn

A Family-First Christmas

———

TARA TAYLOR QUINN

HARLEQUIN
SPECIAL
EDITION

HARLEQUIN®
SPECIAL EDITION™

Recycling programs for this product may not exist in your area.

ISBN-13: 978-1-335-59442-6

A Family-First Christmas

For questions and comments about the quality of this book, please contact us at CustomerService@Harlequin.com.

Harlequin Enterprises ULC
22 Adelaide St. West, 41st Floor
Toronto, Ontario M5H 4E3, Canada
www.Harlequin.com

Printed in U.S.A.

A *USA TODAY* bestselling author of over 110 novels in twenty languages, **Tara Taylor Quinn** has sold more than seven million copies. Known for her intense emotional fiction, Ms. Quinn's novels have received critical acclaim in the UK and most recently from Harvard. She is the recipient of the Readers' Choice Award and has appeared often on local and national TV, including *CBS Sunday Morning*.

For TTQ offers, news and contests, visit www.tarataylorquinn.com!

For my little Morgie. Mima will see you someday.
She loves you very very much.

Chapter One

She was going to do this.

Wasn't she?

Stopped at the light, Sarah Williams folded her hands, tapping her thumbs together.

Her turn was just ahead. A block away on the right. She could see the clean asphalt drive of the upscale fifteen-floor office building that housed the suite of Sierra's Web offices. The tall, perfectly manicured palm trees out front.

Was she really going to do this?

It wasn't illegal. She wouldn't tell any lies. It wasn't against the law to keep non-work-related personal details private.

She qualified for the position. Wasn't planning to steal anything. Or even act upon anything she might inadvertently find out—as long as sweet Kylie was okay.

The baby sister she hadn't seen in eight years, the

baby she'd raised, for all intents and purposes, alone for the first two years of Kylie's life, the baby she'd named, could be in need. Critically in need, for all she knew.

Kylie's adoption case was being revisited for some reason.

If Sarah could believe her mother.

Could she afford not to?

Lily Williams did have a history of telling falsehoods. But generally, they were only to cover up her falling back into addiction. Or to hide a lover.

Either way, what if her mother was right? What if Kylie's case really was being looked at again? Did that mean her baby sister's family life had imploded? Had she been abused? Neglected? Had her adoptive parents been killed in a crash, leaving the ten-year-old sweetheart without a family to call her own?

They were all things Lily had suggested the week before when she'd called Sarah in panicked tears, telling her what she'd heard. *I can't tell you how I know, Sarah. Trust me, you don't want to know how I heard, but Kylie's adoption case is being looked at...*

A closed adoption, to which they had absolutely zero access.

Sierra's Web, the firm of experts who'd assisted the county with the psychological evaluations of potential adopters eight years before, listed an office manager position at the same time of her mother's call. It had been timing she couldn't ignore. Yeah, as a nurse she'd been looking at their open positions for something in the medical field, but...

Being the first of November, it was a little early for a Christmas gift, but when the light turned green, Sarah pushed the gas, signaled her turn and slid easily onto the lot.

Yes, she was really doing this.

"So how did you hear about Sierra's Web?" Winchester Holmes, financial expert, partner in the firm—and the man in charge of hiring at the moment—already knew he was going to offer the woman the job. Her résumé had been, hands down, the best they'd received. All seven partners had taken the time to vet the applications from their various locations across the United States. All had listed her as their top applicant.

And she was available to start immediately.

"I've been checking the job openings boards at the university since my first semester," she said, naming the major institution less than half an hour away. "Sierra's Web has been on there several times, mostly looking for experienced scholars, experts in their fields. Since most of the jobs were not entry-level positions, the firm caught my attention—not because I hoped to get a job here, as I'm definitely entry-level—but because the positions always seemed to fill quickly. So, when I saw an opening for something I was actually qualified to do, I applied." She held his gaze as she answered him forthrightly.

"Universities are a great place to find experts," he told her. "Professors, researchers…" He shrugged, stopped himself from telling her the real story behind Sierra's Web. Didn't mention the college professor who'd helped seven grieving students solve the murder of their friend.

What the heck? He didn't get drawn into personal revelations. To the contrary, his relationships, both romantic and otherwise, faltered due to his lack of sharing.

Except with the other six partners.

And Lindsay—the fifty-five-year-old woman who'd been running their office since the firm's inception.

The seven of them already knew his shortcoming, thus didn't suffer from his lapse...

He noted her bachelor's degree. "What did you study?" he asked, to get himself back on track. The office manager's position only required high school education or equivalent.

"Science, mostly," she said. "And business." Then, with a flick of her long dark hair back over her shoulder, added, "But I worked my way through high school and college in a variety of offices, starting with basic filing and moving up from there. I was employed at a real estate firm first. Then insurance. I spent a couple of summers as a girl Friday at a law firm," naming one of the biggest firms in the Phoenix valley. "And my most recent position was at a medical clinic."

Impressive. And all things he'd already gleaned from her résumé.

"Your variety of experience is a definite plus to us here since Sierra's Web partners all have different fields of expertise."

She nodded, sitting upright, back completely straight in the white blouse she'd paired with navy pants and heeled sandals. Her hands, folded in her lap, were still but for the thumbs tapping against each other.

He noted those thumbs.

Getting the job mattered to her.

Which mattered to the firm.

"You met Lindsay on your way in," he said, holding her gaze directly as she nodded. "She'll still be the firm's contact with our clients and experts. She handles all phone calls."

Another nod, without hesitation or even a blink.

"And…it's quite possible that she'll be somewhat lacking in enthusiasm as you delve into the filing system and other things that have gotten away from us."

She shrugged one shoulder. A slim shoulder. Yet one that gave him the impression of being able to carry much weight. "My feelings don't hurt easily," she said.

"And I need to make it clear, you won't be her boss. The position is office manager, which means we need you to manage the office, literally. The organization, the paperwork, scheduling, phone system, mail…the way *things* are handled, not the people."

Another nod.

"She might disagree with the way you want to do things," he continued, outlining the lay of the land as clearly as he could, as he'd assured his partners he would. Lindsay's delicate positioning was why they'd put off hiring anyone to take over the running of the office for so long.

"We need you to be able to listen, to follow her edicts when they ring true, treat her respectfully, while still doing what you think is best and most efficient in terms of getting us organized."

Kelly, expert psychiatrist partner at Sierra's Web, had given him the verbiage on the phone a few nights before. He'd memorized it verbatim. But had never used it in any of the other interviews. He'd already determined the candidates to be no hires before he'd reached that point.

He waited for comment. Didn't get any.

"You have nothing to say to any of this?" he asked. He'd been prepared for conversation about what could be deemed a somewhat confusing situation leading to a potentially uncomfortable work environment.

The partners had already decided that if they couldn't find anyone who could work affably with Lindsay, they'd come up with some other solution. Like, maybe, the six of them pitching in and getting things in order and then…they didn't know what. Nor did they know who'd help all the hundreds of people they served between them each year if they weren't out doing what they did best.

Still, before they were a firm, the partners were family. And Lindsay was part of it. That's just how it was.

"I don't know what you want me to say," Sarah Williams replied.

"I want you to say what you think," he gave her back. "Not what you think I want you to say."

"I think that I want this job," she told him, her expression earnest. Serious. "If you think Lindsay will be a problem for me, then I can assure you she won't be."

"Have you ever been in a situation when you were both parent and child to the same person?" The words came out all wrong. The partners had discussed feeling that way with Lindsay. The conversation shouldn't have been shared with anyone but the seven of them.

"Every day of my life."

Eyes wide, he sat back. Absolutely hadn't expected that response. Uttered with a truth that couldn't be denied. He wanted to know more. Badly wanted to know more. Figured it wasn't within professional boundaries to ask.

He gave her time to elaborate instead, to explain herself—time that stretched into a long silence. And while a part of him was disappointed not to gain her confidence, at least pertaining to her comment, that same silence told him, clearly, that Sarah Williams was the right hire for Sierra's Web.

She kept her own counsel. Even when she was clearly eager to get something from someone. In this case, a job from him.

"If you ever want advice on how to handle a situation with Lindsay, you can feel free to speak with me or any of the partners. We're all aware of the delicate position we're putting you in, the lack of clear boundaries in terms of powers. We want you to understand that Lindsay has earned her position here. She's like family to us. But that doesn't mean you can't come to us. As it is with family members, we understand that everyone has their issues, and we'll run any interference you need us to run. At the same time, because it feels like I've misled you here in my attempt to get everything out in the open, I also want to make it clear. Lindsay's a sweetheart—she doesn't have a mean bone in her body. She's kind even when she's bothered."

He was babbling like an idiot. Saying far too much. But added, "She's just protective. And might not always be open to sharing...current case files and things...if she thinks you don't need to see them..." *Stop talking. Just stop talking.*

"Does this mean I have the job?"

He almost stared. Blinked just in time, and ruffled the sheets of paper in front of him. Piling them all together and stacking them neatly.

They weren't meant to go together.

That was it? His whole ridiculous soliloquy about over-the-top potential job challenges, and she still wanted to work for them? "It does." He'd run a basic new hire background check, but he didn't have to wait for it.

He might be uncharacteristically off his mark, but he wasn't stupid.

And it would be a very, very stupid move to let this godsend get away.

Sarah liked Winchester Holmes. The man was a little stuffy with his tie and jacket in a thriving metropolis where customs were more laid-back. And the black hair was cropped beyond short.

But she wasn't there to ogle him. She was going to work for him.

She had the job!

As interviewers went, Winchester exceeded expectations. She hadn't even dared hope the meeting would go so well. She filled out paperwork, including a confidentiality clause that she would not break. Offered to head out for coffee and a bagel while he awaited background information. When he called to let her know everything had checked out, she presented herself for her first partial day of work.

Just like that. There she was. Within reach of Kylie for the first time in eight long years.

The knowledge was a breath of air so full and swift that she was light-headed. And it was an excruciating stab in her heart as well. She'd missed so much.

Would be missing it all still, if it turned out that Kylie was in a happy, healthy home and doing just fine.

And she hoped for that. With every fiber of her being she prayed her little baby sister was healthy, happy, well loved.

Her own heartache was nothing if Kylie was well.

No one knew that Sarah had been planning to petition her mother for custody of the little girl the second Sarah had turned eighteen. No one knew, not even Lily, that she'd applied for a job at Sierra's Web, either. And her mother wasn't going to know. Lily's fragile emotions could only handle so much at a time, and Sarah wasn't risking another fall off her mother's rickety wagon.

She also wasn't going to miss the opportunity to get one step closer to finding out what had happened to Kylie, where she'd been taken, by whom. But riffling through files looking for her sister's name couldn't be the first thing she did in her new position.

She wasn't going to lose her sense of self-respect, or compromise her integrity, by not doing the job she'd been hired to do. She was going to work for Sierra's Web to the best of her ability.

And she was going to start with Lindsay Conch.

To that end, as soon as Winchester introduced the two of them, Sarah asked the older woman, "Do you have the time to show me around and let me know what you think I should focus on first?" The lines of concern on the woman's face turned into a smile—one that maybe didn't reach her eyes, but it was there. She showed Sarah the suite of offices, the filing room and the small kitchen with a farmhouse-looking kitchen table and eight chairs, suggesting that organizing the cupboards and figuring out a way to get in groceries regularly might be the best first use of Sarah's time.

She got right on it. Finished that task and assessed the phone system. She researched more up-to-date models, found one at a decent price that would add cloud options to their landline, voice to text, touch screen, cell phone forwarding and Wi-Fi. She wrote a report for Winchester, gained immediate approval for purchase and placed the order.

Then she wrote another report, explaining in detail all of the ways the new system was going to make Lindsay's day easier, more enjoyable and more efficient, and sent that as well. She stayed in the vacant offices after that, making up lists of potential improvements to the furniture—replacing ten-year-old secondhand desks and chairs with more ergonomic options—until she heard the older woman wish Winchester and Hudson, the only other partner in the office that day, good-night.

Sarah had met Hudson briefly, as Lindsay showed her the offices. The married IT expert lived locally and was in the middle of a case he was working with the FBI. He'd had his door shut most of the day. Still had his door shut.

And so, figuring she'd done a fair day's work, and with the office quiet, Sarah allowed herself to make her way to what Lindsay called the filing room. A little bigger than a cleaning closet, the space could hardly be called a room. And the lack of square footage could explain the various filing cabinets she'd seen in partner offices and in the large reception area out front as well.

Heart pounding, she pulled open a drawer marked *W*. She didn't have any idea of Lindsay's filing system. But she figured, with Kylie's case being eight years old, and the firm just a little over ten, chances were good such an old file would have made it to the filing room.

Was it going to be that simple? One day on the job and she'd have…something? What, exactly, she wasn't yet sure. Names of possible adopters who'd been interviewed at the very least. If she was extremely lucky, a note as to what interviewee had been targeted for final recommendation. Or even a couple of them who had been.

She could take it from there. Get on the internet. Do searches.

Something.

Which was better than the nothing she'd had for the past eight years.

Her fingers trembled as she riffled past old, faded and fraying folder edges on her way to the *Wi*'s. *W-i-l*... Wilbur, Wilhardson, Wilmington, Wilson, Wilt...wait.

Where was *W-i-l-l*? For Williams?

Nowhere. It was nowhere. Not in that or any of the other file drawers she went through in that room. She looked under *K* for Kylie, too, and still found nothing...

"I appreciate your willingness to give this job your all, but these files have waited around for years to get any attention. They certainly don't need you to work late on their behalf..."

She heard the words, oddly already recognized the cadence in the voice, and still jumped as Winchester's white shirt and tie took up her view of the doorway.

"I'm sorry," he said. "I didn't mean to startle you..."

Had he seen what she was doing? Seen what, the word *Kylie* in her brain? Even if he'd been standing there watching her the entire time she'd been in the room, it would only appear as though she was doing the job he'd hired her to do. Familiarizing herself with the filing system on her way to a complete overhaul.

And in her search, she had kind of done that. She had discovered that nothing, as it currently stood and was labeled, made logical sense. Things were alphabetized, some by first name, some by last, some by company. None by type of case or expert who'd handled it.

Which is what she told him. In a voice that she hoped sounded like a newly employed office manager should sound.

"Lindsay, of course, would know far more than I do," he told her as she returned a couple of files she'd pulled from an overstuffed drawer just so she could get a look at others. "But it's been a work in progress from the beginning, with new systems outgrowing old, but older systems not being updated. We started out with two tall filing cabinets in this room. Those two." He pointed to a couple of old beige four-drawer units. "Each of the partners had a drawer and there was one left for Lindsay. From there, we expanded as we needed, making use of whatever space was there. Until it was determined that the partners should each have their own files in their own offices, for easy access. From there, each partner has his or her own system. To complicate matters further, some of us managed to get our old files out of here. Some didn't get around to it…"

She smiled, a day's worth of tension sliding off her shoulders for a second. She just couldn't help it. The self-deprecating smile, and more, the affection for his partners that came through loud and clear in the dismal filing tale, just felt…nice.

"You need me," she said aloud, surprised to hear herself. And yet…she was gratified to know that while she was using Sierra's Web for her own peace of mind, she also had something valuable to give back. Not because of her newly earned nursing degree, but from the years of office experience she'd gained while working on that degree.

And give back she would. Whether she found Kylie's file within the first few days of her employment or not.

The nursing job she'd been dreaming about for years was going to have to wait.

She wasn't leaving Sierra's Web until she had their office firmly in order.

Until Winchester Holmes had received what he'd paid for.

It was just the right thing to do.

Chapter Two

Win stayed in town, working long hours at Sierra's Web corporate headquarters, during that first week after Sarah's hiring. Hudson was there for the first couple of days, too, handling a few cases that didn't require an in-person visit. But when Hud was called to Colorado for a job that involved an internal case of corporate hacking, Winchester was stuck. While Lindsay was often the only person in the office, with all the partners being called to other cities and states across the country, they'd determined that for the first week of Lindsay having to share her space, at least one of the partners should be present.

Win had been unanimously elected as the one to stay during the initial phase of the new hire planning. He'd just relocated to Phoenix, had closed on a home and was in the process of furnishing it and unpacking boxes, some of which had been in storage for years.

Everyone had also determined that he'd be the one to host their annual Sierra's Web Thanksgiving dinner—a feast that might or might not take place on the day itself depending on everyone's schedules. The dinner would happen. They'd been joking about him putting it on. He could do it. He was a decent cook. He had service for twelve—Hud could bring his wife and daughter, who were local. Mariah and her husband and newly adopted daughter could join them as well if Harper and Michael wanted to fly in from Arkansas, and he'd still have a place for Lindsay.

Newly married Hud and Amanda could host, too, for that matter. In the past, the partners had always just had the meal catered. They sat around their conference table at work and ate off paper plates. They'd done this since their first year in business together, back when their office had been one big room rented in an old strip mall in a Phoenix suburb. Funny, they'd moved up in terms of office space, but had never bothered to replace the secondhand desks they'd all started with. None of them were generally in the office long enough to notice. Or particularly care. It wasn't like they ever hosted clients or had to woo anyone for business. They'd had more requests than they could handle almost from the first.

But he had to admit, his new L-shaped workstation, complete with wireless computer keyboard, mounted screen and table for spreading out financials was…nice. As was the chair that fit him as comfortably as his recliner at home. The others had moving in to do, but they'd all seen video of their offices with the new furniture in place and were eager to get to Phoenix and unpack the things that Lindsay had insisted on personally

packing—carefully labeling each drawer and space—
so that all the old furniture could be removed at once.

That first week Win saw Sarah every day. Met with
her in one fashion or another as she moved quickly to get
the offices into shape. The real challenge would come
once the working space and facilities were up to par. He
got that. But he couldn't help but be impressed by the
woman's work ethic. Her abilities and attention to detail
were wonderful, recommending that the partners pay
for comfort, and work ease, but not for more than they
needed. And she was wonderful with Lindsay, finding
a way to stay out of the older woman's very busy way,
to not impinge on or hamper Lindsay's responsibilities.
She even enlisted Lindsay's help when it came to learning the partners' habits and preferences.

He also couldn't help noticing that he seemed to be
smiling more as he drove to work thinking about their
new office manager.

And that wasn't okay. The last thing he needed in
his life at the moment was another woman to raise his
protective instincts, which was what always happened
when he started to fall for someone. Or cared for one
in any way, for that matter. It was like he had some hidden superhero gene that, while denying him the hunk
of a body or impressive physical strength, brought out
a drive to protect in him that didn't bode well for relationships.

Or maybe it was his own history, his failure to protect
the women he cared about, that was really driving him.

The idea was more credible than the whole superhero thing. And bottom line was that he had no desire, whatsoever, to be in any way attracted to the new
godsend bringing comfort, order and efficiency—as

well as stocked cupboards—to the Sierra's Web home office. Which was why, on Thursday of the first full week of Sarah's employment, Winchester eagerly accepted an out-of-state job request for a financial expert that could have been handled by any of the freelance experts on his team.

Running away didn't help his newfound predicament, though. Sarah called him on his first night in Washington State, Friday night, reaching him just as he got back to his hotel room laden down with a satchel full of old paper statements and a flash drive filled with newer but still old statements, with a room service order already on the way up.

The new phone system had been installed, days earlier than expected due to a cancellation, and she wanted to let him know to alert his partners that their new features, and access codes, were live.

He had no reason to keep her on the call. A thank-you and good-night would have been most appropriate. Instead, he asked how her day had gone. She'd given him a brief rundown of ideas she had for tackling the filing system, starting with his office as he was the partner soonest to return. From there he'd told her about a couple of open cases he was working and files that shouldn't be touched. Which had somehow led to the possible tax fraud case in Washington for which he'd been hired by the defendant to do an expert audit. The tax filings were the least of his problems. They were already in perfect order on his laptop. But the statements…

"Send me the electronic ones and I'll organize them for you by month, year and type of expense," his new office manager said. Making a perfectly reasonable offer.

His gratitude wasn't so much relative to the offer. It was over-the-top.

"I'm sure you have better things to do with your weekend than pore over pages of numbers and dates," he told her in lieu of the profound thanks he'd wanted to utter at her helpfulness. He could use the help. But it wasn't the offer itself that had him going.

It was that it had come from Sarah. That she, in particular, had offered to help him.

He had to get himself under control or one of them would have to leave Sierra's Web. And since he was a partner...

He couldn't be responsible for losing someone who was turning out to be a powerful asset to the firm.

"I wouldn't have said it if I didn't want to do it," she told him pragmatically—much the way she'd let him know that his Lindsay warnings hadn't bothered her during their interview the Tuesday of the previous week.

He wanted to ask why she wasn't going on a date, or whether she had family and friends who would mind that she was working overtime, and outside the scope of her original duties, after only ten days on the job— mostly because he wanted to know if she had a significant other in her life. But he accepted her help, made arrangements to download the files to her and hung up without any further conversation.

He might not be able to help his overwhelming reaction to their new office manager, but he could damn well make certain that nothing came of it.

That she never ever knew he found her manner disturbingly attractive. That he was drawn to her presence as he hadn't been since Sierra...

He would not fail another woman.

Period.

And if that meant he kept to his own counsel, then so be it.

His own pleasure wasn't worth the cost of possible failure.

Sarah did have other things to do with her weekend than pore over pages of numbers and dates. She had a life.

There just wasn't anything she'd rather do that second weekend in November but give her all to Sierra's Web—a payback for what she was still determined the firm would give her.

Some backdoor way in to find Kylie and know she was okay.

A week and a half of busting her butt and scouring files every chance she got had given her nothing yet, but she'd barely skimmed the surface of the information being stored so haphazardly all over the firm. Kylie's case was eight years old, had been through many filing renditions. There was no telling where it might be. Lindsay had filed by expert for a while, until the firm had acquired so many freelance experts. Then she'd switched to filing by type of case—court or other governmental agency, or private party—and then most recently, by date, changing as the firm had grown and ease of access had grown less…easy.

The older woman was giving Sarah access to all things firm related, other than the experts' desk drawers, but she was watching Sarah like a hawk as well, making it impossible for Sarah to dive into any kind of thorough search for her little sister's file. She'd hoped, with Winchester gone, and Hudson still away, she'd have time in the office to herself, but that hadn't happened.

But she knew that, since the time she was planning to spend looking for Kylie's file would be during working hours, she owed Winchester and the others payback time. And so, instead of heading out when friends from nursing class invited her to a club for some downtime, she sat at home in her little house in Tempe—the university suburb of the Phoenix valley that also bordered Scottsdale—making sense out of years' worth of purchases, payments and deposits. Eventually making a list so that she could get a clearer picture of the person whose accounts she was viewing. While the work was not the medicine she loved, she actually found it quite interesting. Studying a person's habits and lifestyle instead of their bodily functions—but basically looking for the same thing. Something that could be wrong. Or confirmation that all was right.

And on Saturday evening, she found something. A series of random withdrawals that seemed to go nowhere. Why would a man who never paid cash for anything, based on income deposits and credit, debit and check expenditures, suddenly be taking cash and using it nowhere?

The guy paid his bills on the same date every month. Ate at only three restaurants. Bought his groceries from the same retailer on the same day every week. Even at the same time. He golfed. Went to the movies every weekend and took a two-week vacation to various beaches during the summer. He wore nice, though not designer, clothes. Paid to have his house cleaned and his yard manicured.

When she couldn't stand the niggling question any

longer, she dialed Winchester. Listened to his phone ring. She didn't know why the guy Winchester was working for was being audited. She assumed it was by the IRS for taxes but didn't know that for sure. Her boss could have grave need of the information she'd uncovered.

And…she really wanted to please him. To live up to his expectations.

As she did with all her bosses. It probably just seemed more so with him because she felt guilty for having an ulterior motive.

Four rings and nothing…

That's why she'd been thinking of him so often. Wondering about his life. Smiling at things he'd said. Remembering the firm and yet tender grip of his hand when he'd shaken hers to seal the deal on her hiring.

Because of her guilt.

Five rings…

"Sarah?"

Was it wrong…that swirl of warmth that flooded her at his greeting? Of course he'd have her programmed into his phone. She worked for him.

"I'm sorry to bother you…"

"No, it's no bother. I'm just in my suite, working. What's up? Is everything okay?"

Everything? What did he care about her everything?

No one cared about her everything.

Mostly because she didn't give them opportunity to look too closely at it.

She liked it better that way.

"I found something odd I thought might be important," she blurted uncharacteristically. "In the material you sent for me to go over…"

Awkward! For no reason except that she was making it so.

Because of guilt?

Maybe she should just tell him about Kylie.

What? When had she ever told anyone about any of her problems? Or personal business?

And if she told him, she'd lose her chance to find out whether or not her little sister was in need. Because there was no way this man was going to risk his firm, or his partners' credibility, by knowingly turning over confidential information...

Another wave of guilt stabbed her at the thought.

So, should she quit, and abandon a ten-year-old girl? Her flesh and blood? Her sister, who'd become her own baby girl, her responsibility, an hour after she was born?

Thoughts flew so quickly she was confused for a second when Winchester said, "What did you find?"

What? She hadn't found anything yet...

Her gaze settled on the computer in front of her. Right. The job...

She told her boss about the withdrawals. All large amounts. The same amount. Spaced two weeks apart.

"He was being blackmailed..." Winchester's voice trailed off, as though his thoughts had taken him on a road she couldn't follow.

"I just thought you should know. I've made a spreadsheet, can send it to you..."

"He wasn't hiding money...his family, they all said he wouldn't have done that..."

"He's the most predictable person I've ever encountered," she said, because she didn't have much more to offer.

"Was," Winchester said, and then seemed to be off in his own world again.

Wait. The client was deceased? The man who she'd just spent twenty-four hours getting to know?

"He liked steak," she said inanely. "And bought a tux last March." As though those two facts meant the man couldn't die.

"For his daughter's wedding," Winchester acknowledged, and then said, "Daniel passed away six months ago and a business partner has accused him of hiding money in an offshore account. He managed to get far enough in his allegations to have an investigation opened, which included a subpoena for his tax records. Daniel's widow hired us to do an independent audit…"

Her heart rate picked up. "So…what I just found? This might help exonerate him?"

"It definitely puts an entirely different spin on the investigation," he told her. "Who deposits money and then withdraws it if they're attempting to hide it?"

"Sounds to me like he wanted to leave a trail of the blackmail…" Her mind raced along with her heart, and she told herself it was because she liked the work she was doing. "Maybe he was killed," she said, completely unlike herself as she bulldozed ahead with the fantastical thought. "Maybe there needs to be another kind of investigation going on…"

"He died of cancer."

Oh. Deflated, she sat back in the padded chair at her dining room table.

"But this…yes, please send me the spreadsheet, anything you've compiled… I'm going to put it together with the rest of what I've got and see if I can get this done in time to catch the evening flight home tomorrow."

Home. He'd be back in the office on Monday. No reason for that to make the coming week seem brighter.

"And, Sarah?"

"Yeah?"

"Thank you." His tone had softened. No way she'd just imagined that.

She couldn't help that her body filled with warmth as she told him goodbye.

Chapter Three

Sarah had herself better under control when she went to work on Monday. She'd spent Sunday with a couple of nursing class friends, walking the steep path up Camelback Mountain and listening to them talk about their new jobs. One had landed her dream job at Phoenix Children's Hospital, and the other was working in home health care.

They both assumed she was still at the clinic where she'd worked over the summer. They knew she'd had the job offer. And if Lily hadn't told her that Kylie's case was being revisited, that was probably where Sarah would be.

It wasn't her dream job. She wanted to do disaster work. Or something.

At the moment her only dream was finding her sister before it was too late to help her if she was, indeed, in need of help. There were systems in place to keep children safe. She knew that. Reminded herself of child services and school counselors, pediatricians and any number of other resources that watched out for endangered children every night as she lay alone in the dark awaiting sleep.

Lord knew, she'd had enough of the child protection professionals in her life as a teenager to know how invasive they could be when they thought something wrong was happening.

Of course, in her case, it had been happening. She'd just been trying to fix it on her own, would have fixed it, but they hadn't given her the chance.

And…she'd blown the opportunity. She'd known the second she'd lifted the four-can pack of vegetable stew that she'd changed herself. Not in a good way.

But the idea of having four days of guaranteed meals for her and Kylie had just been too tempting…

Yeah, she could have had access to any number of resources that would have given them food. But that would have taken them from Lily, too. Splitting them up.

Which ultimately was exactly what her one bout of shoplifting had done.

Water under the bridge. In tan pants and a lighter tan cropped blouse with long sleeves and matching sandals—Arizona winter attire—she went to work on Monday with a renewed sense of urgency to find what she could about Kylie and be on her way.

No point in liking Winchester Holmes—he'd be out of her life in a blink.

As soon as he found out she'd had an ulterior motive in coming to work for him, she'd be out of his, too.

Keeping her thoughts firmly in check, she strengthened her resolve with the knowledge that the Sierra's Web filing system was up on her full-time radar that week. She wouldn't let herself think about guilt as she started in on a far more thorough investigation of the hundreds of paper files in desperate need of organization.

Yes, she started with Kelly Chase's office because the psychiatrist expert had been the one hired by the county to give testimony on child custody cases when the firm had first opened. But she also began there because the woman wouldn't be in the office until the following week, when all the partners would come to town for their annual fall board meeting and Thanksgiving dinner.

Lindsay had told her about the traditional gathering the week before, though whether she'd been intimating Sarah should be prepared to have something to do with the dinner, or to not be included, she hadn't been sure. And hadn't asked.

Didn't matter, either way. She had her own plans.

The drawers in Kelly's office were in order. Hospital charting order. Which made sense since the woman was an expert medical professional. What didn't make sense was that there was no mention of Kylie anywhere. Nothing under Williams. And nothing for Lily, either.

It was like, as far as the expert witness on Kylie's case was concerned, Sarah's little family hadn't even existed. Crushed with disappointment, she looked again, pulling files out, opening them and reading enough to figure out that they had nothing to do with her sister. Quickly passing over more recently dated items, she opened only those files dated at the time of Kylie's removal from Lily's home. Which had also happened to be Sarah's home, of course. Though no one had given her any consideration at the time of Kylie's placement. No one had interviewed her. Or seemed to factor her emotional duress into their game plan.

Maybe rightly so. As a sixteen-year-old shoplifter, she probably hadn't been the best influence on the toddler. Or didn't have much of a chance of giving the baby a great life. She'd have died trying, though.

One file then another…she perused…she put back.

Funny how the years brought understanding of some things, and yet the new perspective didn't ease the ache of loss at all.

"What are you doing?"

Sarah jerked, startled out of her self-pity as Lindsay's voice sounded from the doorway.

"Trying to get an idea of what type of files are labeled in which ways so that I can get them into one clear and easily discernible order." The words came. She had no idea from where.

Mastering her expression, as she'd learned to do at way too young an age, Sarah turned to face the older woman. "Is there something else you'd like me to be doing?" she asked.

"No…it's just… I spoke to you and you didn't answer."

She hadn't heard.

"Sorry, when I get focused I tend to tune everything else out…"

More likely she'd been lost in her painful past rather than being present as she was being paid to be. "What did you need?"

"Just wanted to let you know that Win is springing for lunch from LaJolla and I was wondering if you wanted the taco salad you've had the other two times they delivered…"

Lindsay's remembering her order almost brought tears to her eyes. Good Lord, she needed to go climb a couple more mountains and find her strength. Grow some of the leathery skin Arizona's hot sun had been trying to give her.

"Yes, that would be great, thank you," she said, but didn't miss the wary expression on Lindsay's face as her gaze lingered on the folder still in Sarah's hands.

Lindsay might suspect that she had stumbled upon something not quite appropriate.

And she was right.

Question was…would the infraction be enough to lose Sarah her job?

How could she have been so blatantly careless?

And yet…wasn't she being paid to go through files? To better organize them? How did you organize unless you knew what you were organizing? Right?

She'd thought maybe at lunch someone would say something, but everyone had eaten alone in their offices—she'd eaten alone in the kitchen. But she'd had her arsenal of defense ready.

She couldn't leave until she found Kylie's file.

Sierra's Web was the only place she had half a hope of finding anything at all about the closed adoption. No court in the state was going to grant her any access. Nor would a police department. Closed meant closed. For a reason.

Didn't matter that a big sister's heart was irreparably damaged.

Didn't matter that Kylie's biological family just needed to know she was okay.

For the rest of the afternoon, Sarah waited for a call to Winchester's office. Or Hudson's. The IT expert was back in town as well. Either one could fire her.

When the day ended, without a summons, she said good-night to everyone and, for the first time since her hiring, was out of the office earlier than anyone else. Breathing a small sigh of relief.

She could still lose her job. The call to a partner's office could come first thing in the morning. But until it did, she wasn't going to borrow trouble.

She was going to change into leggings and a T-shirt and climb A Mountain, the small peak a couple of miles from her home with the university's big yellow *A* emblazoned near the top. She could take the paved path up to the top, but she didn't. With an hour left until dark, she took the rugged, cactus-strewn rock and dirt short way up. Reminding herself with every step that she was made of strong stuff, too.

And trying to pretend that her only concern was Kylie. She didn't need the Sierra's Web job except to find her sister.

And she most definitely didn't care whether or not she'd disappointed Winchester Holmes. Or whether or not she ever saw him again, either.

No, definitely not.

She'd be just fine if she never saw him again.

Would hardly even notice.

Except that, maybe she would.

Win was…eager…when he left a message for their new office manager to let her know he wanted to see her in his office as soon as she got in Tuesday morning. He'd spoken with all six of his partners on a virtual call the evening before. First, to relay to them a conversation he'd had with Lindsay after Sarah Williams had left for the night—a concern that perhaps the new hire had been snooping in their files.

All six of them had lovingly dismissed the allegation—

understanding Lindsay's mother-bear protectiveness. She hadn't come to them a stranger, but rather had been a single mother to a young man who'd lost his life much the way their Sierra had. If only someone had been able to follow all of the little facts that, alone, meant nothing... then maybe...

Shaking his head, he stood at his desk, having just shared with Lindsay the partners' hellos and thanks for having their backs, while at the same time gently letting her know that none of them were concerned that someone overhauling their files was actually looking at said files. She'd replied, as usual, with an acknowledgment that maybe sometimes she got a little paranoid.

She did. Maybe they all did, considering what they'd been through, individually and together. Maybe that was what made them so good at their jobs. And able to help so many people live longer, happier lives.

The second reason for his call to his partners was to get their buy-in for his use of their new office manager on one of his jobs. They all knew the assignment. And as he'd known they would, had all immediately agreed that if there was even a chance that Sarah could help, it would be worth the hourly wage spent on her efforts.

The knock on his door was no surprise. He'd had a text from Sarah letting him know she was in the parking lot and would be right in. The seriously unsmiling expression on her steady features *was* unexpected. The brown eyes that he'd already grown used to looking at him with calm were anything but. Rather, they pinned him with an urgency he didn't understand.

And then thought he'd been mistaken as she calmly shrugged shoulders in another cropped blouse—white this time, over black pants that didn't hide her slim feminine frame—and said, "What can I do for you?" as though she didn't have rooms worth of files waiting for her to unscramble.

One by one.

"I have a request," he told her. Motioning her to one of the two new leather chairs in front of his desk.

"A…a request?" she repeated, lowering herself to the edge of the seat.

He sat down with a little more commitment, settling back in the most comfortable office chair he'd ever had, and slid up to his desk. Picking up a pen, he held it between his hands, end to end, fingers turning it back and forth.

Nervous for no good reason.

And a few bad ones.

Spending time with their new office manager mattered to him.

And shouldn't.

He was her boss, for God's sake. Sexual harassment issues alone meant that he could in no way see her as anything other than a capable employee. And beyond that was the respect she was due. Unwanted attention was not even remotely respectful.

Unless…she initiated something more…human between them?

Was he misinterpreting that look in her eye? As though what he needed might matter to her? Like his opinion of her mattered?

Yeah, right. He was the financial geek whose last girlfriend had lied to him so he wouldn't express concern over the safety of some of her choices and he hadn't even suspected.

Thinking he'd suddenly developed the skills to read women, or this woman, was ludicrous.

"I know you have a lot ahead of you with the filing system overhaul, and while that's important, I wondered if you'd be willing to assist with a current case I'm working. Based on the work you did for me over the weekend, you could be a great help…"

"You want my help on a case?" She sat forward, clearly startled. Even he couldn't misinterpret the raised brow, the complete overhaul of what had been a withdrawn expression.

"If you wouldn't mind." He had more to say. A lot more. Sat there meeting her gaze silently instead. Until he saw himself—the idiot he was acting like—and took charge. Of the meeting. And of himself. "I've been working on the job for a few weeks, thought I'd be in and done, but I've come upon hurdles every step of the way. The client requested me personally, but I've had a couple of other such requests come through in the past couple of days as well and need to get this one cleared."

She nodded. "I understand."

He liked that she did. Yet, how could she? She didn't even know what they were talking about yet.

"I'm tracing the assets of a man who's passed," he told her. A man believed to have been a pimp and drug dealer, but who had, apparently, gotten away from that life a few years before his death, due possibly to a terminal diagnosis. A man who'd appeared to have considerable assets—stating a substantial number in his will. He'd trusted no one with the details of his assets. Not even the lawyer with whom he'd filed the will. Which threw up red flags for Winchester from the get-go.

But the client…the case had come from the county,

back during Sierra's Web's meager beginnings when they'd stayed afloat with a small, local government contract. So Winchester felt…protective.

"The work you did for me over the weekend—most importantly, the way you compiled a character sketch of a man I'd never met—it really helped, and that's the kind of thing I need here."

She nodded again, settling back in her chair. Relaxing? Because she was pleased with his offer?

He liked that she was comfortable with him.

"The work isn't going to be as straightforward as this weekend's was. I've been tracing accounts, but none add up to what they should, and none seem to have any obvious connections to others. That's where I'm hoping your talent will come in—helping me see the person behind the numbers in order to figure out what he might have done with various holdings. His will stipulates that all moneys go to his heir or heirs, and the state only found one. The heir is our client."

"What happens if you don't find all the money?"

"It goes as unclaimed and after a period of time— varies by state and foreign laws—it reverts to the state or government where it's housed."

"I'm in." She didn't show any concern at all. Just a willingness to help.

And he felt compelled to offer, "This is outside your job description, and none of us will think any less of you if you choose not to take it on."

"No." She shrugged. "I'm fine to do it. I want to."

He believed her.

And when she smiled at him, he smiled back.

Chapter Four

She wasn't being fired! Life took on new wings for Sarah as she immersed herself immediately in the project Winchester had given her. Set up in the Sierra's Web conference room, with a company laptop networked to the printer at the end of the hall, she printed off what they had on the man—James W. Milford—and started in line by line. From the few basic accounts—a credit card and a simple checking account—she could quickly determine a couple of things. The man spent top dollar on internet service and an equal amount on every streaming service available. She jotted that information down. Then she started looking at the things that weren't there. Making lists of items she'd found on the spreadsheets over the weekend that were conspicuously absent with her present assignment.

Most of that day and the next were spent the same

way, as Winchester unearthed other accounts through whatever tracing methods he used.

And still, there were more questions than answers. Her character sketch had more holes than clear pictures, and she hated that she was letting Winchester down.

As she passed by his office, and saw him sitting there, his light blue shirt all ironed as usual, the knot in his tie just right and that short hair lying with perfect precision, she paused. Just to look. His fashion correctness, or lack of fashion sense as the case might be, just made her feel good.

For no good reason.

"You need something?" he asked easily, with maybe a bit of a smile on his face as he glanced up from his computer.

Feeling heat crop up her face, she blurted the first thing that came to her. "I've finished with everything you sent." She stumbled through the words. "I just emailed you the spreadsheet, but there's not a lot there." He wanted her insight, her opinion. He wanted her to do what she'd done the last time and notice something significant about the man she was characterizing. "The most I got was that James Milford seemed to be particularly partial to Hometown Bagels. I get it. They're my favorite, too. But over the year of the Liberty Bank credit card use, the man never missed a week without at least one visit to Hometown."

She was making a fool of herself, though Winchester's nod in response, his comment about never having been there himself, didn't make her feel an idiot.

She moved on down the hall before that could change. Instead she turned her attention back to filing on Wednesday afternoon, compiling another spreadsheet as she went, marking each partner's types of cases and filing habits, intending to come up with one universal system that worked for all of them.

And with every file she handled, she was on the lookout for anything to do with her baby sister. She'd found several things completely misfiled. Kylie's case could be anywhere within any of the loaded-down cabinets.

Late in the afternoon, while going through a stack of old files she'd pulled out of a cabinet in the closet, she saw that, with two exceptions, the entire pile was from county cases—all Kelly Chase's. She'd hit the mother lode.

Hands trembling, she looked through one, and then another, all child services cases where Kelly had given expert testimony. Sometimes she'd interviewed kids, sometimes entire families. And sometimes potential adopters. In all that she'd seen so far, Kelly had given final recommendations.

She got through that pile. And then a second. Finished the drawer.

And still didn't find Kylie.

She knew for a fact that Sierra's Web had been on the case. Not just because Lily had told her about the firm when she'd called Sarah, panicked about Kylie's case being looked at. Sarah had known about the independent firm's involvement with her little sister all along. Eight years ago she'd been sixteen. She'd sneaked out of the room where she'd been told to stay after her court arraignment and had heard someone speaking with her mother, telling Lily that a Sierra's Web expert would be conducting the interviews.

That's all she'd heard.

Hadn't had any idea what it meant at the time.

But later, when Lily had driven straight home rather than stopping to pick up Kylie from the friend who'd offered to watch her during the court proceedings, Sarah had learned the horrible, agonizing truth. Child services had taken Kylie from them. And Sierra's Web was somehow involved.

Lily never ever said so, but Sarah knew it had been her fault. She'd drawn attention to their desperate home situation by stealing those cans of stew. The authorities who'd arrested her had obviously sent child services to the home Sarah had inherited from her grandparents— a home held in a trust, with protected rights to live in it, until Sarah turned eighteen.

The house had passed muster.

The people inside had not.

It was as simple as that.

Winchester was waiting for Sarah with Hometown bagels and cream cheese on Thursday morning, though, of course, he'd bought enough for Hud and Lindsay to share as well. And not knowing what kind Sarah preferred, he'd ended up with two of each of the dozen kinds they'd had fresh that morning.

She came in, wearing brown pants and a tailored beige blouse, her long hair flowing in dark waves around her shoulders, just a minute or two after Lindsay, who was already in the kitchen making coffee.

Looking the epitome of professionalism, Sarah gave Win no valid reason to get dry mouthed over her, and he quickly refocused his attention. "I found a cluster of Milford accounts last night," he told her, even before mentioning the bagel gift. "I already sent them to you. But before you go through them, I'd like a couple of minutes to discuss them."

She worked for him. He was doing nothing wrong in requesting her presence in his office. But wanting her there, looking forward to having her there…that was wrong.

In all his years of being a partner in Sierra's Web, all the thousands of people he'd interacted with, the hundreds of offices he'd been in, he'd never ever had such a strong reaction to someone before.

Never, since Sierra, that was.

He wasn't going there.

"Help yourself to bagels first." He nodded toward the kitchen as Sarah moved with him to his office. Hud and Lindsay could be heard from down the hall, discussing cream cheese flavors. Win needed Sarah to join their conversation and give him a minute to get his head back on straight.

He got the minute, five minutes even, but they weren't enough.

The second Sarah came into his office, a small plate bearing a bagel cut into pieces in one hand and two coffee cups in the other, he was right back where he'd been when she'd walked in the office door that morning.

Happy to see her.

"I come bearing treats," she told him. "You said you'd never had Hometown Bagels before and this is, in my opinion, the place to start. It's their basic, plain bagel covered with their homemade honey butter spread. It's so good."

He didn't know if she knew he'd purchased the morning's fare. Didn't care if she knew. The look of pleasure on her face was worth every dime he'd spent. And then some.

To please her, he took a piece of the bounty she'd obviously brought for them to share, since she'd already helped herself to a piece. He wasn't usually a bagel fan—too much bread—and yet, as he sank his teeth into the first bite, his mouth watered.

Physically watered. It was that good.

Or eating it with her was…

Either way, he was in serious trouble.

"I don't in any way want to influence your process, in terms of building this character sketch." Winchester started in even before the bagel was gone. Taking her cue from him, Sarah quit eating and listened. After just a couple of weeks working at Sierra's Web, she'd grown to highly respect every single one of the partners—even those she'd only met through phone calls and going through their files. Their shared focus and dedication, their abilities and the jobs they took on to help ease suffering in people's lives compelled her to want to be a part of them.

And yet…she was a nurse, duping them all for her own gain.

She could only hope that they never knew.

And that, if they did find out, they'd at least understand that her motivation had been as pure as theirs. To make sure her baby sister wasn't suffering.

"This new cluster of accounts I found…they stem from an earlier portion of Milford's life, when he reportedly lived very differently," Winchester was saying, and she gave him her full focus. "It occurred to me that perhaps there should be two spreadsheets—one from before and the one you've been working on."

She was following him, sort of. Nodded. Then asked, "You think there are assets from this 'before time' that he forgot about?"

"I don't think anything yet. For all I know he hid money then and used it later. Or didn't have any to hide. But…there's some history. There are facts I know and other things that I've heard that make me think that maybe if Milford had this 'see the light' moment that it appears he had, then your sketch might need to be of two different men if we're going to be able to use it the way you intend."

"Before the light and afterward," she said, intrigued and agreeing with him. She should definitely make two different spreadsheets. And if they came out similar, that was fine, but at least they would know.

Taking a sip of the coffee Sarah had brought him, prepared by Lindsay—dark with cream and sugar— Winchester sat back in his chair, his full attention seemingly on her.

She liked it. The way his gaze seemed to take her in. And appreciate what he saw.

But the words that came out of his mouth had nothing to do with her, leaving her embarrassed and thankful that he couldn't read her mind.

"This case is particularly close to home for me, and for the firm," he started, bringing her attention fully back to the matter at hand. "The client was directly involved in another job we handled."

He met her gaze—giving her a glimpse of how much he truly cared. And there she was…a sucker for genuine compassion. One of the reasons she loved the medical field so much—it was a career choice that appealed to compassionate people.

"There's a plethora of case files somewhere around here, all together, that pertain to the one and only contract the firm had when we first opened, before we became self-supporting. Kelly was asked by the county to provide expert testimony in child protective custody cases as needed. If you haven't run into the files yet, you will…"

Heart pumping, she could barely breathe.

Had someone seen her snooping? For all she knew they could have hidden cameras…

The thought was quickly followed by a more rational one. He wouldn't have brought in her favorite bagels if he was going to fire her. She'd thanked Lindsay for bringing them in, had offered to pay her share for them, only to be told that they were Winchester's treat…

Because he'd remembered her mentioning them the day before? All the way down the hall to his office, she'd had that thought in mind. Mulled it over. Liked how it made her feel.

No way him buying that particular brand, after admitting he'd never had them, could be just a coincidence.

"This particular assignment came from one of those cases," he said after a pause, as though he'd been reading her mind.

And she came abruptly back to child services and county cases. To Kelly Chase doing interviews that resulted in removing children from their homes.

"I've got the file here," he said, holding it up.

And she stared. Blood draining from her face. She couldn't see the name on the file. Had no identifiers to pull from. Just a faded old file similar to the ones she'd scoured the day before.

But...

The file in his hand...it could be Kylie's.

Made perfect, logical sense.

Would explain why it hadn't been in with the others.

Lily had said the case was being looked at again.

Winchester was working on a case from the same time period.

Kylie's file was nowhere to be found.

Winchester had pulled a county case child services file...

Thoughts flew as Winchester said something about Lindsay being the one who'd brought the file to him.

Cold and hot at the same time, she stared at the file. Knew she had to get her hands on it. To find out the name of the child in question.

She needed to jump up, grab that manila folder to her chest and run with it. To sit in her chair with shaky knees that wouldn't hold her up.

"The child in question was given up for adoption by her mother," her boss continued, and her breath left her body in a gush. Whether he heard or not, she didn't know.

"Her mother gave her up?" she managed weakly.

He nodded. And she took another breath. Concentrated on feeling her fingers and toes. It wasn't Kylie's case.

Wasn't even close.

Her little sister had most definitely been taken from them. She'd been theirs in the morning, and that afternoon, after Sarah's guilty plea, she'd been gone.

Winchester was nodding, seeming not to notice that

his new hire had nearly lost her mind all over the floor between them.

Or to be aware of the disappointment coursing through her. Wouldn't it have been great to know that she was looking for money for her baby sister? That Kylie's case was only being looked at because she'd come into some money?

They would have to know who her father was for that to happen. Lily wasn't sure who'd fathered her second child.

Or her first, for that matter.

When her mother had been on one of her binges…

But that didn't happen anymore.

Not since the day the state had taken Kylie away from them.

"It was the oddest case," Winchester was saying, "which is why we all still remember it. The mother clearly loved the child, but was determined that she be adopted out, in a closed adoption, to protect the child from the father. She'd made a mistake with the man, and she said she'd give up her heart if that's what she had to do to protect the child from him." He paused, his gaze shadowing. That look of sorrow brought Sarah's full attention back to him. "Give up her heart. I'll never forget those words," he said. "Kelly called me after her initial meeting with social services. She was so moved by the self-sacrifice and the heartbreak. Aching for the mother who'd had to pay such a high price due to her own wrong choice."

Sarah had never met the woman, and she felt her pain. Her honor.

And…maybe another mistake? "Did anyone try to help her find a way to keep the child?" she asked, so caught up in the telling, the story, that she wasn't even thinking about why she was there. In the moment, how the things Winchester was telling her related to the current case—but in general, too. For a second, Kylie wasn't the first child on her mind. "A restraining order against the father? Or counseling, maybe?"

What did she know? Except how much a heart hurt when it lost a child it loved as its own...

Winchester was shaking his head. "It was way messier than that. The guy was a drug dealer and hooked girls up with guys who'd give them drugs in exchange for sex. He wasn't technically a pimp as he didn't take money for the hookups, but he made money off the drugs he sold to the guys, who got the sex for free. The girls exchanged sex for free drugs."

Weight filled her veins as she nodded. Now, that she understood. How a woman could get so desperate for a fix that she'd have sex with someone to get it.

She knew it was the story of her own birth—though she'd never been told that specifically.

And the story of Kylie's, too.

Minus the drug dealer hookup.

She didn't know a lot about the times her mom hadn't come home, the times when her grandmother had made sure that Sarah's life had gone as normally as possible even as she must have been worried sick about her only daughter. But she knew that Lily had handled her own trade-offs.

"Did the dad want the child?" she asked softly, in a mixture of professional and personal confusion. The dad—were they talking Milford? They had to be, right?

She'd always assumed that if Lily had known which of the men she'd been with had fathered Sarah, if she'd known how to find them again for a paternity test, if the guy had known that Sarah existed...he wouldn't have wanted her anyway.

It was easier that way. To think that she wasn't missing out on anything by not knowing him.

"The dad wasn't in the picture," Winchester said. "The deal was that the mother traded a closed adoption for a guarantee that the father would never know where the child was or have a chance to get near her."

"But...he would have had to sign adoption papers, wouldn't he?" She was already on the way to asking as the second *her* came out of his mouth.

Her. So the child they were working for—through the parents of the child, who'd hired Sierra's Web on her behalf—was a girl.

Like Kylie in two ways.

A girl who'd been part of the county's child protective services when Kelly Chase had freelanced for them.

A girl who'd lost her mother. Almost two mothers, in Kylie's case.

"His signature wouldn't have been necessary if the court had severed his rights."

That made sense. She tried to focus on this one thing that did. That didn't stab her with the too familiar pain.

"None of that's in Kelly's file," Winchester continued. "Her only contact with any of it was interviewing potential adopters and then making a formal recommendation to the court at the county's request and on their behalf."

Right. Just as it would have been in Kylie's case. Sarah had no reason to think she might resent Kelly if and when she ever met her. The woman had only been doing her job. Likely wouldn't even have known why adopters were being interviewed for Kylie. Wouldn't have been privy to the sixteen-year-old sister, who'd brought the toddler to the court's attention with her own egregious behavior.

Kelly Chase wasn't to blame for Kylie being taken from them.

Sarah Williams was.

All water under the bridge—so why was she suddenly wading in it so much?

"I'm assuming James Milford is the father?" she asked then, determined to keep her feet dry and firmly rooted on the ground from that point on.

Winchester's nod was short. Succinct.

A period at the end of the unspoken order for her to get to work.

Standing, she went to do just that.

Turning at the door to thank him for the bagel.

His smile, his "I'm the one who should be thanking you—it was great" were nice.

Really nice.

Reminding her that there was life ahead of her.

Happiness waiting.

Not with him, obviously, but with someone. At some point.

She didn't see herself all in with a partner, but she wanted to be a mother so badly her heart ached with the need.

She just had to make certain Kylie was okay so she could get to it.

Chapter Five

Win was still at the office after seven that night when his office phone rang with a call from Sarah. Picking up in the middle of the first ring, he said, "Is everything okay?"

"Don't you ever say hello?" Her tone lifted, almost a tease.

Sometimes he did. "Depends on whether or not I recognize the number." Just seemed to him, with caller ID and everyone knowing that whoever was calling could be known to the caller, the whole hello thing like you didn't know was kind of dumb. He told her as much.

"I guess it is kind of insulting, in a way," she told him, which made him smile.

A lot. He sat there grinning from ear to ear, actually, but it wasn't like there was anyone around to see him. Hud had left a while ago, reminding him to at least order in dinner, and he'd barely noticed.

He'd been ear-deep in tracking numbers. Going through shell companies, tracing them in an attempt to find where money had landed and how much of it there was. He'd been expecting to come up with a good number of thousands for the family, but it was starting to look as though there was a whole lot more.

And like James Milford was a lot smarter than he'd apparently been given credit for.

"Anyway, I had a thought and wanted to call in case it was something that would trigger something for you."

Which was exactly why he'd asked for her help.

His enjoying another evening phone call from her wasn't why.

"It's about the bagels…"

She'd been thinking about the bagels he'd brought in for her?

In a good way?

He hoped…

"When I was going through that cluster of accounts this afternoon, starting on the new spreadsheet, I noticed that there wasn't a single charge in the Hometown Bagels column. You have to figure, a guy who eats the same bagels every single week didn't just start out liking them," she said, and he notched himself down a few pegs. She'd been thinking about bagels in terms of the job, not him. "I mean, usually," she continued, thankfully with no way of knowing the wrong jaunt his thoughts had taken, "when someone gets into something new, they go all in, and then maybe enthusiasm starts to trickle off after a while."

Kind of like the couple of serious relationships he'd been in since Sierra…

"I don't know, maybe not, but it seems like that kind

of fondness for something, maybe it's been there for a long time. Which would mean that Milford was eating Hometown Bagels before he saw the light as well. So he must have paid for them. And maybe he paid cash for everything, but if it's legal and all, or you have some way of doing it, maybe you could check with the store closest to where he might have been living and have them check their records. Maybe his name pops up and you can see an account number or something in terms of how he paid…"

Damn!

He was losing his eyesight scrolling through intricate finances on a computer screen, and one of his answers could be as simple as bagels?

The round breads wouldn't have given up offshore accounts or shell companies…but a simple domestic credit card account could help him get there quicker.

Maybe.

It could also point him to a bank that might have a lockbox in Milford's name, with significant information inside.

Finding all of Milford's money wasn't life or death.

But if he could help a child who'd had a rough start, help the family who'd taken her as their own and filled her life with love, then he was going to do so.

Existence wasn't always about life and death.

Sometimes it was just about doing the right thing.

"You've done great, Sarah…" Winchester's words played over her car's audio system as she sat at a stoplight in Scottsdale, still ten minutes outside of Tempe that Thursday evening. She tried not to let the warm tone wash over her too completely. Maybe a little bit of surface cleaning, but that was all. Blinded by headlights across the intersection from her, hating that it got dark so early in Phoenix in winter months, she told him she was glad she could help.

He had no idea how glad.

Guilt was insidious and every little bit of antidote made a difference to its spread.

"I didn't intend for you to take work home with you," he said next. "And certainly not this work."

"I'm not home," she said, before thinking her response through. "I volunteer on Thursday nights and am just driving home now." She made matters worse. Her life was on a need-to-know basis and he most definitely didn't need to know anything personal about her.

More importantly, she didn't need to know that he knew personal things about her.

Or that he might find them interesting.

The knowing would only make her like him more, and liking him was definitely not something she could afford. Not in any more than a casual, impersonal, boss-employee way.

Most particularly not this boss. Not with the duplicity of her employment.

The more she got to know Winchester, and the others, the worse she felt about lying to them. And had already determined that the second she found out what she needed to know about Kylie, she'd quit and fade from their lives. She'd like to come clean, to tell them the truth, but that could make them complicit in her guilt, unless they prosecuted her or something, which...

"Where do you volunteer?" Winchester's question came after a mention that he volunteered at the university, giving personal finance seminars to students twice a month.

She'd never known that. Had attended the school for four years, with him right on campus, and hadn't known.

"At a woman's shelter," she said, more to get away from her own thoughts than because she thought answering him was wise. She gave free inoculations and pregnancy tests, every Thursday night. Her only nursing experience at the moment.

And he absolutely could not know that. Which was why keeping her private life private was so important. The reminder came as the light turned green.

His pause made her curious, though. "You have a problem with that?" she finally asked him. Was he shocked that she'd spend time volunteering? Wondering why?

More likely, her guilt was making her paranoid.

"No." The response was emphatic. "Very much, no. I'm just…a…friend of mine…she went to a shelter once…" He stopped the conversation dead in its tracks, telling her his other line was ringing and he had to go.

She hung up as quickly as he did.

She hadn't heard another line ring.

Didn't think one had.

She also didn't think that whoever the woman had been who'd visited that shelter had been just a friend.

And wished she knew more.

Win called a detective associate of his regarding the Hometown Bagels question Sarah had posed. While he was waiting to hear back, he followed Milford's trails all day Friday. He found no contributions to bogus charities, but he did find an investment trail that led through several shell companies to an offshore account that, while it contained money, didn't have enough to be considered millions.

What the hell? Had Milford been playing them all?

Was there someone alive in whom he'd confided? Someone who wasn't coming forward, but could be spending the guy's money? If the person had access to the funds, and a right to spend them until that right was superseded by an executed will, there was nothing anyone could do about it—legally—except what was already being done. Hire him to try to find the money so that it became an official part of the will.

Someone could fight that execution, fight the will, of course, but that was for the future to figure out. And completely outside of his jurisdiction.

Some of what he uncovered was from the last few years, more from longer ago. As he found accounts and companies, he sent them over to Sarah to add them to her characterization spreadsheets. So far there'd been no connection between accounts opened prior to the past few years and newer ones, other than that the previous accounts had stayed open. Just not seemingly active—other than money streams coming in that, while in the thousands, certainly didn't amount to millions. And so far there weren't enough of them to add up to serious wealth.

Maybe his idea of substantial and Milford's were vastly different, but as long as he continued to find inexplicable account numbers, or money seemingly coming out of nowhere, he'd follow the intricate trails.

When speaking with the partners on Wednesday night, the conversation had turned to Thanksgiving, since the holiday, and quarterly Sierra's Web meeting, were just a week away. As it had turned out, everyone was going to make it for the actual holiday that year, not just sometime over the weekend. Mariah Anderson, their child life expert, had said she'd call Lindsay to make arrangements for the feast to be catered. He'd thought again, then, about hosting the meal in his new home. The gated community was lovely. It was too cold for the pool, but the hot tub had eight seats.

And the place lacked...humanity.

Human beings other than himself.

Life.

It lacked Sarah's having ever been there.

That last point had figured largely in him keeping an invitation from falling off the tip of his tongue. As much as he wanted to host his Sierra's Web family, to have his first home filled with the only close family he'd had since his parents had passed away in a car accident while he was in college, he resisted the temptation to have Sarah there.

But Friday afternoon, when he heard Lindsay on the phone with the caterer, he motioned her to cut off the order. And when she glanced his way, mentioned that they might not need a caterer.

She'd frowned but hadn't argued as she'd canceled what she'd started, and went back to work. It helped that the Sierra's Web phones rang almost incessantly and a call had already been holding for her to tend to.

From there, he went to his desk and whipped off a text invitation to his partners, even Hud, who was in the office, suggesting that they all come to his place for the holiday feast. The responses came quickly...with multiple emojis and jests about possible poisoning, but every one in the affirmative.

As soon as Lindsay was off the phone, he told her about the change of plans, accepting her offer to help with the meal.

And then he sought out the person whose opinion of his home he wanted so badly. He knew it. Didn't try to hide anything from himself.

Just as he knew that, while he might take personal comfort from having Sarah in his space for a few hours over the holiday, he would not at any point, even in his imagination, make it more than the office celebration that it was.

A guy couldn't help how he felt. But he was absolutely responsible for what he did about it. At no point would he and Sarah be alone. His partners would be present every second of Sarah's time there. He'd make certain of that himself, even if he had to out himself and beg them to stay until she left.

The crush on Sarah would pass; he just had to wait it out.

Sarah wasn't in the conference room where he'd expected to find her. And he'd been involved in an emergency call that had come in from local police shortly after lunch until nearly four o'clock, helping them track a suspect through financial records. Lindsay had already left for the day, and Hud was in his office with the door closed by the time he finally got the chance to have a moment of conversation with the woman who was making his life crazier than he wanted it to be.

She gave him a rundown on her progress on the Milford case the second he showed his face in the doorway of the conference room. She'd made it through nearly half the accounts he'd sent to her over the past couple of days, had been busy compiling, but hadn't formed any opinions or had anything stand out to her.

His phone rang as he was standing there… Detective Connolly calling back regarding Hometown…and the news wasn't good.

"My detective contact spoke with the store owner, who said she didn't recognize Milford's picture, know the name, or feel comfortable sharing customer payment information without a warrant," Win told Sarah as he dropped his cell back into his shirt pocket and adjusted the knot on his tie.

More to have something to do with his hands than because it was in any need of attention.

"Which doesn't rule out that he went there before the light," Sarah said. "Because we know he went there at least once a week the past three years and used a debit card to pay, so whether she recognized him or not, or knew his name or not, he was there."

She was right, of course. He and Connolly had already come to that conclusion. But it didn't help him. He wasn't solving a crime. He was simply looking for assets for a young girl who could have a college fund that might give her a boost toward her happiest life.

"So maybe we know we aren't done looking until we find the account from which he paid Hometown?" Sarah said, her frown of concentration partially curtained by the long hair cascading down over her.

"Maybe." The guy could have paid cash. Or not known yet that he liked bagels.

"I'm sorry I haven't been more help on this one. If you'd like me to get back to spending my time on the filing system, I'm fine to do so." Her tone, her words, said she was fine. The depth of expression as she glanced at the work in front of her might be telling a different story.

He couldn't be sure.

As Sierra had probably figured out, too late. If only he'd known, when she'd come to him so harried that day, asking about investing a large, for her, sum of money…

"Don't apologize," he told her with a shrug. Wishing he could say the same to himself. For the rest of his life, he'd be apologizing to the angel Sierra had become. "And I very much need you to stay on this," he assured her. "This is by far the strangest job I've taken on. I don't expect you to figure out where any money is. That's my job. But your outside perspective, the picture you're painting, might very well help me figure out where to look."

The smile that broke out on her face couldn't be misread. There was no doubt that his response had pleased her.

A lot.

Which gave him the impetus to say, he hoped casually, "I'm hosting Thanksgiving dinner for Sierra's Web this year. It's an annual thing, us all getting together, including Lindsay, and the partners would like for me to extend an invitation to you as well." They'd all agreed that he should, at any rate, after he'd brought up the topic. Had he not brought it up…someone else very probably would have done so. "It would be a good chance for everyone to get to know you a little bit, and for you to see how we all are when we're together."

It would be her first step into their family unit.

"Oh, I'd love to," she said, dropping her gaze and then looking back up at him. Which probably meant something. "But I've already got plans."

Of course she did. She had a whole life about which he knew nothing.

Funny how he'd thought his offering the invitation was the only hurdle to having her join him. Or not so funny.

"Got a big family celebration?" he asked her with another shrug and a smile on his face. Last thing he wanted was to make her feel bad.

"No, I don't have a big family. And I'm really sorry, Winchester. I'd have liked to have joined you all." Her gaze was straight on and he felt it inside. Believed her regret.

"Hold on to that thought," he said then. "Christmas is just around the corner and we've got traditions then, too. You'll get stuck with us all in the room at the same time at some point."

He meant to leave then. Took one step toward doing so and heard her ask, "You all were college friends, I know, but don't you have families, too?"

The question stopped him for a second, so used as he was to the seven of them as an understood unit. "Some of us do, but part of what drew us in college was that we were kind of alone, too," he told her, feeling like the nerdy college kid he'd been when he'd first hooked up with the rest of his partners—and Sierra—in a communications class. "Hud, Kelly and Mariah are married now, so they have their families. Hud and Kelly live locally. And Mariah and her small family are coming in for Thanksgiving, but will be back for Christmas, too, so you'll have a chance to meet everyone. Savannah, Glen, Dorian and I all live alone, except when we come to Phoenix. We share the corporate condo then. With this job, traveling as we all do so much of the time…"

"But you just bought a home." Her words were statement, not question, and yet seemed to ask for clarification, too.

Leaning against the doorway, he said, "We try to have one partner in the office at least a few days a week, and because Hud and I spend the least amount of time traveling since a lot of what we do happens over the internet, we were the ones most often here. Him more than me, since he's from Phoenix and settled here. But with his marriage, having just discovered that he has a thirteen-year-old daughter, he didn't want to spend as much time in the office, so I offered to move here from Arkansas, and the house was a good investment."

All true, and probably a bit pathetic sounding. His life was so empty it was no big deal to pick up and move over several states. The place he stayed was an investment, not a home.

And, he guessed, way more than she'd been requesting.

"Real estate here is definitely a good investment," she told him.

Which made him ask, "Do you have a house?" because it went along with the conversation.

"I do."

That was it. Nothing about where it was. Or who might live in it with her.

"Have you been in it long?" She knew he was brand-new to his home. The question squeaked into fitting what they were talking about.

But he was pushing his limit and he knew it.

"My whole life."

Win blinked, raised his brows, stood up straight in the doorway. "You still live at home?"

"Doesn't everyone? You're going home in a little bit. Lindsay already did. Hudson will."

Okay, technically, sure, but, "You still live with your parents?" He wasn't sure what to make of that. Sure she'd just graduated from college, but she seemed so much older. And…like a person who had her own place.

Because he was making her up.

These feelings he was having for her, they weren't real. They were all made up in the person he'd built around her in his imagination. Kind of like the character sketches she built from bank accounts.

Yes, that was right. Relieved, he waited for her confirmation, as though it would solidify that he didn't know her at all.

"I never knew my father," she told him. "My mom had me her senior year of high school, and I was raised in the home she grew up in. My grandmother left me the house when she died."

Rewind. He hadn't known her history, but it completely fit the person he'd thought her to be.

And the situation was exactly why he didn't do relationships. He just wasn't good at the nuances. Which made him overprotective when he did finally manage to get into a thing.

Not that he was looking for a thing with an employee. He wasn't.

He just… Sarah…

"I'm so sorry. How long has your grandmother been gone?" he asked, taking another step into the room, instead of further down the hall as he'd told himself to do.

"Since I was ten."

He stared. A woman left her home to a ten-year-old child?

Instead of to her mother?

"So…who raised you?"

"My mother." She said the words like, who else would have? Like they were to be expected.

He'd assumed her mother was out of the picture. That she'd been raised by her grandmother.

Maybe he'd read that wrong, too.

He didn't think so, though. He did know that he needed to close his mouth and leave the room. That he was in over his head with a situation that he wasn't equipped to handle well.

But if she hadn't wanted to answer his questions, she wouldn't have. In the two and a half weeks he'd known her, he'd learned that much.

And really…all the rest of them, Lindsay included, knew everything about each other. She deserved to be known as well.

The last thought, or rationalization—he wasn't sure—led him to say, "Where is she?"

"California."

"When did she move there?"

"When I graduated from high school."

When she'd become the official owner of the home, he guessed.

"And you've lived alone ever since?"

Another shrug, as though it was no big deal. "I had a couple of roommates when I was in college, when someone needed a place to stay."

Nice. Kind.

And seemed sad to him, too.

"I lost both of my parents when I was in college," he offered, as though that somehow made up for her aloneness. "Car accident."

"Oh, my word, Winchester, I'm so sorry." The wide eyes, the compassion in her tone…they eased him in a way others couldn't.

"Win," he said, needing to get his head back on his shoulders. "No one calls me Winchester."

Except Sierra, a couple of times.

And there they were, her sitting, him standing, both of their insides hanging out there between them…

"Oh, Win, sure, I didn't know…"

How could she know? He hadn't told her. And didn't want to think about why that was.

"I should probably get back to this," she said, nodding toward her laptop—and the accounts he'd sent her to compile for him.

"Yeah." He turned to go.

"Win?"

"Yeah?"

"Thank you for inviting me to Thanksgiving. Even though I can't go…it makes me feel good to have been asked."

He shrugged yet again. "You're a part of us now," he told her, and left before he could do any more damage.

Left with a smile on his face.

Because he'd made her feel good.

Chapter Six

You're a part of us now. Win's words played themselves again and again in Sarah's mind over the next days as she continued to pore over the accounts he sent her. She spent the rest of the time looking for any mentions of her baby sister anywhere in the Sierra's Web offices.

In another life, she'd have loved to be a part of them.

Maybe even wished that Win would ask her out, or just take her right on into bed.

In another life.

Her real life was another matter. In this life she was making her way up a lovely flowered sidewalk in Anaheim, California, heading toward a beautiful carved door that led into an upscale drug rehabilitation center.

If the hotel-like structure with massive, artfully manicured and flowered lawns and an equally exquisite pool area could be called a center. It was. She just didn't think the name fit.

"Sarah!" Lily came out the door just as she was reaching for the long wooden handle. "I thought I saw you walking up!" In designer jeans that fit her lovely frame like a glove, and an equally tight but somehow tasteful black tunic, her long dark hair flowing all around her, Lily had a grin of pure delight on her perfectly made-up face as she threw her arms around Sarah.

And hung on. Tight. For a good minute.

Sarah loved her mom hugely. Hugged her back. And was glad when Lily let go, too.

"I've been looking forward to your visit for ages," Lily said as she retrieved her little overnight bag and walked with Sarah out to her car. "I've got everything prepared for the residents for tomorrow, left full instructions for my sous-chefs and am completely free until Friday morning!"

Lily's energy, as always, was refreshing. A breath of air that had been so sadly lacking during the long, arduous, on and off again addiction-filled years of Sarah's youth. But she'd always had a home, Sarah reminded herself as she climbed behind the wheel and took the short trip from the rich and famous rehabilitation facility to the hotel where she and Lily always stayed when Sarah was in town.

"I was thinking maybe you'd want to come home for Christmas," she said as she pulled into the parking garage. It had been six years since Lily had left home, first for extended rehab—though she'd been sober since they'd lost Kylie, she'd teetered too many times to trust herself on her own—and then to accept the chef's position she'd been offered there after volunteering in the kitchen while she'd been a patient. But Lily had never been back to Phoenix.

She'd used her inheritance from her parents, money that had been invested for more than twenty years, to enter the upscale facility. And spent a good bit of her wages to continue to live on the property.

"No, you need to come here, Sarah!" she said, the same response she'd given any time Sarah had attempted to get her mom to leave the area. "We have so much fun! And what would Christmas be without Mickey?"

Disneyland. Another institution in Anaheim. And her mother's happy place. How Lily didn't get bored with the same attractions twice a year, every year, on Thanksgiving and Christmas, Sarah didn't know, but as long as her mom was sober and happy, so was she.

She'd hoped, with Lily telling her about Kylie, that maybe her mother trusted herself enough, was ready enough to reenter the real world.

She waited the rest of that evening and a good part of the next day while they spent Thanksgiving in Disneyland for her mother to mention the little darling they'd lost to the courts. To ask if Sarah had found out anything about Kylie's case.

Lily didn't.

Just as she'd never mentioned the little girl again after the day she'd come home without her and told Sarah that she was gone forever, to a family that would cherish her and give her everything Lily couldn't.

Standing in line outside "it's a small world," the ride that they took first and last in the park every time they visited, Sarah finally said, "I thought you'd ask about Kylie."

Her mother froze. Not in anger, just seeming to become a statue much like the full color ones all around them.

"I thought when you called and told me that there'd been activity on her case that you'd…that we were ready…"

She'd been hoping for weeks. Had hoped she'd have some good news to bring her mother at Thanksgiving. Had been dreading telling Lily she had nothing.

"Mom?"

Lily nodded. Moved forward in the line, as though moving people had been the reason Sarah had said her name. And then, very slowly, Lily looked Sarah in the eyes and said, "I had to let go of Kylie." That was all. Just that statement. As though it explained…

What?

Lily didn't expound, explain…she just moved forward in line, climbed onto the bench seat of their little boat car when told and, once inside the ride, smiled at the attractions Sarah knew were her favorites.

She was quiet as they left the park, and Sarah worried about keeping her mom at the hotel with her that night, which was ludicrous. Eight years sober didn't just fall away at the mention of a child's name.

Most particularly not when Lily had brought Kylie up between them herself, weeks before.

But Sarah had spent sixteen years living with a woman who, with every loss, every hurt, every heartache, turned to substance as a means of coping. Starting with the desertion of Sarah's father, from what Sarah had been told…

"I'm not as strong as you are." The words fell into the darkness of their hotel room hours later as Sarah lay awake in bed, thinking her mother asleep in the bed beside hers. "I never have been. You take after my mom…"

"Your strengths are different from mine, maybe, but they're there," Sarah said, not for the first time in their lives together. "Addiction is an illness, not a choice, Mom. Not in the end. And you've had the strength to beat it. I have no idea what that's even like…"

"My father was an alcoholic," Lily told her. Something else Sarah knew. She didn't remember her grandfather much, bits and pieces of a smiling man who'd always played with her and whom she'd adored, but she knew that when he'd died, her mother had fallen into a binge that had lasted more than a year. "You're more like Mom."

She'd been told that, too.

"Grandpa lived twenty-one years sober," she reminded Lily, again not for the first time. Or even the hundredth.

"I know, and I will, too, Sarah. I swore to myself, the day we lost your sister, that I would never fall again…"

"And you haven't."

"Because I've learned how not to," Lily said, sounding more like Sarah's grandmother than she'd ever heard before. "I have strict rules, sweetie. So did my daddy, by the way. He talked to me about them when I…after you were born and I was left all alone to raise you. You have to know your limits. And your triggers. You have to be where you feel strong. I feel strong here. I have a good life here. I'm needed."

"I need you." She couldn't remember the last time she'd felt like a child to Lily's mother persona. If ever.

"I know you do, sweetie, but not like I'm needed here.

The people I cook for, they're struggling. I see it on their faces. And when they see me… I give them hope…"

Turning over, Sarah stared at the glistening of her mother's eyes in the dark. "You've never told me that before."

Lily turned, too, until they were facing each other across the small space of floor between them. "Once I knew we were losing Kylie, I had to let her go. Completely. Cut knowing her out of my thoughts. It was the only way I was going to stay sober. But you…you've never let go. That's why when I got the call…" Lily stopped abruptly. "Anyway… I told you what I'd heard about your sister's case for you, Sarah. Because I love you more than life and I know your heart still hurts. But I did it just for you. I don't want to know anything, either way. I can't go back there. I let her go."

Oh. Wow.

Well, then…

She'd thought Lily's call to her had been a plea to fix whatever might have happened. To find out if something had gone wrong. To protect Kylie.

She'd been wrong.

And yet… Lily had called her. She'd done what she could to protect her youngest daughter, whether she knew it or not.

Swallowing back tears, Sarah blinked. Tried for a smile, in case her mom could see it in the darkness. "I love you, Mom."

"I love you, too, baby. More than you'll ever know."

Maybe. Sarah was pretty sure she did know, though. Lily loved her like Sarah had loved Kylie. It didn't ever stop. Or fade. It just was.

"Can I ask you one thing and then never bring it up again?" She had to know.

"I'll answer if I can."

"How credible is the information you called me about?" Was she on a mad hunt for information she couldn't find on nothing more than hearsay? Or gossip?

Would she stop even if she was?

What if the gossip had roots of truth?

"I'd bet my life on it."

Lily's words sealed Sarah's fate.

She couldn't tell Win the truth.

And he couldn't be anything to her other than a means to an end without it.

In his office Friday just after lunch, Win was relieved to have time to himself stretching ahead for the next few hours as all of the partners spent time in their respective offices—five of the seven moving in their new furniture and learning the new phone system. He thought over the morning's quarterly meeting, the more than healthy financials he'd presented, and couldn't help the swell of pride that washed over him. He and his partners, his college friends, really had moved some of the mountains they'd set out to move. There were higher mountains to climb. More than he could count.

But they were there.

Doing it.

As the quiet fell behind his closed office door, he couldn't help but be aware of an emptiness, something he hadn't felt in a long time. Sierra would be proud of them all. He missed her every day.

And…the void was more than that. More immediate. He missed Sarah. That morning had been the first workday without her since she'd been hired. Lindsay was off for the day, too, but...

Straightening the knot on his tie, he reminded himself about the firm's success, about the partners who were all there together—and counting on him to do his part.

So thinking, he turned on his computer and focused on that which he could control, that which served him well, that which he served well—his work.

He'd been at it an hour—successfully—when his phone rang. Glancing up distractedly, he saw the caller ID, and all focus fled.

"Sarah? You okay?" She was off for the day. No reason for her to...

"I'm fine," she said, her voice sounding a bit like she was in a tunnel. Like her phone was a little muffled. "You're at work, right? I'm not interrupting free time..."

Heart pounding, he wanted to be through with the small talk. "Yeah, I'm at work. But I can be available. What's up?"

"I just had something to run by you. I've been thinking about Milford, and I know this is probably way out there, off the wall, but..."

"Wait." He wanted to hear what she had to say, but...

"What?"

"Where are you?"

"On Highway 10, just past Quartzsite, why?"

"You're on your way to California?" It was none of his damned business. None. Period.

"On my way home."

None. Of. His. Business.

She'd been on his mind far too much the day before.

She'd been in California? And was already heading back?

"You had the weekend, you could have stayed," he said. "Milford can wait…"

"I never stay more than two nights," she told him. And then sighed, as though there was more.

He wanted more.

"My mom and I always spend the holidays at Disneyland," she said, sounding as though she was imparting bad news.

He found it…odd. To the extreme. But…

"Why?"

"That's it…why?"

"I'm sorry, I shouldn't have asked." He was way too close to breaking his promise to himself. Letting himself get personal with Sarah. But where did kind human interaction cross the line into more?

"No…it's… I generally don't tell people, but when I do…well, anyone I've told in the past has been…more reactionary… No one's ever just asked why."

A polite way of telling him to mind his own business? He didn't blame her. Was grateful to her, really, for stopping him before he made a mess of things.

"Like I said, I was out of line…what was it you wanted to tell me about Milford?"

"My mom has a heroin addiction."

Leaning back in his chair, he closed his eyes. Rubbed them and then pulled his hand down over the rest of his face.

Professional or no, boss or no, he couldn't just leave that out there as though it hadn't been said.

"How long?" he asked.

"My whole life, on and off."

That's why she'd lived with her grandmother. And why her grandmother had left her the house. The woman had died when Sarah was ten...

It seemed like a dozen things sprang to mind that he could say. Questions he wanted to ask. He didn't want to screw up the conversation. Offend her.

Be too overpowering.

"She'd been clean for a while before my grandmother died, but after that...it was tough for a while. Both of my grandparents had decent life insurance policies, and she was the beneficiary, but the money couldn't be touched, except to pay taxes and utilities on the house, until I turned eighteen."

"They didn't want her to use the money up on drugs."

"Grandma wanted her to have to work because when she was working, she generally stayed sober. She's a chef, a great one, and loved being in the kitchen. She still does. She's the head chef at a rehab resort in Anaheim."

"And she's clean?"

"Since I was sixteen."

Ten to sixteen...hard years for any kid...but dealing with her grandmother's death and a mother who was struggling with drugs...

His gut wrenched with a need to take that away from her. To somehow make it better.

The knowledge that he couldn't ate at him. The helplessness...

"Anyway, she's very regimented with her life, has routines that keep her feeling emotionally healthy, and one of those is to lose herself in make-believe during the holidays..."

He'd been imagining her with a boyfriend. Hoping she was happy with whoever he was. Envying the guy...

And she'd been off with her mother, being an incredibly loyal daughter to a woman who'd given her, at least in part, a really rough childhood.

If it was possible to fall in love with someone you'd only known a short time, and who was only an employee, someone he'd never even been on a date with, he might have just done so. A little bit.

"Sierra's father was an alcoholic." The words were in the air before he'd been cognizant enough to stop them. He needed her to know that he had some understanding of what she'd been through. A frame of reference.

For the most part, he could only imagine. His parents had been the best.

"Sierra's Web Sierra." Statement, not question.

"Yeah," he said anyway.

"No one ever really talks about her."

Turning in his chair so his back was to the door, so he faced the wall and not the faces of partners in the suite, he knew he should give the brief version of the story that they gave to prospective clients who asked, to news outlets when they came to do stories about them. But he also knew he wouldn't. For the first time ever, he wanted to share Sierra with someone.

Sarah had done that for him. He didn't understand. Didn't know why.

"She was special," he said, hearing his voice lower. Had to swallow. "I'll tell you about her, but not now. The others are all here…"

The significance of that would make no sense to her—he knew it as he said it.

"We… I'd just rather tell you about her when…"

"You were in love with her…"

"No one knew." He was near tears. Could feel them

pushing up against the back of his lids. What the hell? He hadn't cried since the day of Sierra's funeral.

"Are you telling me they still don't know?"

"I am." He turned toward the door. Sat up straight.

"Did she know?" The question should have seemed far too personal, coming from an employee of a few weeks. It seemed…natural. Right.

For the first time in ten years, something felt…as though it was as it should be.

"Can we talk about this at another time?" he asked her.

"I'm sorry. I'm the one who's being out of line. Put it down to being out here in the middle of flat nowhere without an exit in sight…"

He'd made the drive, crossing the desert to California, and could picture that two-hour-long stretch of nearly exitless highway.

"Strangely, your questions don't seem out of line at all." He told her the truth. "I'd like to tell you about her. Just not like this."

"I'd like to hear about her."

So…was it a date then? The two of them getting together to talk about his broken heart? Or a boss telling his employee about the person for whom their business was named?

He couldn't ask. As her boss, to do so would be out of line. Could be seen as pressuring her to spend time with him on a personal basis.

"About Milford…"

Right. The reason for her call. Strictly business.

"I'm listening."

"The random scattering of bank accounts you've found…"

He knew the ones to which she was referring. All at various different banks and credit unions. Some with branches in Phoenix, some not. Each account in his name, with two letters separated from his name by a comma coming after, as though they were the man's credentials.

"Like the one at Jasper Credit Union. James W. Milford, HN…"

"It's one of the more lucrative ones," he acknowledged.

"Right, well I was thinking about those bank accounts and the spreadsheets while I'm out here with only coyotes and roadrunners for company. Maybe this is nuts, but can you bring up the Milford spreadsheets?"

He was already doing so. "Of course. Got them."

"Open the one for after he'd seen the light." She'd labeled them "before light" and "after light." When he'd first seen the designations, they'd made him grin.

"Got it."

"Look down the column for groceries. What do you see?"

"Albertos." All the way down the list. "He only shopped for groceries at Albertos." And Win only shopped at his choice of national grocery chain. Partially because it was just a couple of miles from home.

"Right. Now look at music."

"Rock It." Again, one place, but…

"Eating out."

There were four of them. Hometown Bagels. Romocini Pasta. Jose Casita. And Roberts Steaks and Gourmet Burgers.

He was seeing a pattern. Glanced over other parts of the list. Auto repair. Even dental work.

"He doesn't frequent any chain stores at all. Not for anything. He only bought from mom-and-pop-type, one-of-a-kind establishments."

"Yes, but that's not where I'm going with this. It's critical to it, though." Her tone, coming from what he now knew to be the audio system in her car, reminded him that she was out on a desert highway, the sun shining, mountains way off in the distance, and he was filled with a huge longing to be in that vehicle with her.

Just sitting beside her, having the exact conversation they were having.

"Now look at those initials after Milford's name on all those random accounts..."

He was looking at them. They meant nothing to him. There was no professional designation that he knew of for RI, or JE. The list went on.

"Those initials all coincide with the first and last letter of the first name of one of those businesses..."

He had the list—and the spreadsheet—right in front of him. She'd been going from memory. Surely the one or two she'd remembered were just coincidences. But... nope, as he ran down the two lists, he found regular expenditures for a place whose first and last letter corresponded with bank account initials.

What the hell!

"I think that he had to have had some kind of connection with them all," she told him. "I have no idea what. That's not my area of expertise, but it's too much to be just by chance, don't you think?"

He didn't know what to think. The theory was out there.

He didn't want to tell her so. It was Sarah. He only wanted to bring praise into her life.

And…he had to agree that…wow…it was weird, at the very least.

"I've crossed into strange territory out here, haven't I?" she asked, not sounding all that hurt by his lack of response. "It was worth a try, you know. And seemed like…"

"I'm going to check it out," he said aloud as he reached the conclusion. "As I look at the deposits into those accounts, while they came in on different days of the month, every single one of them had deposits either once or twice a month on a regular basis."

"I didn't remember that, but there's a column on the spreadsheet that shows deposits."

"I know. I saw it."

"Don't feel like you have to waste your time on my account, Win," she said then, her tone coming across as easy, as though she truly didn't care.

And maybe she didn't. He was just part of her new job.

"I'm going to look into it because I can't find another explanation for those initials. And, as you say, every single one fits."

"They do? I was only remembering a few of them offhand, but…"

"It could be that Milford was getting payouts from all of these businesses, Hometown included…"

"I was thinking more along the lines of looking up the places he spent money that we don't have corresponding initialed accounts for and go from there to find other accounts…"

Or go to the businesses with a more serious request for any financial information to do with James W. Milford.

Because she was right…while there was most likely

a perfectly legitimate reason for those accounts and deposits—since they were just sitting out there, un-claimed—there were likely more of them. And find-ing them was his job.

"I'm on it," he told her, already calling up Connolly's number in his contacts. "Thank you, Sarah, this could be just what we needed, and even if it's not…this is great work."

He was impressed all over again—which probably wasn't good on a personal level. He'd deal with that later.

"Good. I'm glad I could help."

Telling her to be safe—wanting to ask but refrain-ing from asking her to text him when she was safely across the desert—he hung up, filled with anticipation.

For the work ahead only, he told himself.

But he didn't believe it.

Chapter Seven

Thoughts of Win spun with every turn of the wheel from the end of their conversation, continuing even as Sarah passed through the tip of west Phoenix on her way toward the east valley. From guilt to confession—always landing her solidly back at absolutely not confessing to him—and from there to does he like me, too?

Such a juvenile thing. Not that it was coming across her mind in quite that way, but basically that was what it boiled down to. It seemed that she was developing a serious case of "wants" for her boss, and a part of her was getting the idea that maybe he returned the feelings.

He'd confided in her—sort of—about something he hadn't even told his partners. His best friends. Who were his family.

That was what was keeping her usual mojo out of reach. She'd learned a long time ago how to take life in stride, to keep her head up and her feet stepping forward, without getting into any more potholes.

And it seemed like those feet she'd always relied on had walked her into what might be the biggest ditch of her life.

It didn't go unnoticed that Lily had led her straight to it, either.

With one phone call that Sarah needn't have heeded.

None of which changed the fact that she felt things for Winchester Holmes that she'd never felt before in her life. He seemed to be finding a strange connection to her, too.

And not only was he her boss, but her employment was a lie. She was at Sierra's Web under false pretenses.

Even if there were something between them, the potential relationship's tragic ending had already been written.

And with that last conversation hanging between them—his saying he wanted to talk more to her about Sierra, and her admitting she wanted him to do so—how could they go back and just work together as though they were virtually strangers?

Yeah, right. It wasn't just the talk of Sierra that had her incredibly on edge. Her own big mouth was as much to blame.

She'd told him about Lily, about growing up with a parent with an addiction. About Disneyland! What in the hell had she done that for?

In the six years since her mother had moved to California, she'd never told anyone about their annual jaunts to what Lily still called the Magic Kingdom.

She saw signs denoting that the Scottsdale exits were coming up, meaning that the off-ramp to her suburb would be just a bit further down the highway. Counted down the miles. Thought of Winchester sitting at the office as she watched the miles lessen to that exit in particular.

She was driving past. Off until Monday. She'd determined just west of Phoenix that she had to stay fully involved in non–Sierra's Web activities. Keep Win and all thoughts of him and his company firmly out of her head.

Or…the other option was that she checked to see if, with the partners in town, the office would be open for her to get in and work on the files.

So she could find Kylie and get out.

How ballsy would it be to search the files for her sister with all of them right there?

She'd been hired to go through all the files, organize them. Why wouldn't she be perusing them?

Who, besides Lindsay, might find that odd?

Two miles and the exit would be behind her.

How could she just waltz into the office and get to work while that intimately personal conversation with Win was hanging out there, yet to happen?

Waiting to happen?

With him expecting it to happen?

With a seemingly unreliable part of her wanting it to happen?

She had to talk to him. To put any chance of that conversation happening behind them. Get things strictly back to business.

And if he was put off by her possibly seemingly abrupt change of heart?

Well then, that was all for the better.

Crossing over three lanes, one at a time, she signaled for the Sierra's Web exit.

One thing she'd learned a long time before—when you had a tough job to do, it was best to face it and get it done.

Win was lost in his account hunt. Finding businesses from Sarah's spreadsheet on Milford, then using his various resources to see if he could ping an existing bank account in Milford's name with the appropriate corresponding initials. He was even making some discreet calls directly to businesses, simply explaining what he was doing and why. Up to his neck in success, he had to shake his head and return to the rest of the world as he heard a knock on his door.

A quick double knock, with a corresponding turn of the knob that told him, even before he saw her beautiful smiling face, that his visitor was Kelly Chase. Their psychology expert.

"You got a minute?" the partner he felt particularly close to asked, her loosely curled blond hair filling the doorway on either side of her. Her stretchy tight brown jeans and brown-and-white blouse with white tennis shoes were so…her.

"Of course."

Eyeing his desk as she sat down, she turned that knowing blue gaze on him. "The Milford case," she said, nodding toward the piles of papers and loaded computer screens, recognizing, he was sure, her own file among them.

"Yeah."

"That's why I'm here, actually," she said. "It was such an unusual case. Hard in many ways…but good, too, and so much of it isn't in the file. I know I talked to you about it back then, but maybe I can remember something that will help you in your search."

"I'm all ears."

Focused, pen in hand, he listened as she told him the things that weren't in writing, knowing he had to get it right so that he could pass it along to Sarah for her "before the light" spreadsheet.

"One of the things that made it so odd was that child services didn't initiate taking the child, Cara, from the home. They were called in but didn't see enough reason to remove the two-year-old. To the contrary, they saw a single parent who struggled with substance abuse, but who'd benefited from intervention. They'd been following the little family for nearly a year at the time and were on the verge of releasing them when the mother suddenly came to them wanting to give up the two-year-old, but only with that 100 percent assurance that the child's father would have no rights to see the child or know where she was."

Cara's mother had been protecting her against Milford.

To the point of sacrificing her own heart and soul—giving up her own child—to do so.

She'd thought him that dangerous.

Which didn't completely jibe with the spreadsheets.

Before the light, he reminded himself.

"She turned in a lot of what turned out to be circumstantial evidence on the man, a known drug dealer who police had been watching. But they could never get enough evidence on him, directly, to make charges stick," Kelly continued, then told him something he didn't know. Or hadn't remembered. "James Milford grew up in the system, too, but was placed early in a good foster family and stayed there. He went on to get a degree in business. He wasn't a typical street thug. Just got hooked on heroin in high school, starting with a party he and Cara's mother attended their junior year in high school, where they'd been given the stuff without knowing what it was…"

All news to him. Maybe big news.

"It all went downhill from there. By the time Cara's mother had the attention of child services, Milford was running a drug empire that served mostly white-collar clients and running what amounted to his own prostitution ring on the side, though he never took money for couples having sex."

That part he remembered.

"As I recall, he pimped out women who were hooked and offering to have sex for a fix—college girls mostly. Milford would find a john, the guy would buy the woman her drugs from one of Milford's associates, the sex happened and both parties left satisfied."

"Right."

He wasn't proud of the words that left his mouth then. They bordered on vile and were beneath him.

Wasn't proud that he was taking that part of the case personally.

Sierra's situation wasn't the same, at all, but it had some of the same elements. Sex and drugs.

She just hadn't been into either. Not drugs at all. And sex…not with the guy who'd killed her…

"According to what I was told, Cara's mother never had sex for a fix. She just had it with Milford. She fell in love with the guy in high school and fell back into him any time she went off the wagon."

Feeling dirty as he looked at all the information he'd

compiled on the guy, as he realized just how far he'd let the man into his own psyche in his attempt to think enough like him to find his money, Win felt doubly sick at the thought that he had Sarah doing the same.

Spending so much of her time with Milford when...

Her own mother had struggled with addiction. Still struggled from the aftereffects of it. Shaping Sarah's whole life, still.

Sarah didn't need to live the tragedy again through someone else.

And there wasn't any need for Sarah to ever know the things Kelly was telling him. He'd only thought he'd share if they'd help. He certainly had no obligation to do so.

"Milford had already signed away any rights to Cara, an agreement they'd come to earlier, relieving him of child support. But here's the real kicker, and what's bothering me now that this case of yours has come up..."

There was more?

"The woman had another child, one Milford had fathered in high school, that he didn't know was his. She was reportedly terrified that he'd somehow get suspicious and get his clutches in the older child..."

That was brand-new.

"Did he show any interest in doing so?"

"Not that I ever heard." She paused. Frowned. "But since I wasn't personally involved with that part of it, who knows? I came on board after the agreement with the mother was sealed and only know what I know from conversation with the social worker involved. As you probably remember, my job was just interviewing the potential adopters. I had nothing to do with the legal or criminal aspects of the case. Never even met the toddler. And I can't help thinking now…there's this other kid out there who could probably use some financial security…"

And who was completely out of their jurisdiction. Period.

He knew Kelly knew that. But that shadow in her eyes…she'd come to him for more than just storytelling.

"Did you feel good about being a part of what had happened back then?"

Her shrug was telling. She wanted to feel good about it. "I mostly did. It sounded like the mother was sincere. And that she was right. Given the circumstances, it was absolutely best for the two-year-old not to grow up as the older child had done—with a parent who'd been in and out of sobriety, with and without the ability to provide. I remember that the older kid had already been in some trouble. And frankly, it was probably best for the mother as well. Two kids would have stretched her thinner, making another setback more likely. And I believed that the mother was acting altruistically, that she truly wanted what was best for her child and knew that she was not it."

"Believed?" He caught the word.

"I don't know." That shrug again. And blue eyes turned on him filled with the same doubt he saw in his own mirror when he let himself look that closely.

They'd been wrong before.

And their friend had died.

"Does a drug-dealing father leave everything he amassed to a child he didn't want?" she asked, worry lacing her tone.

He wanted to reassure her. He just wasn't sure he could. He didn't have any more answers than she did.

"Obviously he signed her away or the adoption couldn't have happened," she continued. "It just seems like there's more to the story."

"Did you ever hear what happened to the older kid?" He had to ask. Because he suspected the girl was weighing on Kelly's heart.

Kelly shrugged. "I hope she came out okay. I never met her, of course. Didn't even know her name. All I know is that she'd already been in trouble. Enough to have a record."

"Could you look up the mother?" With the internet, things were different in terms of what you could find, just to ease your mind.

She shook her head. "I never even knew the mother's name. Just had a glimpse of her once, in the courthouse, when she was pointed out to me. The whole point of the adoption was for it to be sealed. Names of the family giving the child up were on a need-to-know basis, and I didn't need to know."

Nodding, he got to his point. "Then there's no way you can find her, no way to know whatever became of her…" He let the words trail off.

"I need to let it go." She gave him the slow smile that always settled his stomach, like the quiet in the valley after a rare storm—a peaceful calm. Kelly had always been that for him…the calm after a storm.

He grinned back. "I have this psychiatrist friend I could hook you up with, but I've been around her enough, listened to her enough, to know that that's probably exactly what she'd tell you."

"Smart-ass." Her smile was full force then, and it felt

good to help her. It was what they did, the partners of Sierra's Web. They'd all been part of discovering their friend's dead body. And would all live with the aftermath of that for the rest of their lives. Out of despair, a bond had been formed that would never be broken.

And he had one last tidbit for her. "You can rest assured that I'm doing all I can for the child," he told her.

"I already know that," she said. She stood and moved to the door, then turned back to look at him. "You seem different."

Nope. Off-limits. Even to her.

"I got my hair cut."

"It's always been that short."

"I didn't shave as well as usual this morning. Rough blade and no time to change it out..."

With a frown, followed by another grin and a nod, she left.

And he was glad to be alone with thoughts of Sarah.

Of what he was not going to tell her about James Milford.

And what he wanted more than ever to tell her about Sierra, for no good or rational reason he could find.

He was on emotional overload.

And needed to get off.

Sarah was nothing if not honest with herself, no matter how hard the practice was sometimes. Since her grandmother's death she'd learned loud and clear that the only thing she could trust in life was herself. And she'd lose that if she started practicing dishonesty with herself.

That thought clearly in mind, she wasn't just thinking of Win as she sat in her car in the parking lot outside the elite high-rise that housed Sierra's Web offices just after three on Friday.

She had to talk to him. To get them out of the muck they'd just made for themselves with their last phone conversation. To get the half of them she had control over out of it. What he did was his business.

But she also wanted to meet Kelly. Who knew when the psychiatrist might be back in town, and in the back of Sarah's mind, the woman had always been the person she'd had to trust to have done a good job with Kylie's placement.

The fact that they'd lost Kylie had been Sarah's fault, not Kelly Chase's. But the choice as to what family Kylie had been forever placed with…that had been on Kelly.

She needed to get a feel for the woman.

To know whether or not she trusted her to have done right by Kylie.

And maybe…just maybe…she could find out more about her sister's whereabouts.

Not with a direct question, of course. That would be ludicrous for all aforementioned reasons. But maybe something…

Yet there she sat, in the navy pants, off-white tank and navy-and-off-white short, cropped jacket she'd specifically packed for the long drive home in case she did decide to go into work.

To meet Kelly had been her original thought. She'd been on the fence about doing it. She'd been leaning toward no, though, pretty sure she hadn't been going to, until that conversation with Win.

Squaring her shoulders, she said aloud, "Get your big girl panties on and get going."

A phrase her grandmother used to say when faced

with something you weren't sure you could do. Or wanted to do.

She wasn't a kid anymore.

Hadn't been for a long, long time.

She didn't call first, didn't want to interrupt the precious time everyone had in their offices together, just intended to slip in and slip out...

And the second she got off the elevator facing the glass door of their suite, Lindsay saw her, jumped up out of her chair and came toward the door.

What, the other woman was going to tell her she wasn't allowed to trespass on their day? Warn her that the partners were too busy to be bothered by her poking around their things?

"Sarah! Come in," she said instead, a smile on her face as she held the door for her. "I had the day off, too, but with everyone in town, I decided to come in. I know everyone was hoping to meet you. Come on, I'll introduce you around."

What followed was a whirlwind of what started out as private office visits, with Dorian first, but quickly turned into a party in the hallway with everyone greeting her, asking her about her holiday, telling her they'd missed her the day before. There were jokes about Win's cooking, which, by the sound of things, had actually been great, and profuse thanks for all of the help she'd been to them already.

Lindsay jumped in whenever she could, answering questions posed to Sarah, if she knew the answers, acting as though hiring Sarah had been her idea all along.

Oddly, the woman's proprietary manner with her was welcome. The protective older woman was showing her acceptance in the way she knew how.

And acceptance, as it turned out, was something Sarah craved.

She hadn't known that about herself. But it was the only explanation she had for the emotion building up inside her, the tears near the surface, due to their kindness.

Completely overwhelmed, she almost thanked them and left. But when the partners started asking questions about phones, a desk lock and new filing cabinets, and Mariah stepped up to say she got to be first as she had family waiting for her to go out to dinner and see zoo lights, and then Kelly called seconds, she knew she wasn't going anywhere.

Not yet, at any rate.

She had work to do.

Chapter Eight

Kelly Chase, while intimidating as hell, turned out to be one of the kindest women Sarah could ever remember meeting. Immediately at ease, Sarah answered questions, explained technical aspects of remote connection and text message transfer and then, before she could lose her nerve, asked Kelly about her filing system as a way to make certain that her overhaul didn't completely confuse the psychiatrist expert.

Of course, she found a way to work in the county cases, wanting to know if Kelly preferred to keep them in a separate drawer or to have them filed by date as a few of the partners had done in their individual offices.

She asked, ostensibly, because she'd noticed a series of them that had been kept together.

And she asked because she hoped to hear where the rest of them were currently being kept. Kylie's in particular.

"As far as I know, they're all still together," the beautiful blonde said, her smile somewhat self-deprecating, and easy, too. "I had them in drawers by date, but then needed access to them by name, not always knowing the date right offhand, and so…"

"And there's why we need them filed by name," Sarah said, changing course midstream on her Kelly filing plan and acknowledging, to herself, that she actually had found a small measure of relief where Kylie was concerned.

Knowing that she'd been in Kelly's good hands.

Didn't mean Kylie wasn't in some kind of upheaval eight years later, but at least she'd started out with a caring and compassionate woman at her back.

"I can make a spreadsheet for you," Sarah half blurted, getting herself back into a conversation she'd technically never left. "I'll cross-reference names with dates so that you can search by date and see what client names you dealt with at what times." She'd helped a doctor at the clinic arrange her files similarly, a doctor who liked to keep paper copies in addition to all the online charting that happened by rote in the medical field.

She'd already worked out a cross-reference plan between digital and paper files for the whole office overhaul. And it was becoming apparent that everyone, regardless of filing by date or job name, would need that same plan applied to their files.

Good. She was moving forward on the job they'd hired her to do.

And had just reached another dead end with Kylie. As far as Kelly knew, all the county files were together. Either Kylie was lost in another file drawer—which could take weeks to find—or she just wasn't there. Neither one was the answer Sarah had been hoping to find.

But it didn't slow down her determination even a little bit. Moving on to the other partners, giving them her full focus while she was with them, she knew she was committing herself to finishing the work she was starting.

And in doing so, she was buying herself more time to find her baby sister's information. Somehow.

She just had to get things straight with Win before that went someplace that derailed everything.

Which was why she kept herself busy until everyone else had left for the day. Several of the partners were meeting up at a club by the condo the firm kept for the out-of-town partners. She'd heard Win say he might see them shortly. And grabbed her chance to realign their association when she knew it would have to be short and sweet.

Knocking on his opened door, she asked, "You got a minute?"

Met his gaze across the room.

Felt as though the conversation happened of its own accord. Without words.

And forgot why she was there.

He'd been waiting for hours to see her. Had come up with a valid, business reason to ask her to stick around until after the others left in case she'd popped in to say she was leaving.

He'd way overstepped his boundaries with her on the phone earlier, and, regardless of whether or not she'd welcomed the conversation—started it, even—he had

to extricate them from a situation that was rife with potential land mines.

The whole boss falling for his secretary thing just
didn't fly anymore.

Did it?

He was pretty sure it didn't.

She'd asked him if he had a minute as though she'd
had something on her mind. And hadn't said a word.

Because things had become awkward between them?

God, he hoped not.

But he knew it made sense.

He was the boss. It was up to him to fix things.

"You were a big hit with the partners today," he told
her, with an aim to get them firmly back on business
footing and sticking his foot in it instead. Trying too
hard to make her feel good, rather than stepping back.
"Not that I doubted for a second that you would be," he
continued, sinking deeper into…he didn't know what.

He just…liked the woman. A lot.

And wanted her life to be as happy as it could be.

He was drawn to her…

And the truth would set him free. While it tangled
him all up.

"Have a seat," he said, thinking they were about to
have a closed-door conversation. But because he was
her boss, he couldn't close the door to have it.

The fact that he didn't need to, since they were alone
in the suite, didn't change the difficult situation he was
in.

When she sat, ramrod straight, on the edge of her
chair, he knew he hadn't misjudged the new awkwardness between them. Hated that he'd helped create it.

"I just wanted to say, regarding…earlier… I apologize for unloading on you, about my mother and all." She flicked back the straight dark hair that had fallen over her shoulder, as though irritated with it for not minding its manners, and then continued without taking a breath. "What can I say? Alone in the middle of nowhere, you tend to get a little chatty. Beats falling asleep at the wheel…"

She was giving him the blow off.

Before he could politely suck himself back in.

She was giving him exactly what he wanted. Making it easy on him.

With her words.

Those big brown eyes…the cropped jacket that looked way too professional for a day-off drive across the desert alone…they were telling him a different story.

"I can say that I was touched that you trusted me enough to tell me the truth."

Had he just made a dig at her? For lying to him about their earlier confidences just being an attempt to stay awake on a long drive?

So not like him.

And yet…oddly satisfying.

Completely off task, too.

The exact opposite of what he was supposed to be doing.

She swallowed. Stared at him.

The truth was there. Waiting.

He was the boss.

"The truth is… I find you… I'm… I relate to you." He ended up with a much weaker rendition of what he'd wanted to say. "I'm your boss. And I cannot in any way, nor do I intend to, make something out of it. I just… relate to you. You need not fear that this in any way affects our working relationship, nor will it have any effect on your job. I don't expect anything from you.

"For that matter," he continued, really gearing up as he got in his stride, "I would turn you down if you indicated that you in any way returned the...sense of connection."

"I return the...sense of connection." She repeated his words—and his tone.

He stared.

She watched him. Seeming to be waiting.

Testing him?

He'd said he'd turn her down.

But she hadn't offered anything...just stated fact.

Or messed with his fact.

God, he sucked at this.

Which was why he stuck to numbers. They always added up, once you found them all. Everything had an answer, and the answers were clear. Provable. Definable.

They just plain made sense.

"See, my way was better," she said then. "Just blaming it on the oddness of the moment. Me out on the road not wanting to fall asleep."

"The truth is always better," he returned immediately. "Because sooner or later, it catches up to you."

Those brown eyes looked almost frightened for a second there. Still wide, they remained glued to him, as though waiting for him to save the moment.

Save them.

God knew, he was no savior.

And he wanted to be.

So badly.

"Just to get this out of the way..." She sat forward

even further, to the point he wondered how she wasn't sliding off the edge of the seat. "No matter what this is here, it does not in any way constitute you coming on to me or being inappropriate. You've been the epitome of proper and have shown me utmost respect. You being my boss, I'm taking that permanently off the table. And I'll put that in writing." She grabbed a legal pad off his desk. And a pen from the leather holder Lindsay had given him for Christmas one year.

"Stop," he said, reaching to take the pad before she got it fully away. "You're not going to put anything in writing."

Her shrug, the resolute look that came over her face, didn't bode well for him. He knew it.

And loved it, anyway.

"I will put it in writing, Win," she said. "Maybe not on that pad, maybe not in this minute, or with this pen, but I have the right to do this. I feel the need to do it. And I will do it."

"I can't just tell you that I accept your assertion and it's off the table and we leave it at that?" He almost smiled, sensing that she was enjoying the moment as much as he suddenly was.

"Depends."

"On what?"

"On what we decide to do about it."

He opened his mouth to send a line right back to her. Nothing came out.

She'd won the round.

This weird thing she was feeling…this…caring for a man she'd so recently met—wasn't just her.

He felt something, too, and she had absolutely no plan

for that. No idea what to do with it. The whole thing spoke disaster.

But she wasn't walking away.

She couldn't. Kylie's happiness could depend on her finding the little girl. And every day longer that it took for her to do that mattered.

"I need you to know that I'm not looking for any kind of relationship—romantic or otherwise—at the moment. I'm not in a place in my life where I'd be good in one." The words poured out of her while she watched him.

His expression didn't seem to change much.

He still looked bemused. And more happy than sad.

Had he heard her?

Was there any chance at all that when he found out she'd been lying to him, he'd forgive her? Any chance at all for a future for them?

Because...why couldn't she be ready for a relationship, once she knew Kylie was okay? She'd worked her way through nursing school! Had her license. Had a home that was paid for and was ready to start her life.

Having someone of her own, someone to come home to, someone to care for, someone to know her, to care if she made it home...she wanted all those things.

No.

She couldn't go there.

Not yet.

"Not that you were offering any kind of... What I'm trying to say is that—" she broke off as he continued to watch her. "I don't know what I'm trying to say."

"I find it hard to resist the temptation to be in your presence."

She stared. "Yeah, that might have been it."

"I also am not open to a relationship," he told her. "Not in a romantic sense."

Well. Rejection sure took energy out of a woman. She'd thought he…well, it didn't matter what she'd thought.

Even though nothing could come of it, even if it was doomed from the start, she'd liked the idea that he was attracted to her.

And what did that say about her? Something pathetic, she was sure.

"That said, I do friendship really well," he continued.

To which she said, "I'd like to do it well."

"You don't think you do?"

"I've never given myself a chance to find out."

"You took in classmates as roommates." She forgot she'd told him that. What was it about this man that she was putting herself out there to him, confiding in him, when she'd never been a person who did that?

"I have friends," she told him, maybe in an attempt to reel herself in, to take back the things she'd given him.

But he already had them. They weren't the kind of things you could just grab back and remove from his possession. Giving yourself…your story…your pain… didn't take it away from you, she realized. It just multiplied it onto another.

"I'm just not…emotionally close with them. Not like you are with your partners, here."

She envied them. So much.

Had been falling in love with the idea of such closeness over the past few hours. Wanting in. Even as she planned to use them all for her own gain.

Which was the antithesis of the type of relationship they all shared.

Because the basis of that bond was trust.

And she...

Would he understand? Forgive her?

"You're what, thirty-two?" she asked him. Based on the math she'd pieced together in the partners' friendships, their graduation from college, the birth of their firm.

"Thirty-three."

"I'm twenty-four." And felt like forty.

"I know."

Of course he did. He'd seen her personal information when he'd hired her.

And it wasn't like the nine years between them mattered. They weren't starting anything romantic.

But they were starting something. She wouldn't be in his office having this bizarre nonconversation if they weren't.

And as awkward as sitting there talking to him was, she didn't want to leave.

"I've got things to do, a life to set up, before I can think about inviting someone else into it." She started in with what she'd meant to say to begin with. A precursor to what he might eventually find out—that she had to get Kylie's situation clarified, in case she had to do something to help her baby sister, before she could focus on starting her own future.

But what if he didn't find out? What if she got her information without anyone knowing and learned that Kylie was happy and loved and healthy? Would he ever need to know that she'd applied to Sierra's Web with an ulterior motive?

The idea had occurred to her more than once since she'd walked into that room. Was it worth entertaining?

"But you… You're set," she said when he didn't respond to her pronouncement. She motioned around the room. "You've got a dream job, are partner in a hugely successful firm, you've just bought a house—a lovely one, I'm told by Dorian and some of the others— Why wouldn't you be ready for a relationship?"

And lest he get the wrong idea… "You're kind and hot and successful, Win. You need to be out there. You'd have your pick of women who'd fill that house with…"

A pang hit her heart and she stopped. No, wait. What was she doing? Pushing him out the door into another woman's arms?

And why shouldn't she be? "You deserve to be loved and adored," she told him. Good. Good. Steering the conversation away from them. That's what she'd set out to do.

Though she'd gone a roundabout way to get there, she was reaching her goal. One that she'd thought through and believed was for the best. Dialing back their earlier move toward becoming…something.

"You think I'm hot?"

"You don't?" He had to know he was. Fishing for compliments didn't seem like him.

He wasn't smiling. His lack of forthcoming was beginning to frustrate her. Or upset her. They had a situation and they needed to deal with it. Figure it out, know what it was and have a plan for moving forward.

She couldn't come to work every day all in a tizzy.

"I'm not open to a romantic, committed, long-term relationship because I know I'm not good at them." His words, when they came, were a shock.

And seemed to be well-thought-out, too. He hadn't blurted them. He'd meant them to be revealed.

His confidence in the truth behind the statement made it impossible for her to argue with him. But she didn't believe him, either.

The words rang false to her.

"How do you know?"

He watched her, loosening the knot on his tie a little. That small movement, his hand at his neck, pulling downward rather than straightening as he usually did…she stared.

Knowing something was happening that mattered. And that they wouldn't be able to go back to who they'd been when she'd walked in the room.

"I know because I've been in two of them," he told her. "And I failed both times."

He didn't sound like someone who was looking for sympathy. Or absolution, either. He sounded sure. Accepting. And…responsible.

Taking accountability for his actions.

Growing up with Lily, Sarah had found that trait to be sadly lacking so much of the time. So she valued it above most others.

"People learn from their mistakes," she said. Something she'd discovered the hard way. "You don't rob yourself of the rest of your life. You just change your behavior so you don't repeat the mistake."

"Some things can't be changed."

"What's so wrong with you that a woman couldn't love you in spite of it?" She didn't care if the question was right or wrong. She had to know his answer. To help him see another side.

The task seemed critical.

"You're already seeing it," he told her. "I see numbers. Facts. Figures. I have an inability to perceive nuances, even when they're right in front of me. I don't read people well."

"You seem to get me."

"Yes, well, that is part of the reason I'm so intrigued by you."

"Part of the reason?" She asked for more, even knowing they were right where they'd set out not to be.

"My last partner, in Arkansas, where I had an apartment before moving here, found me far too protective— her way of saying nicely that I was constantly checking up on her."

"You stalked your last partner?" She didn't believe it.

"Of course not. But I wanted to know what she was doing so I could be prepared to help her if she needed it. She had a history of leaping before she looked, and while she acknowledged that, she still spent a lot of time, which involved a lot of our time, cleaning up behind herself."

"That sounds like her problem, not yours."

"Yeah, and if I could have just left it at that…but I couldn't. I was constantly trying to prevent disaster that I couldn't perceive. I couldn't read her, or a situation, so I'd ask questions, and then I'd see something worrisome and mention it to her. She didn't want to hear it. So she started lying to me, just to get out from under my need to protect…and I couldn't stay in a relationship with lies between us."

Sarah definitely saw a problem in the relationship, but it wasn't Win. And probably hadn't been his partner, either. "You two were clearly not meant for each other," she told him.

One thing did become clear to her though, right then,

like a slap in the face—Win wasn't going to forgive her for the lies she was living at Sierra's Web.

No matter what they decided to do about the attraction between them—one that went much deeper than physical—the end result would be the same.

They weren't going to make it together forever.

Chapter Nine

Win and Emily, the woman he'd left behind in Arkansas, hadn't been meant for each other, but their problems had been deeper than that, too. He wasn't going to argue the point with Sarah.

He was a facts guy. And the facts were, as long as he and Sarah were clear on what they didn't want, as long as they were talking, no more needed to be said.

Sierra—and everything attached to her—was his to deal with. "As long as my enjoyment in spending time with you isn't an issue for you, and you don't feel in any way uncomfortable or harassed by it, then we should be okay here," he said.

"Spending time with me—" Of course she'd picked up on the most damning phrase.

"Being in your company," he interrupted to clarify.

She nodded. Stood. Rested that so-sexy thigh in those navy pants on the corner of his desk. Almost as though she knew full well the effect her nearness was having on him. Physically.

"Here they are, Win, the facts. I'm attracted to you. Your person, your mind, the leanness of your body even when you're hunched over your keyboard. The way you straighten your tie when you're gearing up for something. I'm hoping that what you've been trying so hard not to actually say out loud is that you're attracted to me. Because otherwise this is going to be incredibly embarrassing..."

The word drifted off. She pinned him with those big brown eyes.

He saw the vulnerability there. Something he was pretty sure she didn't let loose very often. If ever.

"I am."

"Good. There. It's out in the open. As is the fact that neither of us is ready for any kind of deep, committed romantic relationship."

He was ready. Just not good enough at it to risk hurting her. Or worse, letting her down when she needed him most.

He let that translate into a nod of agreement to her statement.

"Obviously this...liking of one another...isn't going to go away in the next day or two, so what we need is a plan to move forward through it."

Through it. What in the hell did that mean?

He focused on the plan part. That he understood. And wanted. "I'd like for us to be friends," he said, feeling the words clear to his heart. She wanted a friend. "That I know I can do well," he told her. "I'm new to the area. I could use a friend. Someone to hang out with over the holidays and such—understanding that you're previously committed for Christmas Eve and New Year's."

There was no mistaking the pleasure his words had given her. Her smile stretched all the way across that strong and beautiful face. "Friends with benefits?" she asked, sucker punching him again.

God, yes. But… "Do you want that?"

"Part of me does." There was no shyness in her words, but she was frowning.

"I can guess which part," he teased—shocking himself. Hud would have spit beer if he'd heard that one coming from him. It was more like something Hud or Glen, their forensic scientist partner, would say. "But I'm voting for leaving that one on the table, for now. Until one or the other of us wants it, or doesn't want it, wholeheartedly."

Her grin made him want it wholeheartedly. She slid off the desk—a huge disappointment—onto the chair she'd vacated, relaxing back as though she meant to stay awhile. And then said, "You want to go get something to eat? I'm starved."

He had leftover Thanksgiving dinner waiting at home.

And knew that sex would also be on the table if he took her to his place. Maybe even literally. Apparently once unleashed, his libido was going to be out of control where she was concerned as well.

That part didn't bother him all that much. His sexual desires, while definitely making him physically uncomfortable at times, were something he knew he could control.

"You feel like Italian?" he asked her. There was a quaint eatery not far from his place—one he'd wanted to try out, but the kind you didn't go to alone without seeming conspicuous.

"I love Italian." Of course she did.

And when she said that she'd follow him in her car rather than driving together, he wasn't surprised by that, either.

The woman was made for him.

As long as he didn't start taking more than he could handle.

That Thanksgiving weekend was maybe one of the best of her life. Dinner Friday night was relaxed, fun and…real. She and Win just talked. About foods they liked, movies they'd seen. Mountains they wanted to climb.

And when the meal was over, they walked to their cars, separating as they drew closer to two different driver's doors, and waved good-night. As she reached her car, unlocked it and got inside, she noticed him still outside his, watching over her. And got all warm and fuzzy inside.

He'd paid for dinner. She hadn't argued.

On Saturday, he'd said he planned to work and, excited to have a chance to spend time looking through files without Lindsay at her back, she told him she'd like to join him, and did. She brought Hometown Bagels, which they'd eaten separately in their respective workspaces.

He bought lunch, had it delivered, and after they'd decided to call it quits for the day, her discouragement at not finding a single thing on Kylie eased when he asked her if she'd like to get some dinner.

They went to a Mexican place she'd always loved.

Over chimichangas he talked about his parents, about the vacations the three of them had taken, his dad's job as a firefighter and getting to ride in the truck a time or two. About his mom's volunteering to help with whatever activity he happened to take up, from chess tournaments to a short stint in Little League. Sarah wished she'd had a chance to meet them. And told him so.

She also told him about her grandmother. About Lily having been clean from the time she'd found out she was pregnant with Sarah until after Sarah's grandfather died. About the good times she and her mom and grandma had had during the years Lily was clean. The catering business her mom had been a part of for a while and the functions Sarah had attended with her.

She didn't talk much about the hard times, only alluding to them when they interrupted the good.

And when dinner was through, they walked to their cars, separating as they had the night before, waving good-night, and her turning around to find him watching her from his car.

Not hovering. Not making her feel as though she couldn't get there safely on her own.

Just watching her back.

She got a little teary-eyed at that one.

And didn't want to think about a time when her friendship with Winchester Holmes would end.

On Sunday, he called and asked if she was up for a road trip later in the day. He'd done some research and had found a lot of really cool things to do for the holidays. A couple of them were in Prescott, Arizona, a town an hour and a half north of Phoenix that she'd visited many times with her grandmother. Of course she'd said she'd go. Because of the higher elevation, there was snow on the ground, and she'd had to pull out her seldom-used purple ski jacket to wear with the jeans and black sweater chosen to keep her warm. Also in jeans, black ones, Win was wearing a festive maroon sweater and black outdoor vest when she climbed into his SUV in her driveway shortly after four. He took her to a gingerbread house display she'd never been to before. There were two long rows of tables on either side of an entryway hall, filled with edible entries consisting of a schoolyard, complete with details that fascinated her, a semitruck, a corral filled with horses and even a spaceship, all decorated for the holidays in some fashion.

She took pictures. He pointed out various candies and cereals he recognized as rooftops and details. There were people all around them, families oohing and ahhing, and yet, the strangers seemed to be borders around their twosome, closing them in until she felt as though they were alone. Together.

At one point she stepped back, her heel catching on a barrier setting off the display, and she would have fallen had he not been there, bearing her weight with his body until she could right herself.

The wall of that crowd around them covering up the moment, she took a step forward and leaned in for another photo. She was completely reeling from the unexpected feel of his hardness pressed against her backside during those few seconds she'd been up against him.

Unnerved by how badly she wanted more of him against her. All of him against her.

Taking note of that development, she couldn't quite get past it as he drove them from the gingerbread display to a mile-long drive-through light spectacular put on by a local fire department. The darkness in the vehicle during the drive home down the mountain and through uninhabited desert brought more intimacy she hadn't expected.

Along with a conversation she would never forget.

They'd been talking about the lights and gingerbread houses…keeping the conversation upbeat and friendly, as they'd been doing since reaching their relationship decisions in his office on Friday. And out of the blue he said, "If I wasn't your boss, I'd want to sleep with you."

Yeah, okay, having sex with him had been on her mind since the gingerbread houses, but was she ready?

Could she be?

There were lies between them.

And she felt a growing urgency with each day that passed to find Kylie. The little girl was ten. Should be writing letters to Santa and anticipating presents under a tree.

Did she even still believe in Santa Claus?

Had Sarah ever?

Win wanted to have sex with her.

If she were to write a letter to Santa, assuming she knew Kylie was safe and loved, having sex with Win guilt-free would be the only thing she'd ask for.

"Can we do that, no strings attached?" she volleyed back, her body already responding to his earthy call.

"Probably not."

She didn't think so, either.

"The last thing I want to do is hurt you. I'd never be able to live with myself if I hurt you."

"People hurt each other all the time, Win," she said softly, speaking from vast experience. "It's a part of life.

Part of being human. As long as you don't do it purposefully, willfully, or take pleasure in it, you just need to accept that."

"I let Sierra down."

Afraid to move, afraid that Win would retreat again, as he had any other time the ghost woman came up in his conversation, she asked, "How?"

She had to know about the woman. About what happened between her and Win. Because until she understood, she was never going to fully know him.

Or even understand what was going on between her and Win.

"Sierra and I…we…fell in love the fall before…it all happened."

Before all what happened? "When did it all happen?" she asked in lieu of the question she most wanted an answer for.

"Fall to spring of that year."

They weren't lovers all that long.

"She didn't want to tell the others, thinking that it would mess things up—between us as a group, and maybe between us as a couple, too. Neither of us had ever been in a serious relationship and she worried about the others' opinions getting between us, worried about them giving us advice…"

She let his pause lie there in silence.

"She worried that our close-knit group wouldn't be the same with two of us hooked up…"

"But you wanted to tell them?" she guessed, trying to make the telling as easy on him as possible in light of how difficult the subject clearly was.

"Hell, no. I was relieved. Hud and Glen…they were much more active in the dating field. I didn't need them joshing with me about something that meant so much to me."

"You loved her."

"We all did."

"But you were in love with her."

"I hadn't made that determination yet, but I was pretty sure I could be. I'd started thinking about maybe the two of us having a future together. At some point."

She almost smiled at how tentative he sounded—like a normal college kid not yet ready to commit to more than getting through the semester.

She'd have liked to have known Win then.

Counting back the years, she quickly realized that when he'd been having sex with Sierra for the first time, she'd been dealing with nighttime feedings and dirty diapers.

And loving every minute of it, despite how scared she was by it all.

"So what happened?" She had to ask. Wanted so badly to help him heal. To do something monumental for him while she used him to mend the big hole in her own heart—also stemming from those long-ago years.

"Sierra had been assigned to do a class project with a partner she didn't like. We all knew the guy, weren't all that fond of him either because he was a pompous ass, but she…" He shook his head. "What we each noticed at the time, but never spoke about to each other, was that she'd changed after that project."

He glanced over at her, headlights coming from the other side of the divided highway shining across his face, making it glisten, and she wanted to take those cheeks in her hands, to hold them softly and kiss away the pain she could feel emanating from him.

"She came to me one day, all full of energy, and when I reached for her, she pulled away. She didn't want me to hold her or kiss her. She wanted to know how she could anonymously invest a fairly large—for us—sum of money."

"You didn't know she had that much money?"

"I know she didn't have it or hadn't had it."

"Did you ask her about it? Find out why she wanted to invest it?"

His silence was her answer. And she realized that her question pointed out more critically what he hadn't done. Because it let him know that she'd been sitting there thinking he should have done it. Or would have done it. But only because she wanted to know.

"You were respecting her privacy, Win," she said softly, wishing she could do a rewind and tape her damned mouth shut.

"I just didn't ask," he told her. "She was acting differently...not wanting to kiss or hug even. Maybe changing her mind about us. I figured she'd let me know what was going on when she was ready. For all I knew, the question was for a class and she was nervous about a test..."

"What was really going on?"

"The jerk had raped her."

His words imploded the car like rocks falling from the mountains on either side of them.

"She went to a women's clinic, but she couldn't tell me. And I didn't ask..."

"You couldn't possibly have known."

"I should have been aware enough to figure out that something was seriously wrong. I should have offered my support, even just by asking...letting her know I was there and cared. She came to me, gave me a chance, and I didn't pick up on her need."

"You're being too hard on yourself." It was true. And all she could think to say. Yeah, maybe he could have been a bit more sensitive. "To think that you should have somehow jumped to such a monumental conclusion, to have any idea that your girlfriend had been sexually assaulted…"

He shook his head, cutting off the words as though he couldn't stand to hear them. "I should have asked questions, as you said, but that's not what stops me in my tracks," he told her, staring straight ahead, his face like granite.

"What does?" Her throat caught on the two words in the darkness.

"The fact that she couldn't come to me about it. That she didn't trust me enough or believe that I could be a strength to her. Even if she couldn't tell me about the rape…at least let me know that the guy was giving her a hard time, that she was struggling…anything…"

"She did come to you, Win," she said softly. "She asked for your expertise on a topic she knew you were good at."

"She came to me for factual support, not emotional support…"

Yeah, she was getting that. Understanding so much all of a sudden. More than he probably expected.

And thought that maybe she really could help him.

"You know how you said the other day that you don't get the nuances?"

"Of course I remember. How do you think I learned that?"

"It's not so much that you don't get them, Win. Maybe

it's more that you only see the world through your own perspective?"

"What's that supposed to mean?" He didn't sound angry, exactly, but he wasn't happy with her, either.

"You come from a great upbringing. Idyllic, almost. The loving American family with fun vacations and Christmas traditions that happened every year without fail."

"So I'm insensitive."

"No, you just maybe didn't get that while you grew up in a world where trust was a given, Sierra's world was entirely different. I'm just guessing here, based on the fact that you said her father was an alcoholic. And on my own life experiences. I can tell you right here, right now..." She was getting it as she was saying the words and almost couldn't finish the sentence. "From my own experience," she said, her throat completely dry. "Some of us grew up learning not to count on others to help us."

He stared at the road in front of them and drove, his face straight but no longer stony. She didn't know whether to say more or just shut up.

And another thought came up and slipped out. "My issues were with my mother, but Sierra...maybe she not only learned not to ask for help, but also not to ever turn to the man she loved when she was in need. Not cognitively, necessarily, but emotionally..."

"Kelly once said something similar to that," he said a full minute later. "Not about me, but just one time, afterward, when we were all talking about Sierra, trying to make sense of it all..."

Something she was still trying to do. Without all the facts.

"Did she take her own life?" she asked as gently as she could.

The shake of his head came as a shock to her. She'd been certain she'd reached the tragically sad conclusion… the reason why the seven friends Sierra had left behind were bonded for life, spending every day of their lives honoring her memory.

"She tried to take care of her trouble herself, in a big way," he said then. "She found out the jerk was deeply into illegal gambling, set out to get proof that would take him down and lock him up, without her ever being involved. She had no idea how high up his contacts went. She was murdered by his bookie before she ever had a chance to prove anything."

Her mouth hung open, wordless, as a sting of darts shot all the way through her. What did you say to something like that?

A woman strong enough to be a hero on her own, a woman determined to be the captor instead of the victim, and smart enough to figure out how to make it happen. Sarah sat there, wondering how she had ever thought she could somehow help make it all better.

"We got him, though," Win said, his tone completely different, stronger, almost hard with determination, as he said the words. Showing her a side of him she hadn't realized was there.

A side she respected every bit as much as she did the tender, slightly nerdy brainiac who'd taken such an unexpected hold of her heart.

He told her about Sierra not showing up for a spring break gathering, and the seven Sierra's Web partners coming together and compiling everything they knew about Sierra's life. How they then took everything to their professor, who took the information to a police detective she knew. How the detective worked with them to piece everything together—including the rape, and rapist—ending with the horrible tragedy of finding Sierra's body. Then the ultimate triumph of seeing her rapist and also her murderer found guilty and sentenced to prison, watching both of them being led off in handcuffs. And Sarah knew that she was in way over her head.

And wished Kylie could have someone like Sierra's Web watching over her.

Chapter Ten

He'd told Sarah about Sierra so that she didn't look to him for something he couldn't give. To explain to her, in real terms, why she wouldn't ever have a committed romantic relationship with him.

But based on her reaction to the telling—trying to tend to him, not looking out for herself—he wasn't sure he'd succeeded.

Still, over the next week of work and a trip to a couple of holiday events, he wasn't sorry he'd talked about Sierra. He didn't do it often. Had never told anyone about their sexual relationship. And probably should have. As cliché as the old adage was, talking about it helped.

With that thought in mind, he told Kelly, too, only to find out that she'd already suspected as much. All the partners had—back when Sierra had still been alive. They'd just never been sure. And after her death, when Win stayed silent, they just let it go. They didn't want to ask in case they were wrong. And if they were right, they'd opted, as a team, to respect his right to his privacy.

After speaking with Sarah, he also told his partners that he and Sarah were hanging out after hours, expecting to hear valid and fair warnings to him about mixing business with pleasure. Instead, he was nonplussed by the chorus of "good for yous" that came his way. Along with Hud jokingly warning him about how quickly hanging out can turn into so much more.

Because Hud had been referring to his own recent and very quick marriage to a former client—his own mixing of business with pleasure—everyone had laughed.

But Hud's situation had been very different, too. The client had called him because she'd had his daughter thirteen years earlier without telling him, and the daughter had gone missing. She'd wanted Sierra's Web to help find her, and they did.

Mariah, too, had recently married a client, she'd more quietly reminded Win.

So the whole don't mix business with pleasure thing—off the table with the partners, too, not just Sarah.

One thing became very clear to him throughout it all. Sarah was right that he saw the world through his own eyes, as everyone did, but failed to factor in the fact that others' perspectives were sometimes very different from his.

He'd known the world was filled with varying points of view. He'd just never actually factored them into his equation when he'd interacted on an interpersonal level. He factored in differing opinions. Respecting them.

Just not vast degrees of varying perspectives.

Not sure what any of it meant long term, in the short go, Win found himself looking forward to the holiday season with more excitement than he had since his parents had been killed. For the first time in a decade, he felt hopeful in a personal sense.

Not necessarily hopeful that he and Sarah would someday get married, have kids, become a family.

But hopeful that the future held more for him than he'd allowed himself to believe.

When he came out of his office the following Friday afternoon, five days since their trip to Prescott, and saw her tending carefully to lights and ornaments on the Sierra's Web Christmas tree, arranging everything so that they were evenly placed, he just stood and watched for a second. Like an angel quietly flitting around, she moved, gently touched, stood back and looked, and reached to the tree again, her movement like a tender wisp of air.

In all the years the partners had had that tree, and Lindsay had been bringing it out and packing it up for them, he wouldn't have been able to remember a single ornament on it had he been asked.

And was pretty sure he'd never forget the ones he watched her adjust, the way they glowed just right as she strategically placed them under lights. The little smile on her face as she viewed her work. Hud was still in the office, but Lindsay had gone, and Win wanted the moment to stretch for as long as it could. Didn't want her to know he was there. Was leery to retreat in case she heard him.

The time was hers. He shouldn't be impinging on it.

"You could help, you know," she said, while he stood like a frozen idiot in the shadowed hall of his own firm's offices.

While instinct told him to retreat, he took a step forward instead. "There's no improving what you're doing," he told her, then asked, "Does your tree at home look as good?"

"I don't have a tree."

The words shocked him—considering her loving attention to an old artificial thing that spent most of its life shoved in a box, forgotten.

"You don't put up a tree for Christmas?"

Lowering her chin, she pinned him with a glance over her shoulder. "Do you?" She'd have been looking at him over the tops of her glasses if she'd had any.

"I just bought my first house," he defended, coming closer, actually looking at the ornaments. They weren't bad. Colorful glass renditions of everything from a Santa Claus to a manger.

She reached up, hooking a red-and-blue present with a gold bow to a top branch. And drawing his attention to the breasts covered by the tight red sweater a foot away from his face.

When she lowered her arms, facing him, she must have seen something left of the huge surge of physical desire thronging through him, because she stopped. Stared at his mouth. And then quickly bent to straighten an ornament to which she'd already attended.

"Well, I think you should get one, then," she told him, her words a bit louder than her norm. A bit forced.

She felt it, too.

He liked that she did.

"I will if you will," he volleyed right back at her.

Upright again, another foot or two away from him, she met his challenging gaze with one of her own. "Fine."

"Fine?" He'd expected one of her parries. Wasn't sure what to do with instant capitulation. He had absolutely no plans to put up a tree, or any decorations, in his home.

"Yes, fine. You get a tree, and then I will."

Well, two could play that game. "How about, tomorrow morning, we both get trees? Together. So we're witnesses to each other."

"You don't trust me to get a tree if I say I will?" He couldn't tell if she really thought he didn't trust her or was still just standing up to him for the fun of it, but didn't like the implication, even in jest.

Her question pulled the truth from him. "I don't much want to do it alone."

"Okay." Her expression completely serious. "I have boxes of ornaments and things in the garage attic," she told him. "Maybe, if you don't mind, we start there, get a look at what I've got, and then see what we need to get."

She was inviting him to her home.

To the family heirlooms in her attic.

He felt as though he'd received an invitation to all the vaults on Wall Street.

"You got a tree up there?" he asked, to cover the excited leaping going on inside of him.

"No."

"You want live or artificial?" He was a live guy. Because his parents had been.

"Live," she told him. "Grandpa used to take me, every year, to pick the tree, and no matter what I picked, too big, too small, that's the one we came home with."

Her grandfather, who'd been an alcoholic. And she had good memories.

He liked that, too.

"It's a date, then," he told her, knowingly using the word in the literal context of two people going out because they liked each other. "We explore the attic, and then buy trees."

Half expecting her to correct his "date" term, to qualify, he was surprised again when she turned back to the tree, nodded and said, "What time?"

He faltered. If he named too early a time, would she defer the plans? Or too late, tell him she couldn't because she had something else to do?

"Because nine would work well for me," she said after a pause, not looking at him, but he had a feeling she'd known of his struggle.

Either that or he was just falling so hard for her that he wanted to believe she could read him that well.

Because if she could, then, maybe, his lack of getting nuances wouldn't be such a big deal with her?

"Nine's great," he told her. And went back to his office before anything happened to change the plan.

She didn't need a tree. She'd be in Disneyland for the holiday. And celebrate the Eve with a lovely spread at the hotel where she and Lily always stayed.

They'd have a little plug-in fake tree in their hotel room. Lily brought it every year. Set it up on the table in the sitting area. Put presents under it.

They'd have their celebration. It just wasn't ever at home anymore.

Which hadn't bothered her all that much.

So why now, all of a sudden, was she getting ornaments down out of her attic? And filling with a small bit of anticipation as she thought about having a tree lighting up the living room window again? Like it had all the years of her growing up.

Why did having Win share the experience with her make her want to do it all again? The tree, the watering, the needles…and the ornaments?

Having to pack it all up again when the holiday was over, when she wasn't even going to be there?

The boxes were down out of the attic by eight. She thought about opening them.

And thought about calling Win and canceling, too.

What was she doing? Pretending that life was changing...that Win was really the friend she so badly wished he could be.

How could she be thinking about hauling out ornaments that hadn't been used since the year they'd taken Kylie away?

When another week had passed and she'd still found no sign of her sister's case at Sierra's Web?

In addition to adding more information to Milford's spreadsheets as Win discovered more accounts—she'd been right about the initials standing for businesses—she'd also been through three-quarters of the agency files and found nothing that mentioned Kylie or Lily.

Ten minutes until nine and she'd still not called Win to cancel. She'd put on black leggings and a thigh-length Christmas sweater with a Christmas tree on both the front and back—a coming and going display—that she'd bought for an ugly sweater party in nursing school a couple of years before. She had slid on her favorite black ankle boots—a splurge the previous year—so she was probably just going to go.

But with a firm reminder that she was lying to Win, and friends didn't lie to friends.

And a firm warning to shut up to the inner self who kept nudging her to consider the fact that Win might forgive her lies once he understood the reason for them. False hope only led to crushing disappointment.

A lifetime with Lily's ups and downs had taught her that.

Better to accept what you could see in front of you, to enjoy the moment you had, and not build castles in the air that would inevitably be blown away by the next storm.

Thinking her head was firmly on her shoulders, she answered the knock on the front door and let Win in.

She'd meant only to look through the boxes she'd brought down from the attic in a general sense. To see if she had working light strands, a tree stand, and that enough of the ornaments had withstood eight years of Arizona heat to fill a tree. Win started unwrapping everything. Asking about the artist Santa that plugged into a light strand and lit up and moved from his seat on a tree branch. Listening and then smiling as she told him about seeing it at a festival with her grandmother and wanting so badly to buy it for her mom. Her grandmother had given it to her instead, for Christmas that year.

It still worked.

As did everything else they pulled out of those boxes.

And so did the rest of the morning with Win. They went for bagels. Shopped for lights and ornaments for his place. Bought two trees, complete with stands, which he tied to the top of his SUV. Dropped off hers first. Decorated it together, amid loud Christmas music blaring from the station she was streaming on her television set and cups of hot coffee.

Some of the ornaments she recognized...exclaiming for each rediscovery and sharing little stories with him. Fun things. Tidbits.

Nothing that would bring down the moment.

There'd be enough of that when she returned to the house alone later that afternoon and allowed herself to think about the grandparents who'd purchased most of the ornaments on her tree. The years of celebrations that had filled the walls of her house for so long before she was even born. The baby sister who'd only spent two Christmases with them.

She'd think. She'd grieve.

And she'd move on.

Because that was what life had taught her to do.

For the time being, she was spending the morning with a man she'd accepted as a friend for life, feeling truly happy. Him in her house felt…right. Not an intrusion. Didn't make her feel self-conscious. But it seemed as though he belonged in the space, a sense reinforced by the fact that he made himself completely at home. Win didn't ask where anything was—the refrigerator, cups, the coffee maker or the bathroom. He just found them and availed himself as need arose.

He didn't snoop, either.

She'd wondered as he made his way down the hall to the facilities whether he'd veer off to get a peek at her room before coming back, but he didn't check out anything down the hall beyond the first door on the left.

She'd listened to his steps on the ceramic tile that ran through much of the house.

The tennis shoes he was wearing with jeans and a black pullover made their own special squeak. A sound she'd remember long after he was gone.

The real kicker came when they pulled into his neighborhood, a lovely gated community in Scottsdale, and then up into the three-car garage that opened with a push of a button on his visor. His yard wasn't huge—

most Arizona yards in more recent builds weren't—but the house…it was lovely. The corrugated rock on the outside, variegated tile roof, lovely river rock landscaping with flowering bushes, and out back, along with a swimming pool and fully equipped and covered outdoor kitchen, was a tiny grove of six or seven fruit trees, all wearing semiripened oranges, lemons and grapefruit.

It was every dream house she'd ever had, all wrapped into one.

The ceilings were vaulted, the tiled floors porcelain, not ceramic like hers, and the furnishings, though very brown and masculine, also looked incredibly comfortable, as though they were inviting you to lie back and relax for the rest of your life.

A winding staircase led up to a second floor, with a balustraded overlook to the living room.

She glanced up there, but quickly moved on, not wanting to even know the number of bedrooms, let alone which one was his.

Just as she nosed her way into the largest kitchen she'd seen in person, Win came in through the opened double front door with his tree. She heard the rustle and bumps of one of the doors against the wall—took a quick glance at granite countertops, an island and a sink with a high sprayer handle—before going in to help him with placement.

He'd told her to have a look around if she wanted.

She'd wanted.

And kind of wished she hadn't. Getting the sights she'd just seen out of her head was going to take a lifetime, she just knew.

Any other home she was in, or eventually looked at

to buy herself, would be measured against Win's. And was doomed to fail the test.

He wanted her opinion on everything. From where to place the tree to what kind of tree skirt she thought he should get.

To that last question, she said, "You should get what you like, Win. Or just get something generic until you know what you like, or…have a spouse who knows what she likes." The last was added very deliberately as the day's activities started to play with her.

She'd thought she could live in the moment, enjoy the day and move on. But as she stood there in the middle of Win's massive living room, facing a fairy-tale tree in front of a big fairy-tale set of floor-to-ceiling windows, she felt like a fraud.

In a way, her time at Sierra's Web was like being an undercover agent, on assignment, only without the "department's" approval, and working only under her own orders. In a way.

In fantasyland.

When Win said nothing, just stood there watching her, as though he could read her mind, she said, "For now, if you have a sheet you don't mind using, we can wrap that and fluff it around the stand and it will do just fine…"

She didn't know who'd chosen the tree skirt her family had used for all the years she could remember. It had always just been there.

But she knew how to problem solve.

Win got the sheet. She arranged it. Scooted out from beneath the tree to stand, just as he plugged in the lights.

They'd chosen them together, deciding on multicolor,

and they glistened off the clear glass ornaments he'd picked out, making the entire tree twinkle.

"I love it," she said aloud, not meaning to sound quite so effusive. But she did. The tree was fresh. Brand-new. Full of possibility.

Not hanging with memories that pulled at the heart like hers did.

And yet, the gorgeous tree, all new and generic, with no strings attached—lacked heart.

"It's beautiful," she said then, hating that reality kept intruding on her moments, reminding her that the perfect day she was having wasn't her life.

"You're beautiful." Win's warm, soft tone reached her before his words did. Glancing over at him, she realized that he'd moved closer. Was only a couple of feet away—those brown eyes seemed like two burning pools that pinned her in place.

She couldn't move. Couldn't look away.

Win moved. Taking one step, then another, reaching under her straight, long hair to cup her neck and pull her closer.

"I want to kiss you," he said.

Yeah, she'd gathered that. Couldn't get enough air to say so. Barely managed the nod she gave him.

"You okay with that?"

She wasn't supposed to be.

But it seemed that nods were all she was capable of at the moment.

That and opening her mouth for him.

His lips came closer. Her body melted down low and throughout her veins, too, making her warm and needy. She didn't know what to do with herself.

Sex was supposed to be body parts, pleasure and done.

She'd gone that route way too young and found it far less remarkable than everyone said.

Win hadn't even touched her yet and her body was humming.

Driven by something inside of her that was so much stronger than her resistance, she leaned into him, welcomed him, and when his lips touched hers, she met them eagerly, responded to him hungrily. She hadn't even known she could kiss like that.

That a kiss could make you want to rip off your clothes and press skin to skin as soon as possible.

Instinct told her to press her tightened nipples against his chest to rub them against him, to apply the same tension to the penis pressing against her pelvis.

He moaned. She groaned.

"Oh, God, Sarah, I…"

She stopped his words with a kiss full of tongue. Almost in tears as desperation raged through her body.

Because in the back of her mind, not loudly enough, but there, she could hear a voice telling her that what she was doing was wrong.

That with her lies between them, if she did it with him, she'd be cheapening something she'd never had. Something she'd never even known existed.

But then his hands cupped her breasts and she pushed into his palms, giving herself to him, wanting him to get what he wanted, and she lost herself for another second.

Until she reached for the button on his jeans, felt his hardened penis against her hand and knew that if she pulled down that zipper, there'd be no going back.

"Uh-uh," she said so softly she wasn't even sure she'd made a sound. And then, backing up enough to put an inch between them, she said it again. "Uh-uh." In his mouth.

Her lips kept kissing for another second or two, not getting her message, or believing it, but Win's must have because he lifted his head.

"Too much too soon?" he asked, his hands cupping either side of her face. Exactly as she'd wanted to do with him a week ago. Or two.

Or a lifetime.

Because that was what stretched between them as she took another step back, letting more and more of his pretty porcelain floor separate them—a lifetime.

Hers. Kylie's.

She might not ever find her sister at Sierra's Web. Might not find her at all.

But she'd always have gotten the job there under false pretenses.

Win had to know that before she took any more of his life into her hands.

Into her heart.

Should she tell him?

Trust that he'd help her?

Would she really ask him to risk the reputation of the firm, to risk client confidentiality issues by bringing him into her seedy little world?

Did she trust herself to walk away from all that he was offering her?

She had to think.

"I just...wow...that kind of, no, hell, that completely 100 percent surprised me," she said, pacing a few feet, back and forth, as she caught her breath. "I don't know about you, but I've always thought people who talk about combustible sex were lying, or on the kindest level exaggerating, but that..." She was rambling. Knew. Didn't care.

He came toward her and she knew real fear—of herself. She didn't think she could reject him a second time. Not until she had a chance to…

With a gentle hand on her shoulder, he stopped her in her tracks. "Me, too," he told her, and his grin…it brought tears to her eyes.

"So…you're not angry?"

"At having the best kiss of my life on the same morning I get my very first Christmas tree? Do I look like a fool?"

His grin stole her heart just as the rest of him had been doing for weeks. She knew what he was doing—trying to defuse the situation and let her know that he supported her choice—and in that moment, she loved him for that, too.

"Thank you," she said, not even sure herself what exactly the sentiment covered. His acceptance of her choice to stop, for sure. But there was more.

So much more.

"If you don't mind, I think I should probably get back to my place. I have laundry and other chores on my list for the weekend…"

"You have time for burgers on the way?"

"Of course."

"And we're still on for the concert tomorrow night?"

He'd scored tickets to a nationally renowned Christmas show by a rock orchestra. It crossed her mind to offer him the chance to share the tickets with someone else. But only briefly.

"Of course."

He was her boss. She was going to be spending time with him.

She just couldn't kiss him again.

At least, not until she found Kylie. Or knew for certain that there was no mention of her sister anywhere within the Sierra's Web organization.

And then, almost an hour later, when he dropped her off at her little old house with the pretty yard and leaned over to kiss her lightly goodbye, she broke that last rule, too.

She kissed him back.

Chapter Eleven

Win kissed Sarah several more times that weekend. First when he picked her up for the concert and she came out her front door in a short black figure-hugging dress, Christmas tree earrings and heels. He took his time ruining her lipstick and she helped.

The second time was during the concert when he looked over to see tears in her eyes at a famously moving piece. That one was soft, tender and mostly quick.

And he kissed her when she told him good-night before she got out of his SUV back in her driveway that night, too. He knew he wasn't going to get an invitation inside. He knew why.

But he wanted his kiss good-night.

Her hungry response left him achingly hard, and happier than he'd been—maybe ever.

He was still whistling and grinning when he walked across the parking lot on his way in to work the next morning. At first, when he heard his name, he thought of Sarah, but it wasn't her voice calling across the way to him.

It was Dorian.

He smiled at her, too, as she approached, looking all doctory in her blue pants and white lab coat—obviously she was on her way out to a job.

Or was just coming in from one.

"Love the tie," she said when she first approached.

"It was my dad's," he told her. "It's been hanging in the back of my closet, every closet, for years. I figured maybe it was time I got it out into the sunshine."

The tie was muted, black with little green Christmas trees, but still way more than he'd normally have put on.

Except that now he couldn't get enough of Christmas trees.

He had one in his house.

He'd fallen in love in front of it.

"This doesn't have anything to do with Sarah, does it?" Dorian asked. The question should have been slightly teasing. Curious, maybe.

Salacious.

The frown creasing Dorian's forehead concerned him.

"What's up?"

They'd reached the door of the building, and Dorian nudged him aside and into a courtyard. Sitting on a cement bench attached to a round matching table, she pulled him down on the edge of the bench perpendicular to it, facing him, knee to knee.

He'd just ironed the black pants he had on. And his white shirt didn't need to be smudged by the perennial Arizona dust atop the table.

Neither really mattered. Or would have bothered him.

They were good stand-ins for whatever it was Dorian had to tell him outside the office with such a serious expression on her face.

Oh, God. She was a doctor. Did she know something she couldn't tell him because of patient confidentiality?

"She's not sick, is she?" he asked. A nod was all it would take.

Would she nod at him?

She shook her head.

"I just came from a professional holiday breakfast." She named the function. He'd probably heard of it. Couldn't place it at the moment. "Part of the program was a reading off of the state's top medical profession graduates this year…"

Yeah, fine. What did he care? Well, on some level, he did, peripherally. If it mattered to her, it mattered to him, but…

The compassion that filled her eyes then was unmistakable. Because it was Dorian. And they'd been through hell together.

"Sarah Williams won the top graduate award from the university's school of nursing and health…"

Oh, that was all? A name? "So it's someone else," he said with a shrug. "Sarah and Williams are common names," he explained, as though talking to someone who didn't already know that.

Dorian was shaking her head. And holding his hand, though he didn't remember her taking it. "It's her, Win. Her picture was attached."

Jumping up, Win wiped the seat of his pants. "Why?" he asked the air in general. And then turning back to Dorian, "Why would she do that?"

"I don't know. I'm guessing you should ask her."

Yeah, she was right. He'd ask Sarah.

"It could be nothing," he said aloud. "She said she was a new college graduate. That she studied a lot of science and business. Maybe when she did her clinicals she found out that she didn't like the science part as well as she thought she would." He was grasping. Hoping his words made good sense.

"Or maybe," he said, sitting back down, "she just did the nursing track so that she could better help her mother. She struggles with addiction," he added authoritatively as he met Dorian's gaze. "Her mother, not Sarah. She's clean right now, but Sarah grew up with her in and out of sobriety."

"Like someone else we knew." Dorian's soft tones were almost his undoing.

Except that he wasn't going to be undone.

He was going to talk to Sarah.

One thing he'd learned about her, she had reasons for everything she did.

There'd be an explanation.

And the sun would come out from behind the clouds.

Or it wouldn't.

Sarah wasn't surprised to get a text from Win asking her to come see him in his office when she got in.

He very well could have received more Milford accounts from the various feelers he'd put out to mom-and-pop places around the valley that he needed her to take a look at. It would be the third time she'd had such a summons since she'd started helping him with the case.

But she wouldn't be surprised to find that he just wanted to tell her good-morning in person. To give her one of his kilowatt nerdy smiles and get her smile right back at him.

It's what she would have done after the weekend they'd spent if she were the boss.

And as the employee…she didn't even put her purse down before heading to his door. She stopped her hand in midair before knocking, however, as she heard voices inside, sounding more urgent than friendly.

Backing off, she headed straight back to the reception area, where she'd just waved good-morning to Lindsay seconds before.

"You know who's in with Win?" she asked. "He said he needed to see me, but I don't want to interrupt if something's come up."

"Something has definitely come up," the older woman said. "A local widowed philanthropist married a young model who's apparently been siphoning his money. They need Win's help to figure out how she's doing it and find the money before it's gone for good. He just got the call a few minutes ago. Hud's in there with him now, helping with the IT angle of it, while Win traces the money."

Maybe she could help. Do a spreadsheet on the wife's spending.

"Do you think that's why he wanted to see me?"

Lindsay shook her head. "I'm sorry, I was on the phone when you came in, but Win said to tell you that he'd meet up with you later."

Sending mental good wishes to the man who was more than a friend in her heart, Sarah carried a small smile with her into the workday. There was a chance, maybe small, but a chance, that when Win found out about her subterfuge—and he would find out because as soon as she had what she needed she was going to tell him—he'd understand and forgive her.

She'd spent many sleepless hours since the kiss in his living room on Saturday, fighting with herself about whether or not to come clean immediately. The part of her heart that was becoming his warring with the part of her heart Kylie had owned since the day she was born.

Win. Kylie. Win. Kylie.

In the light of day, there was no question. Win was a grown man. Kylie, a vulnerable child.

But she went into that Monday determined to get through the rest of the files she hadn't seen. She wasn't going to organize, to do the work Sierra's Web had hired her to do, looking as she went. She was just going to look. Like a madwoman.

Time was up. She was falling in love. But he was falling, too. Which meant she'd be able to hurt him. Whether she meant to or not, wanted to or not.

She most definitely did not want to hurt Winchester Holmes.

By midafternoon, she'd seen a couple of strangers, one male, one female, both professionally dressed, enter Win's office before shutting the door behind them.

And she'd found no files on Kylie.

None.

She didn't get it.

Went back to Kelly's office. With the other woman out of state again, she could look more thoroughly in her office. Since the day after Thanksgiving, when all of the partners had been in the office together, Lindsay seemed to have accepted her more as one of them.

Or maybe she was just busy. For whatever reason, Sarah was moving around the suite of offices that Monday without her onetime nemesis randomly showing up behind her. Taking advantage of the freedom, she opened the bottom file drawer of Kelly's desk.

Information in the partners' desk drawers was the one thing she hadn't been privy to in the time she'd been there. Even when the new furniture came, Lindsay insisted on handling the desk drawers herself.

Made no sense that Kylie's file, an eight-year-old case, would randomly be in a desk drawer, but she was getting desperate and had already looked every place that made sense.

Not sure how long Lindsay would actually leave her unattended in a partner's office, she had to be quick. Flipped through hanging files holding random information…vacation spot brochures—Kelly wanted to go on an African safari?—business expense receipts, a hard copy of flight fund numbers. There was a bulging file filled with greeting cards and quotes. And one that said aliases.

Pulling out the skinny green file holder, she extracted the five or so sheets that it held, with a heading of County Social Services.

It had to mean something.

Be something.

Hands shaking, heart pounding, she wanted to run with the papers and hide. To shove them under her sweater and get out of there.

Afraid of being caught with them before she had time to see what was there.

Holding them in front of her, she glanced down the first sheet, struggling to draw full breaths. She didn't find Kylie. Wasn't sure what she was even looking at.

Columns of names. Two of them. Side by side.

The second sheet, and the third, same thing. Kelly had a file of columns of names? *Come on!* Sarah urged herself. *Figure it out.*

And then…there she was. Kylie Williams. Fourth sheet, halfway down, first column.

Kylie Williams.

The second column name came next. Cara Samuels. The name meant nothing to her. Nor did any of the other names on those sheets.

But she'd found Kylie's name.

Her sister existed inside Sierra's Web.

Tears in her eyes, she returned the hanging file exactly as she'd found it, not sure what to do with herself, but knowing she needed privacy.

Time to deal.

Grabbing her purse, she texted Lindsay to let her know she'd be back in a few and left the offices, and then the building.

In her car, she drove to a nearby park, stopped the car and sat there, letting the tears flow unattended down her cheeks.

She hadn't found Kylie yet, had none of the reassurance she sought that her baby sister was okay, but she was a huge step closer.

And twenty minutes later, was on her phone, looking for Cara Samuels. Were the two columns just a way to fit all the names on the pages Kelly had printed, one column having nothing to do with the other? Or, shaking again as she thumb-scrolled, was Cara Samuels the name of the adopter Kelly had chosen on her sister's behalf?

None of the profiles that showed up first seemed to be the right age, or in the Phoenix vicinity, to have been an adoptive parent, but you never knew. She needed more time. She had to look up all of the Caras on social media, to study pictures.

But she had to get back to work.

She'd promised Sierra's Web, and Win, that she'd give them her time and attention, and she would. But the second the workday was done, she was heading home, to spend the rest of the night looking at every Cara Samuels she could find anywhere in any public database on the internet.

She might not find Kylie that way, but she had a place to start.

Something to do.

The day was a game changer.

She'd found Kylie's name on a list in Kelly Chase's desk.

Might even find her baby sister in time to collect on the only Christmas wish she'd had since she was sixteen.

She had the tree up for the first time since then. Was it too much to hope that the present would finally arrive as well?

And, the third game changer, she had the sure knowledge that she wasn't sacrificing her own possible happiness, or risking hurting Win, in vain.

She'd found Kylie's name.

One for the good guys. By four o'clock in the afternoon that first Monday in December, a gold-digging young bride and her boyfriend were in FBI custody in Phoenix, and all the money they'd attempted to steal had been recovered.

Sometimes, when you worked fast and all together, things really did turn out for the good.

Not that there wasn't pain involved. Brandt Young

had been stung. He'd known his young bride was interested in his money as much as or more than she was him. But he'd thought her truly fond of him. Had expected loyalty and companionship for the rest of the days of his life.

Instead, he'd been left feeling like a fool.

Kind of like Win was feeling as he again texted his office manager and asked her to report to his office.

At least Young had figured out his woman's duplicity on his own. Win had had to have Sarah's pointed out to him...

Though grateful for the day's work that had taken his complete focus and turned him away from the news Dorian had given him that morning, now that the day was done, the news was back in front of him.

What possible reason would Sarah have had for failing to tell him that she was a registered nurse? Before he'd had the call on the Young case, he'd already looked up Sarah's nursing license. She hadn't just graduated from the school of nursing at the top of her class, she'd certified herself to work in the profession.

And then hired on as an office manager at Sierra's Web.

He wanted there to be a good reason for that that didn't involve subterfuge, but he'd been unable to come up with one.

He couldn't just fire her, though part of him wanted to do so the second she walked in the door...wanted to just be done with her and have her gone so he could go home and take down the damned Christmas tree.

But she hadn't technically done anything wrong. She'd said she'd graduated, which she had. She'd said she'd had an emphasis on business and science, and she had. She'd given him former work experience, which had checked out the day he'd hired her.

And she'd done an excellent job for them.

Dorian hadn't been concerned for the firm.

She'd been concerned for Win.

He was concerned for the firm.

The knock came on his door, and he wasn't ready. He stood, thinking the position would make him stronger.

Yeah, him, strong, the guy who didn't get nuances.

He got facts, though. And numbers.

And the ones involving Sarah weren't adding up.

"Come in," he said, straightening the knot on his ridiculous Christmas tree tie.

In gray pants and a black sweater with a shiny-looking red scarf at her neck and black pumps on her feet, Sarah looked more like a business professional than a nurse.

That long, silky dark hair, the strength in her features, the big brown eyes that sought his gaze immediately, holding a private welcome that hit him in his private places…they all drew him to her. And pissed him off, too. Setting off a war inside of him.

"What's wrong?" Her expression switched immediately from one of invitation to concern. "Did your case go bad? Do you need my help?"

He wasn't talking cases with her. Not until he knew the truth. The whole truth.

Maybe not even then.

Maybe never.

"I need to know why you failed to tell me that you're a nurse."

The split-second change that came over her killed any hope he'd been surreptitiously clinging to that she'd have a simple explanation that could make everything okay. Even a poor people reader like him could interpret the ashen, wide-eyed, openmouthed expression. The stiffening of posture.

And his merry Christmas died an instant, painful death.

Chapter Twelve

The tone of Win's voice froze every feeling in Sarah's body—leaving only thought. Reason. Calculation.

Truth.

"I was applying for a job of office manager in a firm of experts. I told you the parts about my field of study that I thought applied to the job. I'm an avid in-line skater, too, and have even competed and won an award for it. But I didn't tell you about that, either."

Truth. She hadn't lied to him about her nursing degree, she just hadn't mentioned it, but she had said she'd studied science and business. Which she had as part of her nursing degree.

Feeling as though she was on trial, she waited, her mind focused only on the case at hand. How much he knew, what it meant...they were peripheral to her awareness, no more than that. Giving them any more space would involve feelings, and those were currently out of her reach.

"Why?" he asked.

Truth.

She'd had a breakthrough. Had to have time on the internet to know if there was more she needed before she could walk out Win's door having done all she could do for Kylie.

"Why Sierra's Web?" he continued into her silence.

"I told you why. I'd been following postings on the bulletin board and the job levels you were posting drew my attention because they were so different from most entry-level positions…"

And he'd explained that they were seeking professors, researchers—the types of experts who made livings at large universities.

She hadn't lied to him about how she heard about Sierra's Web. She'd gone to the virtual bulletin board often, to look for job postings. Mostly looking for anything she might be able to do to supplement her income while in college. And the firm truly had stood out as an oddity with the levels of their postings.

All way out of her league.

She'd just failed to mention to Win during their interview that the college bulletin board wasn't the first time she'd heard of them. Or that she'd gravitated to them because she recognized the firm's name the second she'd seen it. It was as though keeping track of the firm's personnel needs in some way would lead her to their dealings with her sister.

And…it had. She was where she was at that moment, having just discovered Kylie's name in a file, because of the office manager posting.

"Why Sierra's Web, and not nursing?"

Truth. "I told you during my interview that I'd most recently been working in the office at a clinic. I also did an internship there and some clinical work, too. And it was too…normal for me. My life isn't Mom, Dad and the kids. It's not sports physicals, colds and pregnancy. I wasn't challenged. I need to be involved in more critical care, and there were no emergency room positions open when I saw the office manager job post…"

His stance didn't change, other than the arms he crossed with concise movement, a clear barrier against her.

"But you still want to be a nurse."

"I am a nurse." Truth.

"You want to be involved in nursing."

"I am involved in nursing. I give flu shots, administer pregnancy tests and handle other medical questions and problems to the level that I am permitted to do so at the women's shelter every week." Truth.

"What are your long-term goals?"

"I live my life in the minute, Win. I told you that."

"But you didn't intend to stay here, did you? You applied for the job knowing you weren't here long-term."

Truth. Truth was, "I had no idea how long I'd stay. I most certainly didn't know how challenging I'd find the work. The spreadsheets I'm doing for you… I'm actually finding them rewarding, like I'm helping to maybe save a life or something, just in a different way." Truth felt good.

He sighed. Threw up his hands. Turned his back on her and then spun around again. "What about career goals, Sarah? Just tell me the truth here! Did you really see yourself as an office manager for the next big chunk of time? Because we didn't hire you on for a month or two. You knew this was a full-time permanent position when you accepted it."

He was mad that she hadn't planned to stay. Her heart went for a small leap but didn't make it off the ground.

"If I had my way, I'd spend my career in disaster relief," she told him. But she rarely got her way. She got life's way. Went where it required her to go, to do the right thing. But, "There are programs where you can get the training... I could be part of the national organization for disaster relief, or any number of state and privately funded programs..."

"Sierra's Web sponsors a disaster relief training program." The words came out as accusation.

"I didn't know that when I applied for the job." Was actually just hearing about it for the first time. But if he thought an in with their program would explain her reason for being there...

It was better than him knowing that she'd taken the job to get access to the firm's files.

"I'm going to speak with the rest of the partners about this."

Surprised that he hadn't already done so, she said, "In my dreamworld, I get the training I'd need, the experience, and eventually be a medical disaster relief expert for Sierra's Web." Just in case he'd pass that on to them as well.

She not only highly respected all of them and the work they did, but she'd begun to feel like a part of their family. A distant relative, of course...but if there was a Santa someplace, and he granted her two wishes...

Kylie first.

Then Win.

Well…maybe three wishes… The third would be to find permanent work at the Sierra's Web firm.

Her face heated up at the thought. And then, as she watched her more than friend stand there so closed off to her, her stomach started to clench. She had to get out of there. To get home.

Be alone.

Think.

"Do I still have a job?" she asked him.

"I can't fire you for not telling me you are a nurse." The answer did not bode well. Not for her fitting in at Sierra's Web. Not for any hope of help or understanding from him in terms of Kylie.

Most definitely not for him as a person to hang out with over the holidays.

Her heart started to crack.

"May I go then?"

"Yes."

He stood there staring at her, as though he expected more from her.

Heart ready to burst, Sarah turned and left.

Win watched Sarah turn her back and leave his office with a wrench in his gut he'd hoped never to feel again.

And there was why you never mixed business with pleasure.

No matter how tempting that pleasure might pretend to be.

He stood at his desk, watching the door, for a good minute after she left. Considered going after her, apologizing for how hard he'd come down on her.

Would he have done so if he hadn't been personally invested?

If he hadn't just come off a relationship where his partner lied to him?

If Sierra's hidden life hadn't also been on his mind so acutely lately? Most particularly because he'd told Sarah about her?

He backed up to his chair, still looking toward the door.

Realized she wasn't coming back in. Sat down.

Pulled the Milford file forward.

Spent an hour on the computer, tracing shell companies associated with so little money they made no sense to him, until he began to recognize a pattern to them. They started out simple, dated back to the time the man had been a kid, barely graduated from high school. And grew more complex as the years passed.

Maybe the companies weren't for hiding money.

Maybe they'd been for learning. Milford, a smart man with no formal education, was clearly a self-taught man.

The thought stopped him. Since when had he started looking at numbers, at accounts, and seeing people behind them? He glanced at his door once more.

And knew he had to apologize.

Sarah had withheld information from him, but he'd been a crap boss when it came to dealing with the information.

And an even worse friend.

He owed her an apology.

And could only hope that she'd forgive him.

Cara Samuels, thirty-eight years old, mother of two Great Danes...

Cara Samuels, thirty years old, recently released from prison...

Cara Samuels, ninety-one years old...

Cara Samuels, friends with Martha Daniels, two children, Damen and Robert...

The list went on. Her spreadsheet list. As she scoured through internet list after internet list of women named Cara Samuels. From social media platforms to people finders, she searched, read, made notes.

Focused.

Because that was what life had taught her to do.

It had also taught her to eat. She needed to get up and find something for dinner. People couldn't survive long without food. And wouldn't grow up healthy and strong without consistent good meals, either.

Which was why she'd stolen four cans of vegetable stew for her baby sister when she'd known better.

Known she wouldn't be good at it.

She'd been right about that.

Hadn't even made it out of the parking lot with the contraband. Whatever Kylie had eaten that night, it hadn't been the stew her big sister had taken for her. By the time Sarah had been released from the police station into Lily's sober-enough-to-get-her custody, Kylie had already been in her crib asleep.

The friend who'd been watching Kylie since Lily's frantic call had proceeded to give her mother a fix and they'd gone off into la-la land together before Sarah could find out if the baby had eaten anything at all.

She'd stored most of the sandwich and fruit she'd been given at the jail in the pocket of her hoodie, and when Kylie had woken up later that night, fussing, she'd fed the little one the rest of her dinner.

The next morning when she'd gotten up, Lily was

gone again. But there'd been a bag of groceries on the counter.

And such it had been, life growing up as Lily's daughter. Two steps back, one step forward.

Cara Samuels, forty-seven years old, widowed school-teacher, no kids associated with her address...

The knock on the door came without warning, sharp. Three loud raps. Startled, she minimized the computer screen as though what she had up there was illegal, reached for her phone and headed toward the front room to look through the peephole in the door.

Win!

In that fun Christmas tie. Looking wrinkled and sexy and...

Bearing white bags with the emblem of a well-known restaurant not far from her neighborhood.

She pulled open the door.

"If you've eaten, then this will all keep until tomorrow," he said, standing there with his goods, not handing them to her, just holding them there.

"I haven't eaten." She didn't step back, invite him in, though every fiber of her being wanted to. Invite him in. And eat, too, once she got a whiff of the bourbon chicken she knew had to be inside at least one of those bags.

"I overreacted and I apologize."

She couldn't accept an apology that she didn't deserve. And she was too close to let go of her quest. If only she'd met him after she'd found confirmation that her little sister was healthy and happy...

But then, she wouldn't have met him, because she wouldn't have applied to his firm for the job to find out about her little sister.

"Would you like to come in?" she asked. The man was a sweetheart, and she couldn't reject his sincere overture, even if she couldn't accept it.

His hesitation lasted only a second. He entered her home, took the food straight to the kitchen table as though they'd shared meals there before. Started to unpack the bags, and because it seemed like the right thing to do in the moment, Sarah poured glasses of wine for both of them.

She knew what he liked. They'd shared half a bottle at a restaurant the previous week. And she knew how much he'd allow himself before driving.

The dinner, one they'd talked about both liking when they'd passed the restaurant on their way back from the lights spectacular, was fabulous, as always. Neither of them said much.

And yet, where she could have felt incredibly awkward, Sarah was mostly just glad he was there.

She got three-quarters of the way through her meal and then pushed the rest toward him, taking a sip of wine and holding the glass on the table in front of her.

"I don't share my life," she told him. Heard how ominous the words sounded, but didn't take them back. She'd been referring to sharing her woes, her troubles, her choices, but, in the end, the meaning came out to the earlier warning she'd given him about only living in the moment.

He nodded without breaking a chew, seemingly more intent on food than any conversation she might be having.

"Maybe I'm not good for you, withholding my stuff, and all…"

Was there a way to break up without breaking hearts?

Because how could she let him apologize for something he hadn't done wrong? The harshness he'd thought he'd unleashed on her earlier had been a walk on the beach compared to what her real actions deserved.

"Maybe let's just be the friends we said we were going to be and cut each other some slack when one or the other of us isn't perfect."

She couldn't believe he'd said the words. Ones she'd hoped, in her deepest heart, to hear if and when he found out that she'd been using him.

Had the man just given her hope for a future? In spite of her sins?

Had the heavens opened up and seen her down there? Finally?

Turning her head, so he couldn't see the tears that had moistened her eyes before she could blink them back under control, her gaze came to rest on the glow on the wall from the Christmas tree she'd plugged in when she'd first arrived home.

Was she really in line for a Christmas miracle, after all?

Or was she just getting soft because she'd met someone who'd brought her long-lost heart back to life?

Chapter Thirteen

Win had heard of makeup sex. He'd just never felt as intense an urge to have it as he did with Sarah that Monday night, sharing take-out dinner in her older but clean and welcoming kitchen. Her place was smaller than his, less fancy, but it felt much more like a home to him. If he'd been a different man, he'd probably have attempted to do it right there on her table, food be damned.

Instead, when dinner was over, he walked with her through her living room to the front door he'd come in less than an hour before. "We're okay?" he asked her, standing there feeling like a schoolboy rather than the thirty-three-year-old financier he was.

She nodded. Her smile oddly sad, but her gaze filling him up as she met him eye to eye. "I've always thought the only relationship that could ever work was one based on cutting each other slack when one or the other messes up," she said softly, her gaze so intent he was kind of confused as to which of them she was talking about.

"Are you apologizing to me for not telling me you're a nurse?" he asked.

"Something like that." She seemed kind of worried, and it hit him just how much his opinion of her might mean to her.

He knew he hoped it meant a lot, at any rate.

Leaning in, he meant to give her the same mostly light goodbye kiss they'd been sharing every time they'd separated since their first kiss. But when his lips met hers, they met fire, igniting him to the point of no thought.

Pulling her fully against him, he put a hand over her tailbone, spanning the backside that kept him up nights, and pushed her into his erection as his tongue plundered her mouth. But he wasn't the only one being aggressive.

Sarah pressed her chest against his as she grabbed his head with both hands and held their lips together. She smelled like sunshine and rain all wrapped up together. Tasted like bourbon chicken and sex. She overwhelmed his senses and made him need things urgently. So much so that he reached for the button of his jeans, to lessen the painful tension there, and…she backed up.

"I'm sorry," she said, her gaze stricken. "I…please don't be mad."

Angry because a woman said no? Never. Disappointed? Hugely. "I will never be mad for something like this," he told her. "You always need to stop what doesn't feel right to you."

"It feels right," she said then, licking her lips, but lowering her gaze. When she looked back up at him, he couldn't read her at all. "Just not now…please?"

"Of course, Sarah. Always. I want you like crazy, but

only when you want it as badly…" That said, he grabbed her hand, pulled it to his fly.

Which was already deflating. "See?"

The sudden smile that lit her face was worth the pain his lower region was going through. He'd go home and take a cold shower to deal with that.

To think…he'd actually considered letting her walk out of his life without a fight…

He leaned in for one more kiss, careful that nothing but their lips touched, pulled back, rubbed a thumb along her cheek and let himself out.

Sarah Williams was a nurse. Not an office manager.

He could live with that.

As long as he didn't have to think about living without her.

She couldn't keep lying to him.

The kiss had done her in.

She could spend weeks, months, researching Cara Samuels, and Cara could just be the name of another adoptee. Someone who was too young to show up on any social media or people search databases.

And the way Win had kissed her—you couldn't fake that stuff. He really was into her. As much as she was into him.

Or pretty damned close to it.

Not because he'd been dry kindle shooting up into flames with one spark, but because he'd stopped the second she'd given an indication that she needed to do so.

Because after she'd given no good reason for hiding her nursing degree from him when he'd hired her, he'd come to her with an apology for being in attack mode when he'd approached her about it.

Though, what kind of crap luck did she have that Dorian had attended some professional holiday something where Sarah's class standing had been honored? You'd think she'd at least have received an invitation to be present for the praise.

A heads-up that Win could soon be privy to the information.

Regardless, after spending a mostly sleepless night exhausting every search she could think of that would somehow pair a Cara Samuels with her little sister to no avail, she lay down for a couple of hours. Then she took a long hot shower, pulled out her black dressy legging pants, topped them with a long off-white tapered sweater that belted at the waist, slipped on black pumps, took the time to blow-dry her hair and was careful with the light makeup and eyeliner she always wore.

She chose earrings—Christmas trees because…well… because—three pairs, larger to smaller trees going up her ears, in piercings that, in the past couple of years, she'd grown used to leaving empty.

And then, feeling as though she was sixteen again and going off to court for sentencing, she texted Win to ask for an early morning meeting at the office and went to work.

Already at the office when Sarah's text came through Tuesday morning, Win still didn't like the idea that she'd kept something as simple as her being a nurse from him. Mostly because he truly didn't understand the reason for the secrecy, but at the same time, he felt like the incident had brought them closer. Like, perhaps, they were on their way to being something permanent.

Maybe she'd even be working with him at Sierra's

Web as a disaster expert someday. Yeah, the thought was fanciful for a numbers guy like him, but in the weeks she'd been in his life, he'd begun to see possibilities he'd never have entertained before.

Hell, he had a Christmas tree up in his home!

Had he known she was coming, he'd have stopped at Hometown Bagels on his way in. As it was, he had two cups of strong, hot coffee waiting on a tray in his office when she texted that she was in the lobby downstairs and on her way up.

He'd toned down the tie choice from the day before, but the maroon knot he loosened as he waited for Sarah to come up in the elevator was still a bit bolder than he generally wore to work. He'd liked the festive feel of it against his white shirt and black pants as he'd stood at his bathroom mirror that morning and tied the thing.

He liked knowing that Sarah would notice.

He liked that, with her, he noticed so much more than he usually did.

Like the second she stepped into his opened office door, his gaze went to the Christmas trees dotted up her ears.

"Nice earrings," he told her, watching them as she moved her head, and then took in her equally festive attire. The woman was beautiful to him in every way.

"They were a gift from my mom," she said, touching one of them as she sat down on the edge of the seat in front of his desk, rather than taking a step further to kiss him hello.

Frowning, he wasn't sure if he should retreat to his seat behind the desk or not, but chose to prop his hip against the edge of the desk. "What's up?"

Her gaze, when she looked up at him, was…he wasn't

sure what. Not good. Troubled, at the very least. "I have something to tell you."

Right. She'd said she needed to see him. Which explained why she was there half an hour before even Lindsay generally arrived.

"Okay."

"Before I do—" her chin trembled as she continued to meet his gaze "—I want you to know that this…you and me…or even me telling you something private in general…this isn't how I operate."

Thinking of Sierra and her secrets, of Sarah's growing up, he nodded, flooding with compassion for her.

Feeling honored that she was about to give him something she normally kept to herself.

And remembered the secrets Sierra had kept.

If someone had hurt Sarah, the way Sierra had been hurt…

Leaving the desk, he sat in the vacant chair next to her and pulled it closer.

He wanted to take her hand but chose caution instead.

"You were right to question the secret I kept when I hired on here, Win." Not moving, he listened to the words a second time in the privacy of his head. A bit confused.

Or unwilling to accept what he knew they meant. The lapse hadn't been an omission; it had been part of a cover-up. Some kind of purposeful hiding of information.

His initial instinct had been right after all.

Or not.

What possible nefarious scheme could involve hiding the fact that you'd just graduated with highest honors from nursing school?

He waited.

Pushing off the arms of her chair with both hands, she stood, started to pace, making him want to do the same. Whatever she had to say…she just needed to get on with it.

Hanging in limbo was a far more difficult position for him to maneuver his way through than the unrequited sexual desire he'd taken home with him the night before.

As she rounded the edge of his desk, he resisted the instinctive urge to shoo her away from there. From the private Sierra's Web business strewed over the entire face of it.

He came into the office at dawn to work—had always found that those early morning hours were his most productive…

And…Sarah had already had access to every single file in the company, he reminded himself.

Her gasp drove him straight up out of his chair. Too much suspense for him. He needed to know what was going on.

Couldn't force her to talk.

And didn't want to do anything that would stop whatever confession she'd been about to give him.

"What is this?" The question was half whisper, half shriek. The whiteness of her face, the shock in her gaze, was so evident even he got it loud and clear.

And shook his head, confused. "It's the Milford case," he told her, seriously concerned for a second about her mental state. Had she been drinking?

Taking something?

Was an addiction what she'd been hiding from them?

Though the nursing degree wouldn't point that out, maybe someone at the school had found her out?

Made sense, growing up as she had, but...

"It's what?" She stood there over the opened file folder, staring. Her gaze hadn't lifted from it for more than a minute.

"That's Kelly's file from the client who hired us for the Milford case."

"Cara Samuels is the adopter whose child's biological father just died?" Her voice sounded dry. Croaked.

"Cara Samuels is the little girl who was adopted."

Mouth open, she stared at him, looking sick enough to have him thinking he might have been right about her being on something. "Kelly has a list in her office, in a file...it has two columns on it. Both columns have names. What's it for?"

He shook his head, shrugged. "I have no idea."

Without a word to him, she walked out. No explanation. No finishing of her confession. He couldn't just let her go like that.

Couldn't let her drive under the influence, if nothing else.

He followed her to Kelly's office. Started to protest as she reached for the unlocked bottom drawer of his partner's desk, reminding himself she'd already had access to everything that might be there.

She didn't filter through anything. Reached in, grabbed one file, pulled it out, opened it and handed it to him. "Two columns. Labeled B and A. All names. If they were all adoptees, then why two columns? Why the labels? What does it mean?"

Was she some kind of undercover detective? As well

as a nurse? Being a nurse was one of her covers? An alias?

As ridiculous as the thought was, he was ready to believe it. Sierra's Web worked a lot of law enforcement cases. They'd dealt with the dregs of humanity many times.

Had private investigator experts on retainer who worked undercover more often than not.

Did he know her at all?

Had their friendship…the combustible desire…all been an act?

Oh, God, what had he done?

Fallen in love with a fake?

"What does it mean, Win? Are the two columns related to one another? What does A and B stand for?"

He might not have known, if not for the Milford case. He hadn't actually seen the spreadsheet. But when Kelly had given him the Samuels file, she'd told him that…

"I'm guessing that B is before and A is after."

"Before and after what?"

What the hell did it matter? Was she about to accuse Kelly of some nefarious activity? Because if she was…

"Adoption!" He hadn't meant to raise his voice. Never raised his voice in the office. Rarely outside it, unless he was home alone and pounded his thumb with a hammer.

He'd like to be pounding with a hammer right then. Get rid of some of the tension building inside him.

Sarah dropped the file. It splattered to the floor, its contents spilling out, as she fell back into Kelly's chair.

No other way to put it. She didn't sit. She fell.

And looked like she'd seen a ghost, or a glimpse of

hell as, head against the back of the chair, she stared up at him.

"Cara Samuels used to be known as Kylie Williams?"

"I have no idea. I didn't see the list. I just know that she had it. And that she files cases by the adopted names because future reference will always include them. She just keeps a sheet of..."

He stopped as Sarah's eyes filled with tears. She shook her head and said, "It can't be. Makes no sense."

She was making no sense. About to call Dorian—because what other medical personnel would he call so early in the morning—he hesitated. Assessed the woman he wasn't sure he'd ever known.

He didn't need an ambulance squad there. Just someone to pinch-hit for him...

"It can't be," she said again, wiping her eyes brusquely and standing up.

Without a glance in his direction, she strode purposefully back to his office. To his desk. To the file spread open.

Right behind her, he snatched it away from under her gaze. Gathered papers and shoved them haphazardly inside, different angles, bending some.

"Mind telling me what's going on?" he demanded, so not himself, as he stood there with the paper mess held with both arms at his chest.

"I applied for the job here because I saw the Sierra's Web posting on the college bulletin board, exactly as I told you. I'd been watching the firm, exactly as I told you. What I didn't tell you is that I'd been watching the firm since the first posting I saw my freshman year because I recognized the name of the firm, not because of the high-level job postings. Although I was honest when I said that those intrigued me."

Her words came in a rush, her gaze locked on the file in his possession.

"There's been some huge mistake," she said, shaking her head, reminding him of the woman who'd pulled out of his arms the night before.

Vulnerable and strong all at once. Wanting. Denying herself.

Raising in him the protective instincts that were always too little too late.

"You need to start explaining yourself," he said, at a total loss. Not sure if he needed the police, if she *was* the police and he'd been made a fool of, putting the firm at some unforeseen risk, or if she was having a substance-infused breakdown...

While her behavior was odd, she seemed to be cognizant, for the most part...

"Kylie Williams, Win." Her words were almost harsh in their fierceness. *"Williams,"* she repeated through gritted teeth. "She's my baby sister. I took the job here because I saw the posting shortly after I'd had a phone call from my mother telling me that someone was looking at my sister's case again, and we knew Sierra's Web had been hired by the county to vet and recommend adopters. Lily didn't know if Kylie was in trouble, hurt, sick, with social services...or...she didn't know. Only that someone was looking at the case. I had to know. I'm so sorry, but if she was hurt, unhappy, a ward of the state... I'm somebody good now. I could help her..."

Her words broke when her throat gave out and tears started to roll down her face. She didn't sob. Didn't fall apart. Just stood there while he watched her, processing...

"You had no desire to work for Sierra's Web. You just wanted access to our files?" He was reaching for facts. Pulling out what he thought he was seeing.

She nodded. Shook her head. Wrapped her arms around her middle and stared at his chest. The file pressed against it.

He wasn't delving into that information yet.

"Actually, that's not true," she told him, adding more confusion to the situation. "I really have been intrigued by the idea of an expert firm, and by being that great at something…and I really do want to focus my career on some kind of emergency room or disaster relief…"

He wasn't being sidetracked by personal associations that shouldn't have happened. "Did you or did you not hire on here specifically to gain access to our files?"

I'm somebody good now. I could help her. The words from Sarah's speech floated up at him. And he had a flash of Kelly telling him something about another sibling… one who'd been in trouble.

Oh, God.

Oh, great God.

What in the hell did he do?

What should he do going forward?

"I did."

"Then, Sarah *Williams*, I must demand that you collect any personal items you may have in our space, put the laptop you were given to work with on Lindsay's desk and leave. Immediately."

"But…"

"Now, Sarah." He could speak though gritted teeth, too, when desperation pushed him hard enough.

He had to get her out of there. Had to think. With his head, not his heart. Had to alert the partners.

And wanted to take her in his arms, hold her tightly and never let go.

He followed her as she moved silently through the quiet hallway to the kitchen, where she gathered a coffee cup, and then back to the front of the suite, where she pulled a laptop out of the bag she'd had on her shoulder when she'd come into his office. Holding the laptop, as though it were some kind of hostage, she looked up at him.

"Please, Win…"

Feeling as though his heart was actually splitting inside his chest, he said, "Leave it on the desk."

She set the laptop down in the center of Lindsay's desk. Then turned to him, her expression blank. Her manner resolute.

"I deserve what you're doing here," she said, meeting his gaze head-on, eyes wide-open. "I understand it. And there's a mistake, Win. No way Kylie is Cara. You said that the mother in the Milford case gave up the child for adoption…"

"She did."

"I'm not saying she didn't. I'm just saying that it's not the same case. Kylie was taken from us. My mother was as devastated as I was…"

He hadn't been there. Couldn't argue without facts.

"What I know is that you breached our trust, Sarah. You put this firm, our hard-won reputation, at risk by breaching client confidentiality…"

When she shook her head, he almost turned his back on her and walked away. Probably would have if he wasn't the one responsible for seeing that she left and then locking the door of the suite behind her.

"That's one of the reasons I didn't tell you the truth,

Win. Not any of you. I would never have put the firm at risk…"

"We hired you. *I* hired you. That makes me culpable." And sick to his stomach.

"Not in the eyes of the law it wouldn't. You went through the proper channels, did a background check…"

According to Cara's case, the older sibling had been in trouble. There'd been no police record for Sarah. No charges. Could she be right? That two cases were interchanged?

Did it matter? Whether Cara Samuels was her sister, or someone else was, she'd still come to work for them under false pretenses.

"You need to leave," he said again. Sure of only that one thing at that moment.

She blinked. Nodded. Turned her back and walked out of his life.

Bowing his head, Win stood there until he heard the elevator bing just outside their door, gave it time to suck her up and whisk her away, and then he looked up, his vision blurred by tears.

Chapter Fourteen

Why in the hell didn't anguish get any easier? Her lips curled in between her teeth, where she held them steady, Sarah made it to her car. And then around the corner.

Hands shaking, she pulled into an upscale hotel parking lot. Thought about checking in, pretending to be someone she wasn't.

She took deep breaths.

Tried to shut out all the thoughts and recent conversation storming through her mind. To remember who she was.

And who she wasn't.

She'd done this to herself. Had known going in what she was risking.

And while she hadn't planned to fall in love, most particularly not in a matter of weeks, she'd known that allowing feelings for Win to flourish hadn't been a good move.

She'd made it anyway.

Seemed a penchant for wrong choices, albeit made for good reasons, was part of her character.

Or her curse.

The choice to steal food had lost her Kylie.

And the choice to join a firm with an ulterior motive had just lost her the man who could have been the love of her life.

"I don't really believe in such a thing," she said aloud in her little six-year-old car, watching as a couple loaded suitcases into the back of an SUV. They looked young.

And weren't using valet service.

Probably on their honeymoon, her morose frame of mind concluded.

And a clear thought surfaced. Reaching for her cell phone, relieved to have a legitimate reason to make the call, to connect with Win, she pushed his speed dial. Listened to two rings and then heard the click to voice mail.

Either he was on the phone, or he'd just ended her call.

With butterflies in her stomach, she sat there another five minutes. Figured he'd be talking to the partners. Needed to get him before he reached them all. Dialed again.

Went to voice mail again.

There were six partners in addition to himself. At even just one minute a call, five minutes wasn't enough.

After another five, she tried again.

And then, seeing truth in place of hope, sent her message via text.

I took nothing from the firm, and never intended to use any information I found, other than for my own peace of mind, and to ensure that my sister is safe. Were she not, I would go through proper authorities, starting with Sierra's Web, to consider options to help her. I did not, at any time, intend to contact her, or her family.

She read. Fixed a couple of typos. Deleted a line. Re-read. Put the line back. And hit Send.

Maybe she'd hear back from him.

Maybe she wouldn't.

And Kylie?

She'd basically gained nothing. The confirmation of what she'd already known—Sierra's Web had been associated with her sister's adoption case. And she now knew that Kylie's name had been mistakenly listed with her adopted name.

It was up to Kelly Chase to sort that one out.

And when she did, Sarah could pretty much bet her life on the fact that she'd never know about it.

Sarah wasn't giving up. She'd never give up on Kylie.

But starting over again…was getting old.

So much for Christmas wishes. Christmas gifts.

And based on the pain roaring through her, hope was hugely overrated, too. It just made the inevitable end result that much more agonizing.

She'd come to him. Sitting in his office later on Tuesday morning, Sarah's text message box was open for the umpteenth time. Win tried to focus on work, to step away from the pain of betrayal, from feeling like an imbecile, only to come back each time to one fact.

She'd come to him.

There was no reason for Sarah to have outed herself. He'd accepted her explanation for not telling the firm she was a nurse. They'd moved on.

Clearly, he had, with his blatant show of besotted-ness at her door the night before.

And then, that morning, she'd come to him.

Something that was not protocol for her—exactly the opposite of the way she worked.

Something Sierra had never done.

He'd told her how badly that had hurt him. She knew he carried Sierra's inability to tell him she'd been raped, to let him help her, with him still. That it affected the way he saw himself, his relationships, and was shaping his future.

She'd come to him. And had had nothing to gain by doing so, but everything to lose.

He had to fire her. He'd do it again, every time.

As his partners would expect him to do.

A niggle of guilt crept up on him. He needed to call all six of them. Let them know that Sarah was no longer with them. He'd have to tell them why.

And he would.

Just…she'd come to him.

That had taken a lot of guts.

Self-sacrifice.

Risk.

The move deserved some kind of acknowledgment. A thank-you at the very least.

And as he calmed down, managed to climb outside his own personal heartache, he had questions, too.

What information did you gain about your sister's case from our firm?

He read the text. Let it sit there for a while in case he thought better of sending it. Then hit Send.

None. The response back was immediate, as though she'd been sitting there staring at her phone waiting to hear from him. Then his text app dinged again.

No files, nothing. The only mention I ever found of her was that list in Kelly's desk. And if that's what you think, a list of before and after names for adoptees, Kylie's listing is wrong.

Kylie Williams.

Sarah had a little sister who'd been taken from her eight years before. She'd have been sixteen. Dealing with an addict mother.

So who'd cared for the baby? Done the proverbial midnight feedings?

He knew who. The same woman who spent every Thanksgiving and Christmas in Disneyland, basically forgetting rather than celebrating, because it was what her mother—her family—needed.

Kelly had told him that Cara Samuels had a biological sibling who'd been in trouble. On a hunch, and because he needed all his ducks in a row, all of the information he could get, before he went to the partners, he sent another text.

Were you ever in trouble as a youth?

When a reply didn't immediately shoot back, he told himself it was a good thing. That he needed to focus on moving forward, not looking back.

Half an hour later, his phone rang. He looked at the screen before answering. *Sarah.*

He didn't think it a good idea to speak with her. Personally. His nonprofessional self, the one with the heart involved, didn't want to talk to her.

But the professional who'd hired her, who needed to have answers to questions his partners would likely ask, should do so.

"Yeah," he answered. No *Hi, Sarah.*

If she noticed the difference—and Sarah would— she didn't indicate as she said, "I will answer any questions you have as a partner in Sierra's Web, but I will not put it all in writing. Nor do so electronically where I could be overheard without knowing who's listening."

Wow. Her caution was a huge peek into the life she'd led. And a kick to his heartstrings.

"I'm here alone," he told her.

"We do it in person or not at all."

His first thought, to wonder what she had to gain from doing so, was quickly quashed by the obvious answer. Nothing. She'd lost all access to what she wanted—anything to do with her little sister.

She was cooperating with him, knowing he had to answer to his partners, but she was going to do it on her terms.

Tatters of the respect he'd had for her seemed to appear at some of the rattiest edges.

And there was another thought to consider—one all of the partners would come to on their own, he was sure—where was Kylie Williams and was she okay?

Not that he intended to share that with Sarah.

"When and where?" The question was succinct.

"I'm at the base of Camelback Mountain, getting ready to head up," she said, naming a famous mountain right in the middle of the city, not far from Sierra's Web offices. He had done the walking trail to the top the first time he'd visited Arizona years before. "Meet me in the parking lot at the base in a couple of hours."

Agreeing, Win hung up, with a strict admonition to himself not to fall for any emotional crap when he was with her. His own, most of all.

Even as he knew he'd have climbed the damned mountain with her if she'd asked him to do so. Sarah Williams had somehow managed to get her hooks in him after just a few weeks. Something no other woman in more than ten years had been able to do.

Now he was going to have to find a way to free himself.

She climbed for an hour. Coming down took half that time. In black leggings, a long-sleeved white T-shirt, black quilted vest and black-and-white tennis shoes, Sarah adjusted her sunglasses, found a warm rock in direct sunlight and sat, increasing the serotonin that would help stave off anxiety and depression. She was an Arizona native, and her body knew what to crave.

She was many things.

The product of her mother's choices, yes, but of her own as well.

Win wanted to know if she'd been in trouble...her juvenile record was sealed. She didn't have to tell him.

But she would.

A choice she was making to atone for the decision she'd made to deceive him in the first place. The choice she had to make to be able to live with herself and move on.

She'd hardly ever let herself think about what it would feel like to not move on. To be able to stay where she was for the rest of her life.

Ironic that she thought she didn't know. She was the only person she knew still living in the house she'd been born in. If that wasn't not moving on, nothing was.

And yet…how would it feel to have a real family? One that didn't leave. One she didn't have to leave. One that she could come home to every night.

It was her own damned fault she'd let her guard down with Win. She'd told him not to expect permanence, and then she'd gone and let the thought in.

"You look like a goddess…"

At first she thought she'd imagined his words, but when she heard steps crunch on the hard ground beside her, she opened her eyes to see Win there, still in the clothes he'd been wearing in his office that morning, hands in his pockets.

"A moderate amount of sun, with sunscreen protection, is good for you," she told him inanely.

"Did you make it to the top?"

"Almost. I chose not to." Time meditating in the sun had been more important. As her heart rate sped up at the sight of him standing there in the desert, looking so out of place and so right, she figured the added exercise might have been the wisest choice. She hadn't expended enough of the nervous energy that coursed through her any time he was around.

Unless it bred in his presence, which was the possibility she was going with.

Perching his butt on the edge of a boulder a couple of feet from hers, his hands loosely linked in front of him, he said, "So were you in trouble?"

The first words on the tip of her tongue were to ask him to define *trouble*. But they weren't there to parry. Or to play games.

"Once. I was arrested for shoplifting. I pleaded guilty in juvenile court. Was sentenced to community service. Served my sentence. And the record was sealed."

She looked him in the eye. "And that's why my sister was taken from us." She gave him the rest, voluntarily. Waiting for him to pull it out of her would be too excruciating. "Mom and I left her with a neighbor while we went to court for my hearing. Mom was pulled out of court while I was waiting for my turn to appear. I didn't know it at the time, but it was to be told that Kylie had been taken from us. She heard mention of Sierra's Web being given the job of finding a new home for her. All I knew was that when we got home that night, she was gone. There in the morning, gone that night."

"And that makes sense to you? That an older sibling pleads guilty to one count of minor theft and the younger child is removed from the home?"

If he was trying to make her feel better, as she'd tried to do when he'd been blaming himself for Sierra's inability to come to him for help, he'd succeeded a little, in that it eased her heart to hear him try, but...

"Child services had been to the house before, when Mom had had issues, went into work high, that kind of thing. But they'd come to the house, see it all picked up, clean, well cared for, same for us kids, and off they'd go. With me showing signs of delinquency, that's all they needed to rescue the toddler before Mom had a wrongful effect on her, too."

It didn't sound as strong a case out loud as it did inside her, but he'd have had to have been there, as she'd been, to get the full picture.

"Did your mother tell you it was because of you?"

She shook her head. "Lily's not like that. She'd never

say anything harmful like that to me, no matter how true it was. She just told me they'd taken her from us, blamed herself, actually, because of her inability to stay away from drugs whenever life dealt us a blow. She'd actually been clean for a couple of years before my grandmother died, and she hit the skids again and ended up pregnant. Then she stayed clean through the pregnancy and I thought...you know...maybe...but right after the baby was born, she was back at it.

"Until they took her from us. As far as I know, she hasn't touched an illegal substance, or alcohol, since that day."

His gaze felt kind. She couldn't really tell, though, with the sun's glare hiding most of it from her. Just as well. If it wasn't, she'd be hurt. And if it was...

She didn't need any more emotions pulling at her, warring inside of her.

"Do you know who Kylie's father was?"

"No, and neither did Mom." And there he had that ugly truth. "She'd been with a few guys during a week-long binge and wasn't even sure who they were." She'd finally got that truth out of Lily a couple of Christmases before when she'd told her mother that all she wanted for Christmas that year was the truth.

"I'm sure all of this is in Kylie's file, but I couldn't find it anywhere," she told him, because she was there so he'd know that she'd taken nothing from the firm. Had not compromised them. Not from lack of trying, but from lack of success. "It's not with the county files, and not anywhere else, either. I've made it through all of them now..."

He wanted the truth. She was giving it to him.

"Actually, none of it would have been," he told her.

"Personal information on the adoptee is not given to the placement counselor, at least not in Kelly's cases. She only interviews prospective adopters, and since, based on my math from you saying earlier that you were ten when your grandmother died, Kylie would have just been a toddler, right?" He paused.

"Two, right."

"So, with her being just a toddler, it wasn't like there was any community that she'd fit better with than another, so there was no need to know…"

She'd been a "no need to know" in her sister's life. Sarah felt the pang. Knew she'd cry about it when she was alone.

And knew, too, that in the long run, it didn't matter.

She didn't matter in Kylie's life. Because while she'd loved the little one with every fiber of her being, Kylie wouldn't even remember her.

And she'd given Win all that she had. "Is there anything more you need from me?" she asked, standing.

"Not at the moment." He walked beside her toward the parking lot, his hands in his pockets again. Safely contained, the thought occurred to her.

"May I contact you again if something comes up?" he asked as they reached the sidewalk.

So formal. So clearly not asking for personal reasons. "Of course."

They'd reached her car. Pulling her keys out of the pocket on the water bottle carrier strapped to her waist, she headed toward the driver's door, needed to get in the seat and take control of steering her life.

"Sarah?"

Telling herself not to look over at him, she did it anyway. Couldn't really see his eyes with the sunglasses and glare.

"I'm sorry."

"You didn't do anything to be sorry for."

"I'm sorry for all of it. The way you grew up, losing your sister. Just...you're a good person. Don't ever doubt that."

His words started to warm her heart, which made her angry. Mostly with herself, but since he was there... "I don't need your pity, Win. I'm a big girl and I've made a good life for myself, despite how it might seem to you."

With that, she got in her car, shut the door, and if he tried to get her attention again, he failed.

Because she was in the driver's seat, and because seeing him in person hadn't brought the comfort she'd hoped it would. Because being with him hurt so much, she had to be done with him. She just couldn't take any more.

Chapter Fifteen

Win spoke to Kelly first and then Dorian and Hud, before letting Lindsay know that Sarah would no longer be working for them. That he'd be hiring someone to finish her work with the filing system.

To his surprise, the older woman expressed regret at Sarah's departure, and displeasure at not even being able to say goodbye. He hadn't told her why Sarah was gone—only that she'd had something come up in her personal life.

He phoned the rest of the partners, one by one, and was surprised to receive the same response from every one of them—while they didn't condone Sarah's duplicitous reasons for signing on with them, they understood her reasons and trusted that she'd had the firm's well-being in mind the entire time she'd been with them.

They also concurred with his firing of her. She'd hired on under false pretenses.

The morning passed, and then half of the afternoon. He couldn't get Sarah out of his mind.

Thought about phoning her when he should have been trying to wrap up the Milford case. Whether Sarah's sister could be found or not, Cara Samuels still deserved to receive the funds due her.

Several of the accounts they'd amassed over the past weeks showed the same expenditures to a company that existed in name only, which paid another company that existed in name only, which paid into an offshore bank account, and that account came back into various accounts in the States, at amounts always less than what had to be reported to the federal government to go...where?

He'd never seen so much money movement for such small amounts.

Had Milford turned it all into cash? He bought a lot of clothes.

A lot of clothes, he noticed, looking at Sarah's spreadsheet against some of the accounts that had just come in.

He made small donations to various charities. And spent a load of money having his boats cleaned and maintained.

The boats weren't his concern. It was up to the courts to see that they got title to them. Assuming he owned them outright. If not, the vessels could be repossessed for nonpayment if the Samuelses couldn't sell them for more than what was owed on them and make a few dollars.

But...looking at the spreadsheets, thinking as Sarah had taught him to think, he stared.

And had a legitimate reason to call her.

When she didn't pick up, he texted, telling her he really needed to speak to her. That it was important. A minute later his phone rang.

"I'm so sorry to bother you, and you can hang up if you want to, but you have nothing on the Milford spreadsheets to do with boating. Did you put marine gasoline under regular fuel? Or docking fees on parking? He saw substantial amounts spent on both the fuel and parking, but…"

"Hello to you, too," she said dryly. "There was nothing to do with the water anywhere in what I found," she told him. "Why?"

"Because all the accounts I showed you emptied into various offshore accounts and I've found where they came back into different accounts in the States, and ultimately the money is ending up paying a legitimate company that maintains boats. He pays them enough to maintain a fleet of them."

Silence fell on the line, and he sat there, feeling like an insensitive fool.

Milford and Sierra's Web were no longer her concern.

"I apologize, Sarah, I'm no longer paying you for your time on this matter."

His thumb was on the End Call button when he heard a sniff.

"Are you okay?"

"Fine."

And the call ended.

She hadn't thought the plan through far enough. As Sarah sat on the couch in her living room late that afternoon, Christmas tree lights glimmering, tablet on her lap, looking for a job, she realized that having taken a job under false pretenses could follow her into the rest of her life. Obviously, she couldn't put Sierra's Web down as a reference, but they would be a part of her official employment record. She'd been fired from a job.

Of course, she hadn't been there long. Could explain away the six weeks between getting her nursing license and applying for jobs as time spent looking for the right job for her. Or as family leave time.

And start the next job off on a lie, too?

And that was the problem with being duplicitous. Much like addiction to drug fixes, lies bred at an alarming rate, one leading to another and another, and there was no magic cure that would kill off the need for them.

She was more like her mother than she'd thought.

Except that she wasn't.

Picking up the phone on the cushion beside her, she glanced at the screen. Pushed for recent calls.

He'd called her after firing her, asking for work assistance.

She pushed Send on the call.

"Sarah, what can I do for you?"

The greeting was better than the "yeah" with which he'd greeted her earlier in the day.

"I'd like a chance to resign," she said. "For the official record. I realize that I do not have a stand-up argument to defend the request, but I was fully cooperative this afternoon when you called needing my professional opinion on a Sierra's Web business matter, without compensation. I'd like to propose that in exchange for any such information you might need in the future, I agree to make myself available to the firm, free of charge, and keep my right to resign."

"I already marked your employee file with a no fault, mutual party split."

Oh. Well. Good. But, "I was at fault."

"You also, as my partners pointed out, protected the firm's interests and performed your job duties far above expectation."

She had done that.

And, "I'm sorry, Win. I felt so guilty lying to you, from the very beginning, and more critically after we, after you and I…well, anyway…with my sister's well-being in question, I did what I felt I had to do."

She'd already apologized. Repeating the gesture wasn't going to change anything. Especially since, given the same set of circumstances, even knowing the ending, she'd do the same again. She wasn't giving up on Kylie. She just had to find another way in.

"Can I ask an admittedly just curious question?"

"Why not?" She'd bared herself to him. Had nothing left to hide. If he wanted to know if any of it had been real for her, if she'd cared about him at all, she'd tell him. What would it hurt at that point for him to know that he'd managed to breach walls no one in her life ever had?

"What did you steal?"

Seriously? She'd been thinking heart and soulmate and…he wanted to know her crime.

"Four cans of vegetable stew. Lily had used the month's grocery money on a binge—the trust my grandmother set up for her paid the household bills automatically and gave my mother spending money each month for food and incidentals. Anything she made at work was for vacation, presents, car payment, that kind of thing. Anyway, I'd had to quit my job months before to take care of the baby and she needed to eat."

"You didn't think to ask for help?"

"And risk someone calling social services?" Which was exactly what she'd risked, and caused, by her stupid, stupid move. "Funny thing was—" she sat there with the glistening lights, remembering back "—from the moment I was arrested, Lily straightened up. Two months later, when I went to court to be sentenced, she was completely clean."

"Almost as though your arrest finally woke her." Win's voice sounded softer than it had all day. Almost as though he was her friend again.

"I think it was the very real threat of losing Kylie that did that." Not that they'd ever know for sure. Lily had made it very clear at Thanksgiving that there would be no more talk about that time in their lives.

Sarah sure as hell wasn't risking another setback for her mother by forcing the issue. What was past was past. She wanted Lily's future to be healthy and would do whatever she could to help make that happen.

What was she doing? Trying to get him to be her friend again? Residual hope waiting to trap her some more?

"Is there anything else?" she asked abruptly.

"Not at the moment."

The call was going to end, and he'd be gone. He might understand her motive, but she'd lost his trust. She'd knowingly deceived him even after he'd told her that his last girlfriend had done the same.

"Thank you for the no fault mutual split," she said.

"It was the right thing to do. Take care, Sarah."

She heard the call beep but didn't look to verify it had ended. Glistening lights blurred into a collage of colors as tears filled her eyes.

Win could do without the constant lump he'd been carrying in his chest since his talk with Dorian in the courtyard outside work.

Two days had passed since his last conversation with Sarah, and he still couldn't get her off his mind. Maybe because he was finally wrapping up the Milford case.

He'd found the money. A load of it. All safely tucked away in a company Milford had created under his first and middle names, with a legal tax identification number, that was ostensibly in business to offer boating maintenance, but which he just used to pay himself from all the various accounts he'd amassed. Hidden in the company's papers of incorporation was the definition of the term boating maintenance. *A man's boat is a vessel by which he carries his assets. Boating maintenance is defined as maintaining those assets.* He'd paid all taxes on the business's income from himself. Made charitable donations and some safe investments with it, too. There was nothing illegal about what he'd done. The man had been incredibly inventive, and perhaps cautious, to the point of paranoid.

And the upshot was that Cara Samuels was going to be a very rich little girl.

That thought was growing the lump in Win's chest. Along with other nonmoney or number-related facts that were slowly sorting themselves out in a way that built their own portrait.

Kelly had said that she'd seen Cara Samuels's birth mother in the courthouse for a brief moment—that the woman had been pointed out to her by the social services worker on the case. And Kelly would only have been there if she'd been appearing before the judge to render her expert opinion and recommendation for placement. Often that final appearance had been a formality, as Kelly would have already given her opinion to the county, and the family was notified and present in court to take custody at that time. Sarah lost her sister the day she was in court with her mother, and her mother said she'd seen Sierra's Web there.

According to Sarah, that was how she had heard of Sierra's Web in the first place.

It could be a huge coincidence, but...

Kelly never made mistakes when it came to her paperwork. She triple-checked herself, with wait periods in between, to make certain of her accuracy. At least she had back in the beginning, which had been when she'd worked for the county.

No one was perfect. Including Kelly.

But...he had to get past the lump. Couldn't seek out Sarah's sister. Doing so would be a definite conflict of interest for the firm that had recommended her placement in confidentiality, for a sealed adoption.

Milford's will stated that his assets were to go to his heir or heirs.

Heirs.

What if Sarah was one?

The lump would dissolve. Win would have helped her as she'd helped them. He wouldn't need to feel bad for her, would find her dissected from his system and start discovering his future.

The chance of Sarah being an heir to the client they'd been researching was a trillion to one. In math world.

In the strange universe in which he'd been unwittingly catapulted...she'd come to them because she'd heard her sister's case was being looked at. She'd been there specifically because of movement with her sister's case. With them because of their association with her sister's case. She'd been through every file in the firm and had found no mention of her sister.

She'd never been through Cara Samuels's file.

Because it had been in his possession.

He could call her, offer her the chance to go through the file, to see if anything stood out to her.

No, he could not.

Legally, if his out-there suspicion proved true, she deserved half of the money he'd found.

Oh, good God. He could just see it. *Merry Christmas, Sarah! Look what Santa left under the tree for you!*

The woman had been struggling when most kids were taking their parents and security for granted. She'd had to steal stew to feed her baby sister.

Everything she'd accomplished in life had been because of her own tenacious hard work.

If anyone deserved a windfall, it was her.

He'd been hired by the other heir to find the money. They'd allowed him access to Kelly's file on them, as part of proving their legitimacy so he'd take their case. How could he be the one responsible for that girl possibly losing half of her inheritance?

The amount tallied on a report in front of him could easily be split among four children and have them all be taken care of for life.

Sarah had come to him. She hadn't found any information at the firm, had gained nothing from them to use, had zero chance of being found out, and she'd come to him with the truth.

Her example made the lump grow, not dissipate, which was his goal.

He picked up the phone, dialed the number for Jason Samuels, the man who'd hired him on his adopted daughter's behalf, and did what Sarah had done. He told the truth.

* * *

Sarah had received calls for interviews on all four applications she'd submitted. As Christmas gifts, those calls were pretty noteworthy. And she'd had a call offering a dream job, as well, working in the emergency room of the largest children's hospital in the valley. Apparently, the gathering that Dorian had attended had gained her recognition among top health professionals, so while that meeting had set in motion the eventual loss of the job she'd loved, with a man who was probably the love of her life, it brought bounty, too.

Kind of how life worked. The extreme bad produced good. Like her arrest and subsequent loss of Kylie. It had borne her mother's sobriety, and her own attention to job, schooling and work ethic, which was granting her the opportunity to have her pick of jobs.

And, she hoped, it had brought Kylie a better life than being raised by her sixteen-year-old sister in a home with their mother vacillating back and forth between being clean and higher than a kite.

On Friday of that week from hell, she'd just hung up the phone after making the interview appointment for the ER position for the following week, less than two weeks before Christmas, when her phone rang. Win's identification information showed up on the screen. She'd snapped a photo of him at the gingerbread house display on their first official date, had had it as a picture identification, but had deleted it the night before, after a couple of days of hoping she'd hear from him and then not.

The lack of a picture made her sad. And strengthened her backbone, too. She had five interviews scheduled for five jobs that would be great forward moves for her.

On the fifth ring, after debating letting him go to voice mail, she said, "Hello?" As though she didn't know who was there.

"I have some information to discuss with you." He started in without any kind of greeting, as usual. She was equally glad and annoyed by that. They weren't personal anymore. He needed to be more professional. And he felt close enough to her to just start right in without any preamble.

But then, he'd done it with her so early on in their relationship, chances were, he did it with everyone. Win wasn't at the head of the class when it came to people skills.

One of the things that endeared her to him.

Maybe because putting people at ease was something she'd always thought she excelled at. A born nurturer, her grandmother used to say.

"You there?"

He could see she hadn't disconnected.

She could have put the phone down and walked away. Thought about it. "Yeah."

"I'd like to schedule a time to meet."

He couldn't compel the meeting. Not professionally at any rate. But she wasn't even going to try and pretend that he hadn't already compelled it from her heart with the phone call.

"I'm free now," she said. Five o'clock on a Friday afternoon. He could take it or leave it. If he had other plans, some social engagement, he'd have to make a choice.

The firm's Christmas gathering was on Saturday. And as of Monday, he had nothing else. She knew he'd had invitations from various banks and financial institutions, but Win wasn't that guy. He didn't excel at hanging out in a crowd of smiling people, holding a drink and making conversation.

He'd told her so on the way to the orchestra. Had hoped they didn't run into the client of his who'd helped him get the great seats during the intermission.

"You want me to come there?"

Absolutely not. Because she couldn't help but think... yes, please. "I'll come to Sierra's Web," she told him, challenging him to tell her she was no longer welcome within the hallowed doors.

"I'll be waiting."

Well, crap. She had to put on going-out clothes and drive in rush-hour traffic.

Copying behavior from him, she hung up the phone and ran for the shower. Flannel pants and unshowered was not the way she was going to see him again.

She couldn't reverse what he thought of her, but she could leave him eating his heart out.

The thought was beneath her. Unlike her.

But she didn't change her mind.

Chapter Sixteen

"You really love this woman."

Pacing the reception of Sierra's Web, perching on the arm of a chair, and then pacing again, Win shook his head. "I can't love her, Kel," he said, throwing his partner a glance, and then, straightening the plain black tie he'd chosen with black pants and a pristine and pressed white shirt that morning, he continued to pace again. "I can't trust her not to lie to me if she determines that it's best for her. I know she's not Emily…" He'd barely thought of the woman he'd left behind in Arkansas over the past months, but he'd had her duplicity on his mind all week. "But she made the same choice."

Leaning against the corner of a wall, looking all professional in a blue suit with a cream blouse, Kelly's loosely curled blond hair fell around her as she turned those compassionate blue eyes on Win. "She's got you all wound up," she pointed out softly.

Why couldn't he have fallen for Kelly? She was gorgeous. Smart. Generous. Compassionate. And a best friend or sister to him.

"I feel for her." He tried to explain the tragedy playing out inside him. "The woman was born into a bit of a bum rap—although, thankfully, she had her grandmother for the first ten years of it. Then there she is, no more than a kid, dealing with her own grief and having her mother off on binges, getting pregnant, bringing the baby home… She was fourteen when she basically took up full responsibility for Kylie's care…"

Kelly knew everything he was telling her. She'd flown in that morning specifically to meet with Win and Jason Samuels. And had been counseling Win on what to say when he met with Sarah.

His partner had mentioned calling Lily Williams, but he'd vetoed that one straight out. If anyone contacted Lily, it would be Sarah.

Period.

Just as he'd rejected the plan to have Kelly present when he met with Sarah. No way he was going to make her feel ganged up on.

He'd relented, though, at the idea of having Kelly present in the suite, just in case. Once it became known that Sarah was insisting on meeting him there.

"She's made something great out of her life," he said then. "Not just going to nursing school, but graduating at the top of her class. She's loyal to the mother that made her life pure hell at times…"

And she'd done it all alone. How much more could Sarah take?

"Maybe we should just leave well enough alone," he

said again, a stab of panic hitting his gut as he stopped walking and stared at his partner. "What would it hurt?"

Kelly's shrug did nothing to encourage him. "It might not have hurt anything," she said. "But the choice isn't yours to make now."

Because he'd opened his damned mouth. Talked to Samuels, who'd talked to his wife, who'd talked to their lawyer, who'd…yada, yada, yada.

"I can meet with her, Win."

No. As much as Sarah trusted anyone, she trusted Win. Even an emotional imbecile like him got that one.

No way he was pawning her off. Or hiding from the tough stuff. He'd wanted Sierra to let him share her burden, to protect her where he could, and she'd refused to give him that right. He wasn't walking out on Sarah's needs.

If nothing else, there were the financial ramifications to maneuver, not that she'd be overly fazed by that.

Family was all that mattered to Sarah Williams, and hers was about to be imploded.

The elevator bing, usually a minimal sound in the office, blared so loud it shot lightning through him.

He glanced at Kelly, who straightened. Gave him a concerned smile, and said, "I'll be in my office."

His nod was meant to be in her direction, but ended up being delivered to the front door.

The elevator door opened.

Sarah stood there, dressed pristinely in black leggings—that left no part of her mouthwatering womanly shape to the imagination—a tight lavender top that practically screamed out that her breasts were too sexy for words, and a calf-length long-sleeved sweater thing that was partially see-through and revealed as much as it concealed as it tipped up against tight black leather boots. Her hair seemed to glow as it caped around her, and the makeup, deep burgundy lipstick included, begged to be photographed.

For the page of some very private, accessible only to him, hot sexy Sarah magazine.

Or he could just kiss it off…

When she stepped off the elevator, managing the high heels of her boots as though she'd been born to them, he moved forward to hold the door for her, reminding himself that her visit was strictly professional.

His heart and body were a minor nuisance and would settle in a second or two.

His mind would take over, as it always did, the job would get done and he'd move on to the next challenge that life would bring him.

Leaving Sarah Williams and his brief time with her in the past.

The plan was solid.

Smart.

Good.

He just wished he felt a bit more confident about his ability to bring it through to successful implementation.

She was a fool to have insisted that they meet at Sierra's Web.

His territory.

He'd offered to come to hers. She could have chosen someplace neutral. But no, she'd insisted on making her way as difficult as possible. Shooting herself in the foot.

Just as she'd done the day she'd shoplifted four cans of stew.

Seemed she hadn't learned after all.

Win stood there, looking so solid, so…like she wanted to walk into his arms and pretend life hadn't happened to her.

The thought, so unlike her independent self, scared her. Straightening her shoulders, stiffening her backbone, she felt her heart start to pound as she walked through the door he held open for her. Whatever he had to speak to her about couldn't be good.

Not with that pinch to his face.

And the fact that she hadn't even been allowed to walk through the front door unescorted.

"Sarah, thank you for coming," he said, not even seeming to notice that she'd dressed to the nines.

So much for making him eat his heart out.

As if she'd ever had that much allure where he was concerned.

Without another word, he turned and headed toward his office. She could have stood her ground. Made him invite her to follow him. Wanted to be in some kind of control where he was concerned. Lord knew, her heart had deserted her on that score. She loved the man. If she hadn't known it before, or been ready to admit to such a disaster, the past couple of days had shown her the truth.

And because she loved him, because she trusted him and wanted to attend to whatever business he had for her so she could get out of there and back on the road without him so she could begin to heal, she followed behind him without a word.

"Have a seat." Leaving his door open, he motioned toward the chair she'd occupied every other time she'd been in his office.

"Is someone else here?" Almost six on a Friday night…

"Kelly's in town for the night and catching up on some work."

Kelly Chase. Should she stop in and see if the woman would speak to her?

And what would she ask?

Hey, would you mind compromising your ethics and helping me climb out of a hell of my own making?

Win sat behind his desk. Touched a file lying there. Stood. Came around the desk to lean one hip on the corner of it. Then stood again and took his seat.

His agitation making her uneasy, she asked, "What's going on?"

Fear struck through her. She batted it down. Was Sierra's Web going to press criminal charges against her? Wouldn't she be talking to the police if they were?

Unless Win was feeling guilty and wanted to give her a heads-up.

But…was failing to disclose the full reason for your hiring a crime? She hadn't accessed anything she hadn't been authorized to access, and she hadn't taken anything.

Except a name. Cara Samuels. She'd done a full people search of the name on her computer. If that was illegal, she was cooked…

Didn't matter that her motives were selfless and pure. They'd been pure when she'd stolen stew, too.

"I've got some things to tell you and I'm struggling to get it out." His words sent another stab of fear to her gut. The uncertainty claiming his features calmed her some.

"It's like taking off a Band-Aid, Win. You just do it quickly so it hurts less."

Her knees felt weak, and her hands started to shake. "Please," she said.

When he came around to sit next to her, leaning his elbows on his knees, bringing him closer to her than he'd been all week, she wanted so badly to touch him. To hold his hand or something.

"Your mother gave your sister up for adoption."

The words fell around her. She heard them. Didn't compute them, though. What did Lily have to do with anything, and how did Win know her?

"She planned to turn her over to her adoptive parents the day that you were sentenced on your shoplifting charge. She met the adoptive parents. And thanked them for giving her baby girl a loving home."

"No, she didn't."

He was just going where he didn't belong. Talking about stuff he couldn't possibly know. He meant well, she was sure, but...

"There's more, Sarah."

Head shaking, she stared at him. "I was there, Win. I know my mom. She did not willingly give Kylie away."

He sucked in his bottom lip, chewed it a second and said, "I have proof that she did."

Proof?

Glancing around the room, as though people would be lining the walls, nodding that he was right, or signs would be hanging there, or something equally hideous and obvious, she realized that she wasn't just talking to Win. She was talking to an expert. In a firm of experts. Investigators included.

Kylie hadn't been taken from them? Lily had willingly *given* that baby away? But...

"You didn't see my mother's anguish, Win. She was as devastated as I was..."

"I'm sure she was. That doesn't change the facts.

Child protective services had chosen to allow Kylie to remain in your home on the condition that your mother went into rehab and was monitored on a weekly basis with no setbacks. A neighbor was to stay with you and your sister during that time."

"But…" She heard him. Understood. Just couldn't find acceptance within herself for his version of things. Didn't believe. "She didn't do it, Win. I'm telling you. My mother might have been a terrible caregiver after Kylie was born, but she loved that baby as fiercely as I did. She wouldn't have just given her away."

"She did it, Sarah."

He sounded so completely sure of himself. So…strong in his belief.

So…Win.

He wouldn't lie to her.

"But…why?" she finally asked.

"I haven't spoken with her to ask that question, Sarah." Win's tone came through a cottony fog, sounding more distant. "None of us have. I knew you'd want to make that call."

None of them. So… "The partners, Lindsay, they all know about this?" Why that mattered she couldn't say. But it was something she could grasp hold of.

"Kelly, Hud and Dorian know."

She weighed the news. Was okay with it.

"I know what the adoptive parents told me about your mother's motives." He sounded hesitant again. "I don't want to tell you, but as much as I hate things being withheld from me, I can't then allow myself to with- hold information."

She met his gaze, her eyes stinging. "I wanted to tell you, Win. I hated not telling you. But if my little sister's in trouble…don't you see? I'd have put you in a compromising position by telling you, and I couldn't not look for her…"

He held her gaze. And then said, "Your mother did love Kylie, enough to know that she didn't want her to grow up as you had, seeing her in and out of addictive episodes. You had your grandmother, but Kylie…"

"Only had me. After the arrest, Mom didn't trust me to be a good enough influence on Kylie." The truth hit like rocks to the head. It wasn't the state that hadn't found her worthy. It was her own mother.

"No, Sarah. Please. Listen." With a finger to her chin, he lifted her gaze to him. "This is not your fault. It never was. What your arrest did was showed your mother what she, what her addiction, had done to *you*. She gave up Kylie for you. Because she would not let her errors in judgment ruin another second of your life. Seeing you in custody is what scared her straight, according to what we've been told. She adored Kylie, but she loved you more, and she was going to do whatever it took to see that you got the best life you could make for yourself in spite of her."

She blinked at the tears that filled her eyes but didn't fight them. She knew she wouldn't win. Her heart ached so bad she wasn't sure the pain would ever stop.

Her own mother had…

All those years of anguish…missing that precious baby girl…

Lily had given up her own heart for Sarah?

Her mother had sacrificed her own baby to take care of Sarah?

"There's more." Win sounded like a judge handing

down a sentence. The facts were there. Had to be delivered. It was his job.

Wiping her eyes, she looked at him. "Tell me." Get it over with.

"You remember that story I told you about the mother who gave up her child in a closed adoption, with the stipulation being that the father could never get close to the child again?"

She frowned, shrugged. "The Milford case..." And went cold. Blood drained away. She felt it go.

"There was an older sibling," Win said. "Same father, only he didn't know about it. Hadn't seen the mother for some time before Kylie was conceived. The mother didn't want the father or the older child to find out about each other." He paused. She sat there, filling with horror. "The child had been in some recent trouble and the mother feared that..."

"The drug-dealing father could somehow come into the picture and the older child would be lost..." Who couldn't see that one coming? It was low-budget film at its worst.

"Something like that."

What in the hell was he telling her?

He expected her to believe that...

"Your mother and father were high school sweethearts, Sarah." The soft feminine voice came from behind her, an angel, coming to take her out of hell, to end her earthly life and just let her go up into the clouds, where there was plenty of blue skies, sunshine and... gentle breezes.

An angel of sorts on earth. It was Kelly Chase. Right there in the room. The expert psychiatrist kept talking. "She and James went to some parties, smoked what they thought was really good marijuana. It was laced with heroin and they were addicted before they even knew they'd touched the stuff. Your mom's parents stepped in, did what they could. Got her into rehab, where it was discovered that she was pregnant with you. James was a foster kid and he was sent away. He never knew she'd been pregnant. He was placed with a good family in California, finished high school, went on to college, managing his addiction well, but getting into dealing, too…"

Kelly was sitting in the chair Win had occupied. He leaned on his desk, facing her. Sarah focused on the soft, feminine voice. The strong, compassionate blue eyes. She took a deep breath and said what had to be said. "James Milford is my father?"

There was horror in her tone. In her heart.

Kelly nodded.

And just when Sarah thought she'd had enough for one lifetime, just when she was ready to let the weight of it all crush her, something else finally got through to her.

Cara Samuels. It was like her mind had had to have its moment to digest, her heart had had to accept, before they could move forward. *Cara Samuels.*

"Cara is Kylie."

She wasn't talking to anyone. Wasn't sure she'd have heard anyone had they responded. All that mattered was that she'd found her baby sister.

And the ten-year-old was in a happy, loving home.

Eight years of anguish, of worry, rose up within her. Gushed out. Ugly sobs pushed at her ribs, ripped through her throat and left her body, one by one, another after another.

She felt a hand at her back. And a larger one gently

running through her hair. Two hands took hold of hers, one smaller than the other.

She held on through the storm. Let it all out. Let go. And was thankful.

Her Christmas wish had come true.

Chapter Seventeen

Win thought when he'd heard what Sierra had suffered at the hands of the fiend who'd caused her death that he'd never again know such despair.

Not so.

Standing there in his office, hearing Sarah's pain, helpless to do anything to ease her anguish, he'd never felt so debilitatingly useless.

Swallowing back his own tears, he held her hand, stroked her hair, wanting her to know that she wasn't alone.

That she was remarkable and special.

He wanted her to know that he loved her. Not for him, but so that the love would ease into her heart and give her comfort. Fill tattered remnants with light.

As Sarah's sobs finally relented, leaving her washed out and hiccuping for air, he listened as Kelly started to talk to her.

.Not to counsel. Just to talk.

Like she'd talked to the rest of them in college.

As a friend who understood. And could sometimes help others understand themselves better.

He didn't take in all her words, was too focused on Sarah's breathing, her colorless cheeks, to do that, and then, suddenly, it was like Kelly was yelling straight at him.

They hadn't told her about the money yet, and she'd have no reason to ask. From what she'd known, Cara Samuels had been the only heir in the will. Jason Samuels already had his lawyer working on having the executed will brought back to court for further ruling and had asked that Win let his attorney handle any dealings with Sarah.

Win had tried to assure the man that Sarah wasn't the type to give a darn about the money, or to cause any trouble over it, but he understood the man's caution where his vulnerable ten-year-old daughter was concerned. The family could suddenly be brought into the limelight over the huge windfall they would likely be splitting.

As it was, Kelly had her work cut out for her helping Sarah accept that she had a right to be free from the guilt she'd been carrying far too long.

"Maybe it's time you quit spending your life making amends," his partner said, her tone still low, but firmer. "Maybe it's time you started asking for something for yourself. Not providing it for yourself, but asking for it."

He swallowed. Glanced over to see if she was pinning him with that look she had, the one that demanded one pay attention. But her focus was clearly all on Sarah.

"I'm not sure what I'd ask for." Sarah's tone sounded

foreign in the room. Cracked. Hoarse. And timid, like a child.

"So that's where you start," Kelly told her. "You ask yourself what you want. And be open to the answer, no matter what comes."

Sarah sort of smiled. "Disappointment is what comes," she said, trying for a chuckle that mostly failed. "It's not like I've never wanted anything."

"But have you ever believed you'd get what you asked for?"

Sarah's lack of reply seemed kind of telling, even to him, prompting him to give in to what he wanted to tell her.

Hoping it wasn't too soon.

Or too little.

Looking at Kelly, Win raised his brow, and at her nod, said, "There's more, if you want it." He was finding it easier to get words out to her.

"Might as well," she said, seeming a bit self-conscious as she looked between the two of them. "I sure don't want to go through this all over again."

"When Kylie, Cara as she knows herself, first went to live with the Samuelses, she went through more than a year of failing to thrive…" He saw the stark fear on Sarah's face and quickly continued. "She's doing great now, but something that came out then, all the time, was her calling out for 'sha sha.' At first they thought it was a blanket, or a toy, something that hadn't come home with her, but after time with a counselor, they began to think that it was a person…"

Sarah was crying again, but staring at him, seeming to be hanging on to his words, so he just kept talking.

"Lately, she's been struggling a little bit, being adopted

when her siblings are not, and a couple of times she's woken up from nightmares calling out 'sha sha.' When I told her parents about you, they wondered if maybe Sarah came out as…"

She was sobbing again. And smiling. And nodding. "That's me," Sarah said. "I'm Sha Sha."

He'd known. Was finding that feelings, life, had a way of lining up, coming together, just like numbers did. He needed only to get out there in the fray to find that out.

And was tripping over his words, his heart caught in a deep breath as he said, "They don't want to tell her about you, Sarah. Not if it's going to set her back…"

She was still nodding. "I get it," she said, her voice stronger. "I'm a nurse, Win. I wouldn't risk it, either. Wouldn't even want them to…"

"But they spoke to Cara's counselor today, in case they were being selfish—they'd been back in touch because of the recurring nightmare—and she suggested that maybe you just happen to be someplace where Cara is and see what happens."

Her mouth hung open. Win noticed Kelly's grip on Sarah's hand tighten.

Had he pushed her too far?

"Chances are she won't know you," Kelly said. "You'd need to just walk by and keep on walking. But if you'd like to see her, they're willing to facilitate that."

"If you'd want that." Win jumped into the silence that fell. "If not, I can…"

"I want." The words that cut him off were firm. Maybe a bit too loud. Almost demanding.

And Win took his first easy breath since Sarah had left him at the base of the mountain.

* * *

Dazed, dehydrated, shaky, yet strangely lighter, Sarah thanked Kelly profusely as the woman excused herself to an appointment shortly after Win had made the call to the Samuelses to set up a meeting at a mall in Scottsdale for the following day. They'd be taking Cara and her siblings to see Santa, would be standing in a line, and Sarah could just walk by. She'd know them by the green sweaters with white holly leaves and red berries the family of five would all be wearing. After her earlier call with Win, JoAnne Samuels had purchased them at a local box store that afternoon, just in case.

There was nothing left to do then but leave. Drive herself home. Get through the night first, and then the rest of the hours she had to wait to see for herself that her baby girl was happy and healthy. To see the child Kylie—Cara—had grown into.

Cara. She liked the name. A lot.

And was fine to retire Kylie, and all of the residual pain the name brought to her heart.

Retiring her guilt and culpability for her own part in the loss of Kylie would take longer.

Maybe forever.

Win walked with her to the door of his office, and she wanted to wrap her arms around him and hold on. What he'd done for her…

That he'd made it all happen…sought the answers…

The others had probably helped, but she knew in her heart that Win had set it all in motion.

"Thank you," she said, needing to tell him so much more.

"I'm glad I could help."

A send-off. She heard it. He was done.

Yet, he was still holding her hand. Hadn't let it go since he'd taken it while she'd been crying. He'd loosened his hold. Had caressed her palm some, rubbed his thumb against the top of her hand, but he'd never completely let go.

Just as she hadn't pulled it away.

Maybe it's time you started asking for something for yourself. Kelly's words weren't an order. Maybe weren't even right. She'd said *maybe.*

"You want to have some dinner?" she asked. Not quite the 'Will you please have dinner with me?' asking for herself would have entailed. But she'd put it out there. Basically.

"I do plan to eat, yes," he said, his gaze not leaving hers.

"Could you see yourself doing it at my place?"

He stepped closer. "I could."

She lifted her face to his, saw his lips coming down and said, "Maybe we should go now?"

He kissed her anyway. Deeply. Passionately.

Then he was gone, leaving a chill where his warmth had been. But only long enough for him to grab his keys.

Nothing was resolved between them, she knew that. She'd lied. He'd turned his back on her. She'd had good reason. He'd given her the one thing she'd been after—finding her sister.

The math he was so fond of added up.

They just had to figure out the sum of it all.

After dinner. Which, considering how many times they'd kissed as he rushed her out the door and they hurried to the parking lot, might be after sex.

She'd ask for what she wanted.

And listened as he did.

And if all they ended up having was one great night, she'd never be sorry she'd asked for it.

Heart pounding, Winchester Holmes climbed on top of Sarah Williams, settled himself between her legs and in one sure, swift thrust, slid himself home.

One thrust was all it took. All he got, before she pulsated around him and he shot his goods in the condom he'd barely gotten out of his wallet and on before mounting her.

Afterward, lying there on a throw rug that barely camouflaged the hard tile beneath them, with only the glow of the Christmas tree lights she'd flipped on when she'd unlocked the door to see by, he didn't know whether to laugh, or die of embarrassment.

Doing her on her living room floor hadn't been his plan, or even an option up for consideration. But when she'd asked him to take her right then, right there, as they stumbled inside her front door, he hadn't been able to consider that she might have meant right then as in before dinner, and right there, as in in her home.

He'd thrown off his clothes, grown explosively hard as he'd watched her ditch hers, lowered to his knees as she had and then had climbed on top of her.

They hadn't even kissed.

"You want to do it again?" Her saucy tone of voice as she posed the question had him hard all over again.

"I want to do it again and again," he told her, rolling off from her. "But I want you comfortable, because I intend to do it right this next time. My lips need to travel all over you. My hands, too. And I want your hands on me. Most particularly on key parts of me…" Where the words came from, he had no idea. He'd never talked like that in his life.

But then, Sierra had been his first lover. And he'd never let himself care that deeply again in all the years since.

They made love twice more before reaching a mutual decision that they needed some sustenance. And over dinner—salmon in a bourbon sauce and red potatoes in butter, all of which they had made in under half an hour thanks to the fact that she'd already had the salmon marinating—they talked some.

About Sierra. And Cara. About love that didn't end. And love that you had to move on from, too. He talked to her about things he'd never voiced before, not even to himself, feelings of inadequacy in the emotional department. And listened to her relive some of her happiest moments raising Cara as a newborn, a crawling baby, learning to talk and then walk.

He had much to learn in the relationship department, but didn't feel rushed to do so. Wasn't sure she'd wait around for him to figure it all out, but didn't worry about that right then, either.

They were there, together. In her home. Spending the night with each other.

And in that moment, it felt right.

Sarah alternated between sleeping soundly and lying awake with her mind reeling. Snuggled up to Win— the first time she'd ever spent the entire night with a lover—she'd relax and drift off, and then something would wake her and she would lie there trying to make sense of her life.

Her world had changed completely, and she wasn't sure how that changed who she thought she was.

By morning, she was het up. Emotionally jumbled. Eager. And dreading the future, too. What if seeing Kylie—Cara—brought back all the anguish? What if she couldn't bear just walking by and moving on?

She'd do it. She knew herself well enough to know that. No way would she create any kind of scene that would upset the child. Or even get her attention.

And she was going. There was no negotiating that one. Even if it killed her, it would be worth a glimpse of her baby sister.

Win left before breakfast, saying he had to get home and shower. Get into fresh clothes. She'd asked if he was coming back.

He'd wanted to know if she wanted him to do so.

She'd hated that he'd had to ask. Hated the awkwardness that fell between them.

And had told him to come if he wanted to.

She had no idea if he would.

If he was having regrets. Or worried that she was.

She wasn't.

She was crazy in love with the man.

Just didn't know how to tell him. It felt too much like asking to be loved, and that wasn't something she knew how to do.

She wasn't even sure she wanted to know how to do it.

While her world hadn't been perfect, it had been nice. Peaceful.

She'd been content.

She wanted more sex nights with Win.

The thoughts rambled through her mind as she took

a long hot shower, blew her hair straight and dressed in three different outfits, before settling on the leggings with the Christmas tree sweater she'd worn once already that year. She thought she'd never wear it again after the ugly sweater party but had held on to it because of the money she'd spent.

She wasn't starting a new life with her little sister in it, but she *was* getting what she'd most wanted. To see for herself that the little girl was well.

Truthfully, she acknowledged to her gaze in the mirror as she applied the light eyeliner she always wore, she hadn't even dared hope she'd actually get to see Kylie. Her dream had only gotten as big as knowing that Kylie was fine.

She'd told Win she was planning to leave around noon, wanting to be inside the mall, scoping out Santa's workshop and throne, getting the lay of the land with plenty of time to spare before the Samuelses were supposed to be getting in line. She'd told him that if he wanted to go along with her, he should be at her place by a few minutes before the hour.

His place was a good twenty minutes from hers. More with Saturday holiday traffic. He had the Sierra's Web holiday gathering that night. A fancy dinner with good wine in a top-tier resort in Scottsdale. The partners all got rooms so they could have a few drinks and not worry about driving. Knowing Win, with his head in numbers and spreadsheets all the time, he'd probably left his gift buying until the last minute and would need to spend the afternoon taking care of his own affairs, not tagging along for hers.

And really, she couldn't blame him. She was going to walk by a line. Soak up the sight of a ten-year-old girl in a green sweater that matched those the rest of her family was wearing. Her family. Not Sarah's.

She and Sarah might share biological parents, but the little girl didn't know that. Would never know that.

Sarah wasn't even sure she believed it yet.

James Milford was her father?

A drug-dealing sort-of pimp?

She'd known her mother had gotten pregnant in high school. Simple math had told her that much. She'd known her mother had never told the father. She'd just built this hope that her dad was some football jock out there who might have loved her if he'd known she existed.

She'd told Win as much the night before.

"You never wanted to look him up?" he'd asked against her neck as he held her, naked in his arms in her bed.

"I didn't want to find out I was wrong about him." She'd told him the truth buried deep in her heart.

They'd lain there silently with the day's activity between them. With the fact that Win had killed that fantasy for her hours before when he'd told her who her father really was.

But the good news was, she reminded herself, as she watched the clock and tried to find things to do with herself as the morning dragged slowly by, the man's last deed had been a great one. He'd left the daughter he'd known about a fortune.

Staring at the containers in the refrigerator, she thought about cleaning it out.

Kylie. Her Kylie. She would be taken care of for life.

Smiling, Sarah closed the refrigerator door and glanced at the clock. Eleven o'clock. She couldn't wait much longer.

Pulling her cell phone out of the waistband of her leggings, she dialed.

"I'm on my way," Win said.

And she smiled. Started to tear up a little and admonished herself. She was not going to show up as a passerby to a line of kids waiting to see Santa with her makeup smudged.

And she wasn't going to show up alone, either.

Chapter Eighteen

Christmas fever was almost overwhelmingly in the air as Win stepped into the mall with Sarah. He'd suggested they get lunch at the mall, at one of the quaint eateries that were almost hidden in between posh boutiques and expensive department stores.

She'd agreed immediately, but as they sat with their quiche and scones, she barely got half a bite to her mouth.

He wasn't hungry, either, as it turned out, and they ended up with a doggie bag to go. So much for that suggestion. The failure had him second-guessing his next plan as well. Because, of course, he'd mapped out a series of events that would add up to a successful day for her.

Seeing her baby sister was going to be grand. Nothing he could do would equal it. But seeing her and not being able to meet her...that would be agony.

He was hoping to ease some of that, if he could.

His plan was bizarre. Crazy even for a fun-loving crazy guy. Which he most certainly was not. *Maybe it's time you started asking for something for yourself.* Kelly's words had been haunting him since they'd flowed from her mouth.

Maybe it's time you quit being afraid to ask for something for yourself, he translated as he walked with Sarah through the mall, dodging the shoppers thronging through the halls.

Even if it was crazy?

He looked at every store that passed. Every store ahead that he could make out. Looking for one particular store. Saw it. And averted his gaze. She kept walking, bringing them closer to it. She was talking about ugly Christmas sweaters. He heard her. Could hear the nervous tension in her voice and told himself it would be way too selfish to distract her attention at the moment. The store was almost upon them and he was going to let it pass.

His nerves settled, his system filling with relief.

And a curious disappointment as well.

"Do you believe in love at first sight?" she asked him.

At first, he thought the fates were giving him a sign— as though he'd ever in a million years been open to such a thing. And then he saw the advertisement that had caught her attention. A couple with a huge diamond and a caption of Love at First Sight. He suspected the ad was meant to refer to the diamond, but said, "I've never thought about it." Which wasn't completely true. "Until recently."

His words hung there, as though the huge high-ceilinged hallways had just evacuated, leaving a deadly silence.

"Do you believe in soulmates?"

Wait. What? Didn't he get to hear what she thought of love at first sight?

"I kind of do," he said. He'd thought Sierra was a soulmate. Partially because she'd told him he was one of hers. Kelly had been one, too. For all he knew, all the partners had been. He could see them all as soulmates to each other. Family.

And Sarah? With her...

"I think it's the kind of thing you don't believe in until you come face-to-face with it," she said.

They'd passed the store.

"Have you come face-to-face with it?" he asked.

"I think I have."

He might be dense, but he was not a fool. And he was tired of settling for the nice high of satisfaction numbers gave him. He wanted heaven.

After his first taste the night before, how could he not?

Turning so abruptly that he ran into a couple close behind them, he stepped aside, grabbing for Sarah, catching her shoulder for a brief second. He backed up to the wall as she turned and saw him.

"What's wrong?" she asked, weaving her way over to him.

"Nothing." His throat was dry. But a grin broke out on his face. What the hell. Better to live big than die small.

Grabbing her hand, he pulled her to the edge of the store. Into the store. And started slowly perusing the cases of glittering gems as though he could tell one quality from another.

"Win?" Sarah frowned. "What are you doing?"

"Just looking."

"Win." She'd stopped walking with him. And her tone brooked no argument. The woman could be tough when she had a mind to be.

And so he did what he wanted to do. He got down on one knee and asked for what he most wanted. "Sarah Williams, I know that we haven't known each other long, but I do believe in love at first sight because I met you. Because from day one, you have been familiar to me, from things we had in common, to those we didn't. The way you take my world, my numbers, and add a whole dimension to them…" He was peripherally aware that a crowd was gathering around them, but he didn't much care. Sarah was still there. She didn't look angry. In fact, her eyes were brimming and those beautiful generous lips were trembling.

"So, I'm going to ask for what I want. Sarah Williams, will you pick out a diamond, let me buy it for you and agree to marry me?"

He should feel out of his mind.

He didn't.

"You don't think it's too soon?"

"What I think doesn't matter. Ask for what you want, Sarah."

He could be wrong, but he didn't think he was. Not after the night they'd just spent.

Not after she'd come to tell him why she'd applied at Sierra's Web when she'd been home free. That was love.

"I want you to tell me you love me."

The crowd was outside the store. He didn't give a damn. He did care that he'd failed once again to catch all the right nuances. "Oh, my God, woman. I love you so much it hurts."

"I love you, too, Winchester," she whispered. Then

dropped to her knees in front of him, put her arms around him and said, "Yes, Win, yes. I want you to buy me a diamond, I want to wear it and I want to marry you."

Then she kissed him. Right there in the middle of the store with a crowd all around them. He heard the clapping. Some cheers and catcalls, but he didn't care.

"I love you, Sarah," he told her again. And wanted to keep telling her. "I know it's going to hurt, seeing Kylie today, but you aren't doing it alone. And hopefully, someday in the not-too-distant future, we'll have a baby of our own for you to love to distraction."

She smiled, kissed him again and pulled him to his feet, leaning in to whisper, "I want to continue this conversation tonight, when we're home alone."

Right, that would be much better. With a grin, he turned to the case of diamonds. "So, which one do you want?"

He'd buy them all for her, not caring if they cost him the entirety of the very hefty investment account he'd amassed for himself.

Her love was worth far more.

Wearing her brand-new solitaire diamond on the ring finger of her left hand, Sarah held Win's hand as they approached the hallway that led to Santa's Workshop.

"I can't believe you picked such a small diamond," Win was saying, for the third time since they'd left the store. "Truly, Sarah, Kelly was right—you need to learn to ask for more."

"I asked for what I wanted," she told him, her smile wavering a bit as she contemplated the turn they were going to make in less than a minute, and then the line waiting at the end of that road. "My grandmother wore a diamond like this one. She said it wasn't the size of the diamond, but the glitter, because love was like that—it glittered in your heart even when things weren't jump-up-and-down great."

And her grandmother had been right. About so many things.

Love, loyalty, family…they were the real wealth in life. Even with their imperfections.

They turned the corner. She saw the line in the distance. Didn't even try to look for green sweaters yet.

Anticipation swirled in her stomach, and yet, as she held Win's hand, she knew that she'd be okay. She'd get her gift, finally see her little sister again, know she was okay, but she wouldn't be leaving with an empty heart.

"Do you know if her hair is still dark?" she asked Win.

"I don't."

"Or if it's long?"

"No idea."

She'd have asked the questions while making plans for the meeting. Win was probably never going to. Obviously not those particular ones. But not a lot of the ones she'd ask. He was who he was. And she adored him.

And he'd have her to ask the questions for them.

Just as he'd have their backs every minute of every day, paying attention to life details, to the numbers, protecting them from whatever life might send their way.

They'd reached the line. She couldn't believe it had come up so quickly. Squeezed Win's hand so hard it probably hurt, but she couldn't help it. Her other hand was equally clenched.

He didn't seem to mind. Or even notice.

"There they are," he said instead, pointing out the

five green sweaters. She hadn't even started to look for them.

And that was Win, her detail guy.

The plan was for them to walk around from the opposite side, so that the family would be facing them. So, hopefully, she could see Cara's face. If Win had given the Samuelses any way by which they could recognize her, she didn't know.

Didn't need to know.

She just had to see Cara.

As they drew closer, she started to shake. "It's okay, my love, I'm here," Win said. "I'll guide you through the people. I'll hold you up if I have to. You just watch her for as long as our slow walk can give you."

Yes. The green sweaters had become full bodies. The tallest child, that was her. Cara. She saw dark hair and teared up. Long. And couldn't breathe.

Her face was turned away as her little body hopped from foot to foot in anticipation of her imminent visit. Holding her mother's hand, she looked up, said something, and then, after her mother's lips moved, presumably in response, she bent to the body closest to her in size. A boy. Probably six or so. Said something to him. Gave him a hug and then stood, hopping from foot to foot again.

Tears in her eyes, happy tears, Sarah turned to Win. "We can go," she said. And meant it. Cara was… beautiful. Perfect.

Clearly loved.

Happy.

And, "Sha Sha!" The shriek came so loudly everyone around them stopped for a second. The busy mall, the Christmas excitement, the chatter all just stopped, as a little girl hurled herself through the few people separating her from Sarah. "Sha Sha?" she asked, stopped a foot away, staring, and then looking back at her parents, as though she'd just realized what she'd done.

And wasn't sure what to do next.

Sarah looked at the couple who'd followed their daughter, each with another child's hand in one of theirs. They met her gaze, and both nodded.

Sarah knelt, putting herself lower than the child in front of her and said, "Hi, sweetie, yeah, it's Sha Sha, and I'm so glad I get to see you again. I've missed you so much."

Just that. No identifiers. She'd be an old babysitter. A nanny. She'd be whomever the Samuelses wanted her to be.

To Cara—to Kylie—she was Sha Sha.

A name, a title, biology didn't matter.

Love did.

It had bound two sisters' hearts from day one.

And would hold them forever.

Just as it had bound her and Win in such a short time.

Love didn't follow convention or culture. It was bigger than all of that.

Stronger than all of that.

It was all she'd ever needed.

Kelly had told her to ask for what she wanted. She didn't have to ask.

She already had it all.

Epilogue

Win wasn't going to make it. No way. No how. Sarah's pain attacked him from all angles. Tensing his muscles. Scraping his nerves. Stabbing his heart. And there wasn't a damn thing he could do about it.

"Back up, I need air…" The words were slightly slurred, reeked of suffering, and he instantly stepped away from the bed.

This idea of his…his wife suffering so…she should have told him no. She was a nurse. She'd known. They could have adopted.

"Push!" Dr. Knowles, Leslie Knowles, a woman he'd previously thought calming and capable, was pissing him off. Telling Sarah to do something she clearly did not want to do.

She'd been trying for hours to get that baby out, and little Rachel Marie, named for his mother and her grandmother, was apparently more determined than her mama.

He'd suggested removing the baby surgically, hours before, and had been given an adamant "no" from his wife. And a less intense but still negative response from the doctor, too.

"Push!"

"I…can't." Sarah huffed and puffed and, closing her eyes, lay back against the bed. "Just let me rest a minute."

"We don't have a minute, she's crowning…"

Tears trickled down the sides of Sarah's face.

He'd known it was going to be bad. He'd been through the classes. Seen a movie.

But this was worse than anything they'd seen. And… this was Sarah.

Her face red with exertion, tired beyond anything he'd ever imagined. After more than twenty-four hours of labor, she'd reached her limit.

During their three years of marriage, he'd seen her devastated and exhausted, cut and bruised, in a hotel room after a day of disaster relief as Sierra's Web's youngest expert, even sick in bed with a deadly flu. She'd never ever seemed as vulnerable to him, as worn out, as she did at that moment.

"Are you sure everything's okay?" he asked the nurse who'd been keeping a watch on Sarah's vitals over the past few hours. The fourth one to do so.

"Just fine." The nurse smiled. "She's almost here!"

How the woman could sound cheerful in the midst of his wife's agony he had no idea, but…

"Win?" Her tired voice called out to him.

"Yeah?"

"I need you up here, right next to me," she said, holding out her hand. He was there in an instant, grabbing hold. And then, as she sat forward, he supported her back as he'd learned to do.

"Push!" the doctor said again.

"I can't."

"Push!"

"I…"

Win pushed Sarah's back as she went to lie back down. He held her up. And said, "Cara's waiting to meet her new niece."

The Samuelses, with help from Cara's counselor, had determined that it was best for Cara to know Sarah for who she really was, and had gladly welcomed Sarah and Win into their family. Lily knew.

And chose to remain apart.

Win figured her for a much wiser woman than Sarah had given her credit for. And made a point of calling his mother-in-law once a week just because.

"For Cara," Sarah gritted through clenched teeth.

Three seconds later, there was a cry. And then Dr. Knowles saying, "She's here!"

Things happened so swiftly after that, he could hardly compute through the cacophony. But he would never forget his first sight of his baby girl, so beautiful and perfect straight from Sarah's womb. As beautiful and perfect as her sweaty, exhausted mother as they laid the baby on Sarah's chest.

Just as he'd never forget the moment when, later that night, after everyone had gone—every single one of his partners had come to town for the occasion, and the Samuelses had hung around for hours at Cara's request—Sarah looked up at him with tears in her eyes and a smile on her face and said, "I want to ask for something."

"Of course, my love, anything."

He didn't care what it was. He'd find a way to lasso the moon for her if she asked for it.

"Promise me that if I ever say I want to go natural again, you insist on an epidural."

He burst out laughing.

"Shhh, you'll wake her," Sarah said, pointing to the bassinet by her bed. And then, yanking his arm, pulled him down to the bed beside her.

"I love you, Winchester."

"I love you, too, Sarah. More than life."

"We have our family."

"Yes, we do."

"And the love lives forever."

He knew that now.

Something she'd taught him.

Something he'd never forget.

"Win?" Her voice was laced with fatigue.

"Yeah?"

"Merry Christmas."

Christmas. He'd completely forgotten. Christmas Eve, they'd been packing to head to California when Sarah's water broke. He'd called Lily then, and again when the baby was born, but had completely spaced on the holiday...

"Merry Christmas, Sarah."

"Thank you for my present. She's the best Christmas gift ever."

She was thanking him for the gift she'd given him. Such a Sarah thing to do.

"And the two of you are most definitely mine."

Holding her in his arms as she fell asleep, he thought about the tree they'd put up weeks before in the living room of the home they'd purchased together for Christmas the year they'd gotten engaged. Every year their Christmas tree stood tall in front of the floor-to-ceiling windows in the living room and proudly bore all her grandmother's ornaments, and the ones they'd bought for his first tree, too.

And he thought about the money she'd received from her father's will. She'd had him put it into an investment account with all gains going to yearly donations to a local addiction clinic.

He thought about Kelly saying people had to ask for what they wanted. About how he'd lived for more than a decade being afraid to do so.

He'd needed that time to grieve. And to grow.

To be ready for the incredible burst of strength and new perspective that Sarah brought to his world.

He still had a lot of growing to do. And might never fully grasp the nuances of personal interaction.

But he knew how to love.

And Sarah knew how to love him.

That…he figured…was the true meaning of Christmas.

* * * * *

SPECIAL EXCERPT FROM

◆ HARLEQUIN
SPECIAL
EDITION

Time to rewrite their story?

He'd always simply been her best friend. But when
Noah Cahill moved back to town, bookstore owner
Twyla Thompson knew something was different.
Was it holiday nostalgia for the loss they both
shared or Noah's surprising decision to reignite a
dangerous career? Their solid friendship had been
through so much, yet now Twyla grew breathless
every time Noah was near. Why wasn't Noah—
handsome, fun but never-one-to-cross-the-line
Noah—showing any sign of stopping?

Read on for a sneak preview of
Once Upon a Charming Bookshop
by Heatherly Bell.

Chapter One

Twyla Thompson was thrilled to see a line out the door on the night of *New York Times* bestselling author Stacy Cruz's book signing. This was exactly what Once Upon a Book needed—an infusion of excitement and goodwill and the proverbial opening up of the wallet during the holidays for a book instead of the latest flat-screen TV. Even if Stacy's recently released thriller wasn't exactly Christmas material, the timing was right both for her, the publisher and certainly Twyla's family-owned bookstore.

The reading had been short due to subject matter—murder—and Stacy took questions from the crowd. As usual, they ranged from "How can I get published?" to "I have an idea for a book. Would you write it for me?" to "My mother had a *fascinating* life. It should be a book, then a movie starring Meryl Streep." Stacy was a good sport about it all since the Charming, Texas, residents were her friends and neighbors, too.

Twyla, for her part, would never dream of writing a book. She barely had time to read everything she wanted to. Which was basically…everything. The heart of a bookseller beat in her and she recommended books like they were her best friends. Want an inspirational book? Read this. Would you like a tour de force celebrating the power of the human spirit? Here's the book for you. A little escapism with some romance and comedy thrown in? Right here. Want to be scared within an inch of your life? Read Stacy Cruz's latest suspense thriller.

The very best part of Twyla's day was getting lost in the worlds an author created. Her favorite books had always been of the fantasy romance genre, particularly of the dragon-slaying variety. She adored a fae hero who slayed dragons before breakfast. But honestly? She read anything she could get her hands on. Owning her four-generation family bookstore had made that possible. She'd grown up inside these four walls filled with bookshelves and little alcoves and nooks. She read all the *Nancy Drew* mysteries, Beverly Cleary and, when her grandmother wasn't looking, Kathleen Woodiwiss.

Twyla stood next to Roy Finch at the register as he rang up another sale of Stacy's latest book, *Vengeance*, that featured a serial killer working among the political power brokers in DC. Twyla had read it, of course. She could not deny Stacy's talent at terrifying the reader and making them guess until the last page. You'd never expect this from the married, sweet and beautiful mother of a little girl. She was as normal a person as Twyla had ever met.

"Nice crowd tonight," Mr. Finch said. "Too bad Stacy doesn't write more than one book a year."

Too bad indeed. Because while hosting yoga classes and book clubs, and selling educational toys had sustained them, it would no longer be enough. For the past two years, the little bookstore, the only one in town, had been in a terrible slump. Her grandmother still kept the books, and she'd issued the warning earlier this year. Pulling them out of the red might require more than one great holiday season. Foot traffic had slowed as more people bought their books online.

"I've got a signed copy of Stacy's latest book for you." Lois, Mr. Finch's fiancée, set a stack of no less than ten books on the counter by the register. "And I grabbed a bunch of giving tree cards."

The cards were taken from a large stack of books in the shape of a Christmas tree Twyla set up every season. Instead of ornaments, tags indicated the names and addresses of children who either wanted, or needed, a book for Christmas.

"We can always count on you, sweetheart." Mr. Finch rang her up.

It was endearing the way residents supported the Thompson family bookstore. They might have been in this location for four decades, but they'd never needed as much help as in the past two years.

Mr. Finch, a widowed and retired senior citizen, volunteered his time at the shop so Twyla could occasionally go home. For a while now they hadn't been able to afford any paid help. Her parents were officially retired and had moved to Hill Country. Their contributions amounted to comments on the sad state of affairs when a bookstore had to host yoga classes. But the instructor gave Twyla a flat rate to rent the space, and she didn't see *them* coming up with any solutions. They didn't want to close up shop. Of *course* not. They simply wanted Twyla to solve this problem for the entire Thompson family by selling books and nothing else.

"I don't know what I'd do without either one of you," Twyla said fondly, patting Mr. Finch's back. "Or any of the other members of the Almost Dead Poets Society."

Many of the local senior citizens had formed a poetry group where they recited poems they'd written. It had all started rather innocently enough—a creative effort, and something to do with all their free time. Unfortunately, they also liked to refer to themselves as "literary" matchmakers. Literary not to *ever* be confused with "literally." They'd failed with Twyla so far, not that they'd ever give up trying. Last month they'd invited both her and Tony Taylor to a reading and not so discreetly attempted to fix them up.

You're both so beautiful, it's a little hard to look at you for long, Ella Mae, the founder of their little group, had said. *Kind of like the sun!*

The double Ts! Lois had exclaimed. *Or would that be the quadruple Ts?*

Quadruple, I think, Mr. Finch had said.

You won't even have to change the initials on your monogrammed towels! Patsy Villanueva had clapped her hands. *I mean if it works out, that is.*

But no pressure! Susannah had held up a palm.

Twyla didn't own anything monogrammed, let alone towels, but she'd still exchanged frozen smiles with Tony. They'd arranged a coffee date just for fun. Unfortunately, as she'd known for years, Tony batted for the other team. He even had a live-in boyfriend that the old folks assumed was his roommate. It was an easy assumption to make since Tony was such a "man's man"—

a grease monkey who lifted engines for a living. And he hadn't exactly come out of the closet, thinking his personal life was nobody's business. He was right, of course. But...

"You really *should* declare your love of show tunes, Tony," she'd teased.

"I'm not a cliché."

"Well, you *could* get married."

"I'm not ready to settle down." He scowled.

Still, they'd had a nice time, catching up on life post-high school. He'd asked after Noah Cahill, and of course she had all the recent updates on her best friend. In the end they'd decided she and Tony would definitely be double-dating at some point.

When Twyla could find a date.

This part wasn't going to be easy because Twyla had a bad habit. She preferred to spend her time alone and reading a book. Long ago, she'd accepted that she wouldn't be able to find true love inside the walls of her small rental. But accepting invitations to parties and bar hops wasn't her style. She wanted to be invited, really, but she just didn't want to go. An introvert's problem.

This was why she'd adopted a cat. But, she worried, if she didn't get a date soon, she was going to risk being known as the cat lady.

"That's the last copy!" Stacy stood from the table, beaming, holding a hand to her chest. "My publisher will be thrilled. I honestly can't *believe* it."

"I can." Twyla began to clear up the signing table. "You're very talented and it's about time people noticed. I just wish you'd write more books."

"So do I, but tell that to my daughter." Stacy sighed. "She's a holy terror, just like her father. Runs around all day, throwing things. I'm lucky if I get in a few hundred words a day."

"That's okay." Twyla chuckled. "We can't exactly base our business plan on how many books you write a year."

Stacy blinked and a familiar concern shaded her eyes. "Are you…are you guys doing okay? Should I maybe ask my publisher whether they can send some of their other authors here for a signing?"

As a bookseller, she knew everyone in the business was suffering, and publishers weren't financing many book tours. Stacy did those on her own dime, hence the local gig. Twyla didn't like lying to people but she liked their pity even less. She constantly walked a tightrope between the two.

"As long as we have another great holiday season, like all the others, we should be fine!" She hoped the forced quality of her über-positive attitude wasn't laying it on too thick.

But Stacy seemed to accept the good news, bless her heart.

"What a relief! We can't have a *town* without a bookstore."

"No, we can't," Mr. Finch agreed with a slight shake of his head. "It would be a travesty."

One by one the straggling customers left, carrying their purchases with them. Not long after, Stacy's husband, the devastatingly handsome Adam, dropped by to pick her up and drive her home. Everyone said their goodbyes.

Mr. Finch and Lois brought up the rear, wanting to help Twyla close up.

"You two go home!" She waved her hands dismissively. "I'm right behind you."

"I'll be by tomorrow for my morning shift promptly at nine." Mr. Finch took Lois's hand in his own.

"Are you sure you don't want to take a break? Take tomorrow off." Twyla went behind them, shutting off the lights. "You worked tonight."

"I'll get plenty of rest when I'm dead," Roy said, holding the door open for Lois.

"Roy!" Lois went ahead. "Please don't talk about the worst day of my life a second before it happens."

"No, darlin'." He sweetly brought her hand up to his lips. "I'll be around for a while. You manage to keep me young."

These two never failed to fill her heart with the warm fuzzies. Both had been widowed for a long time, and were on their second great love.

Which meant some people got two of those, and so far, Twyla didn't even have one.

Twyla arrived at her grandmother's home a few minutes later, having stopped first at the bakery for a salted caramel Bundt cake. She and Ganny usually met for dinner every Saturday night and she always brought dessert. Was it sad that a soon-to-be thirty-year-old single woman didn't have anything better to do on a Saturday night? Not at all. She had her cat, Bonkers, waiting at home. He was mean as the devil himself, but he'd been homeless when she adopted him from the shelter, so she was all he had.

Twyla also had at least half a dozen advanced reader copy books on her nightstand waiting for her. There were also all the upcoming Charming holiday events she'd agreed to participate in because that's what one did as a business owner. Ava had told her about a rare angel investor offering a zero-interest loan to a local Charming business. On top of everything else, Twyla had to prepare an essay this month to be considered. It wasn't as if she didn't have anything else to do. Too much, in fact.

"Hello, Peaches."

Ganny bussed Twyla's cheek. Occasionally she still referred to Twyla by her old childhood nickname. Once, she'd eaten so many juicy fresh peaches from the tree in Ganny's yard that she threw up. It wasn't the best nickname in the world.

"How was the book signing?"

"A line out the door." Twyla followed Ganny into the ornate dining area connected to the kitchen and set the cake on the mahogany table.

Ganny had been widowed twice and her last husband, Grandpa Walt, a popular real estate broker, had left her with very little but this house. It was too big for Ganny, but she refused to leave it because of the dining room. It was big enough to accommodate large groups of people, which she felt encouraged Twyla's parents to visit several times a year.

"It was a good start to the month."

"Good, good. Well, that's enough book business talk for tonight." Ganny waved a hand dismissively. "I've got a surprise for you tonight. An early Christmas present."

"You didn't have to get me anything."

But a thrill whipped through Twyla because her grandmother was renowned for her thoughtful gifts all year long. It could almost be anything. Maybe a trip to New York City, where Ganny had promised to finally introduce her to some of the biggest booksellers in the country. People she'd met over a lifetime of acquiring and selling books. Twyla had wanted to go back to New York for years. She could still feel the energy of the city zipping through her blood, taste the cheesecake from Junior's, and the slice of pepperoni pizza from Times Square.

"Why wouldn't I give my only granddaughter the best present in the world?" Ganny smiled with satisfaction. "He should be along any minute now."

All the breath left Twyla's body. Just the thought of another blind date struck her with a sadness she had no business feeling during the holidays. Everyone in town was conspiring to fix up "poor, sad Twyla who can't get a man."

She could get a man, but she wasn't concentrating her efforts on this.

Please let it not be Tony again. And yet there were so few single men her age left in town. Hadn't her grandmother always told Twyla she'd do fine on her own? If she couldn't find the right man, she didn't need *any* man? Twyla had embraced this truth. She wanted the perfect man or no one at all.

"Life with the right man is wonderful. But a life with the wrong man might as well be lived alone. So many things in life can replace a spouse. Work, travel and books, to start with," Ganny had said.

Twyla, then, *could* lead a happy and fruitful life without ever being married.

"Oh, Ganny." Twyla slumped on the chair. "You didn't fix me up with someone, did you?"

"Of course not, honey!" She patted Twyla's hand. "But speaking of which, you're not going to meet anyone special if you don't get out more."

"I'm just like you. Books are my family."

It seemed to have skipped a generation, because

though her father, Ganny's son, had loyally run the family bookstore, it wasn't exactly his happy place.

"Yes, but keep in mind I made myself go out and meet people. It wasn't like it is today. Certainly not. I used to have three dates on the same day. No funny business, of course, but your mother already told me things are different."

Twyla couldn't imagine going out three times in one day. She'd be lucky to go out once every three years. Okay, she was exaggerating. But still. Men weren't exactly lining up to date her. One of them had said she'd look prettier if she'd stop wearing her black-rimmed glasses. Twyla refused to go the contact lens route because if glasses stopped a guy from being interested in her, it wasn't the guy she wanted anyway.

"Fine, I promise I'll go out! But please don't fix me up." Her friend Zoey had bugged her to go out with her and her boyfriend, Drew, and Twyla hadn't yet.

"No blind date. This is someone you actually want to see."

"I can't even imagine."

There was only one "he" she'd like to see, and he was all the way in Austin, at home with his girlfriend. Probably planning their wedding.

"That's it. I'm having dessert first." Twyla opened the cake box.

The doorbell rang and Ganny rose. "You stay here and close your eyes! Don't open them until I tell you to."

Oh, brother. It was like being twelve again. She clasped her hand over her eyes, but not before taking a finger swipe of salted caramel frosting, feeling…well, twelve again.

"Okay, fine. My eyes are closed."

Twyla heard the front door open and shut, Ganny's delighted laughter, but no other sounds from this "he" man. Nothing but the sounds of boots thudding as they followed Ganny's lighter steps.

"Can I open my eyes now? I would really like to have a piece of cake. Whoever you are, I hope you like cake."

"I love cake," the deep voice said.

Twyla didn't even have to open her eyes to recognize the teasing, flirty sound of her favorite person in the world. She didn't have to hazard a guess because she knew this man almost as well as she knew herself.

And Ganny was right. It *was* the best present.

Ever.

"Noah!"

Twyla stood and hurled herself into the open arms of Noah Cahill, her best friend.

Chapter Two

There were few things in his life Noah enjoyed as much as filling his arms with his best friend. He held Twyla close, all five feet nothing of her. Her dark hair longer now than it had been a year ago when he'd left Charming. Today she was wearing her book-pattern dress, which meant the store must have had a signing. The outfit was a type of uniform she wore for those events. She had a similar skirt in bright colors with patterns of dragons, swords and slayers.

God, she was a sight. The old familiar pinch squeezed his chest. He almost hadn't come home this Christmas, thinking it would be easier. There was already so much he hadn't told her when he normally told her everything.

Almost everything.

Then he'd narrowly missed death, or at the least a devastating injury, and everything changed in the course of days. He would not waste another minute of his life doing a job he no longer wanted to do.

"I thought you weren't coming home this Christmas!" Twyla said, coming to her tiptoes to hug him tight. Her arms wrapped around his neck.

Automatically and before he could stop himself, he turned his head to take in a deep breath of her hair. She always smelled like coconuts. He set her down reluctantly, but he was used to this feeling with Twyla. It was always this way—the push and pull always resulting in the distance he'd created due to guilt.

And loyalty.

"Things have changed."

"Noah isn't just *visiting*," Twyla's grandmother said, sounding pleased. "He's come home to stay."

Bless Mrs. Schilling's kind heart. She'd always been pulling for Noah, against any and all reason, even if he could have told her a thousand times it was useless. He was destined to pine after Twyla forever. What he wanted to have with her would never work and the door had been slammed shut years ago. Now the opening might as well be buried under rubble. Like the roof that nearly fell on him.

"You're here to stay?" Twyla brightened. "But what about your job in Austin?"

"I quit." He held his arms off to the side with a shrug. "It's not for me. Not anymore."

"It's *exactly* you. You've been an adrenaline junkie since you were a boy. How is it not for you?"

Yeah, best not to tell her about the roof that fell inches from him during a building fire. His entire squad had been lucky to escape with no fatalities. Three had wound up with minor injuries.

Noah could have sworn something, or *someone*, had shoved him out of the way. In that moment, with the heat barreling toward him and unfurling like a living thing, he'd felt his brother Will there in the room with him. Will, shouting for him to get out of the way.

His long-dead older brother was telling Noah, in no uncertain terms, to stop trying to be a hero. To, for the love of God, stop rescuing people and start living his own life. Noah had first worked as an EMT, and then later a firefighter in nearby Houston for the past few years. He'd saved some people and lost some, but "imaginary Will" had called it. No matter what Noah did, he'd never get another chance to save Will.

And he was the only save that would have ever mattered. Now it was high time to honor his life instead. Noah may have always felt second best to his much smarter and accomplished brother, but that feeling wasn't one encouraged by Will. His older brother had always had Noah's back. Even on their last day together.

"It was good, for a while, but it's time to move on."

"But—"

"Let's have some of that delicious cake." Mrs. Schilling urged them to take a seat at the table. "We have plenty of time to discuss all this."

"I never say no to cake." Noah took a seat, avoiding Twyla's gaze.

If he looked too directly at her, she'd see everything in his eyes, so at times like these he had a system in place.

Don't make eye contact.

Three serving plates were passed around and Twyla sliced off generous pieces.

"No matter what, we're glad you're home," Mrs. Schilling said. "Aren't we, dear?"

"Yes, of course. It's just such a surprise. So…unexpected." Twyla took a bite of cake.

Using an old trick, he purposely looked at her ear, to make it look like he was meeting her eyes.

"It's a career choice. I have a really great opportunity here."

"Where are you staying?"

It was a fair question since he'd given up his rental when he'd grown tired of the memories that haunted him here and moved to Austin to start over.

"I rented one of those cottages by the beach. Just temporary until I find a place. The place where I'll be living is far less important than what I'll be doing." Noah winked.

This was his biggest news: the culmination of a long-held dream. He'd squashed it for so long after Will's death that he'd nearly forgotten it. But in that fiery building, he'd *remembered*.

"What *are* you going to be doing?"

"Taking over a business here in town." He'd start with the easy stuff first.

"Wonderful!" Mrs. Schilling clapped her hands. "Obviously, I have always loved the entrepreneurial spirit. Why, it's the reason the Thompson family started Once Upon a Book."

"What kind of business? Fire investigation? Teaching safety? You would make a *great* teacher." Twyla smiled and took another bite of cake.

He hoped the news wasn't going to kill her like it might his own mother. But he couldn't live the rest of his life in fear. Or worse yet, accommodating the fears of others.

"No. I'm taking over the boat charter. Mr. Curry is

retiring, and he's been looking for a buyer for a year or more."

When his news was met with such silence that he heard Mrs. Schilling's grandfather clock ticking, he continued.

"He actually wants someone local to take it over, so he'll work terms out with me. I have enough hours on the water, so I'll be taking the USCG test for my captain's license. I've obviously already had first aid training and then some. Until I get my license, I'll have Finn's help and he already has his license. Mr. Curry said he'd be around awhile longer, too, if we need help." He filled his mouth with a big piece of cake.

Twyla sucked in a breath, and Mrs. Schilling's shaky hand went to her throat. Other than that, Noah thought everything here would be okay. Nothing to see here. Sure thing. They'd all get used to the idea. Eventually.

Just give them a couple of decades.

"Are you serious?" Twyla pushed her plate of unfinished cake away.

Only he would fully understand the significance of the move. For Twyla not to finish a slice of cake meant that in her opinion, the world just might be ending.

"Yes, I'm serious. Ask yourself whether if anyone else said the same thing, you'd have this kind of a reaction."

"That's not even funny. You're *not* anyone else." She took a breath and whispered her next words. "You're Will's brother. You…you almost died out there, too."

"Now, Twyla…let the man finish." This from Twyla's grandmother, thankfully, the voice of reason.

She didn't let him finish.

"If this is my surprise, I don't like it." Twyla stood.

With that she walked right out of her grandmother's kitchen.

"Twyla!" her grandmother chided. "Oh, dear. Noah, I'm sorry. She's had a rough year. The bookstore isn't doing well, and—"

"Let me talk to her."

"Noah? Are you sure about this? If Twyla reacts this way, you can only imagine how your poor mother—"

"I know. *And* I'm sure."

He found Twyla outside on the wraparound porch's swing, bare feet dangling as she stared into the twinkling sky. Without a word, he plopped himself next to her and nudged her knee.

"Hey."

"Hey." She leaned into him, and he tamped down the rush of raw emotion that single move brought. "I'm sorry. I may have…overreacted."

She couldn't stay angry at him for long. Neither one of them could. Not since they'd been kids.

"You think? It's not that I don't understand the concern but everyone seems to forget I grew up boating. Will and I both did. I'm going to be careful and follow all relevant safety practices. Probably go overboard with them." He chuckled and elbowed her. "See what I did there?"

"Funny man."

"I just…can't pretend anymore."

Starting over had served its purpose. He'd lived in a city in which no one knew him as Will's younger brother. A new place where he'd excelled and never been second best. He'd tried to settle down into a stable relationship with Michelle. But he hadn't been happy even before the roof collapse.

"What are you pretending?"

"That I'm okay living someone else's life. I don't want to live in Austin. I want to live here. You do realize the ocean is not the only danger in life?"

"Sure, I'd prefer you do something normal like… I don't know, real estate? You'd make a killing. *Everybody* loves you."

Wind up the only surviving brother after a boating tragedy and you're bound to get a lot of sympathy. He was tired of that, too. Another reason he'd left town.

He grunted. "Real estate is not going to happen. Too much paperwork."

"Why now? Did something happen?"

While he could tell her, letting her realize that it wasn't only water that could kill a man, this didn't seem like the right time. Later, he'd tell her about the roof collapse. Later, he'd tell her about Michelle.

And everything else. Someday. Just…not now.

"I think Will would want this. And I want this. This was our dream when we were kids. We'd wake up every day and go fishing. Every day would be like a vacation."

"I know he would want you to be happy."

"*This* is going to make me happy. I'm tired of living for other people. You only get one life. This one is mine."

They both sat in silence for a beat. Will had been only eighteen when they'd lost him in the accident that nearly took Noah's life, too. Their family had never been the same. When Noah's parents divorced, his father left the state and now rarely spoke to Noah. His mother still lived in Charming and had never truly gotten over the loss of her oldest son. She'd laid her dreams at Will's feet, who had done everything she'd ever asked of him. He'd been the good son, the strong academic. Noah had been the classic bad boy, unable to live up to the impossible standard that Will set.

"Remember when you, me and Will would lie under the stars at night?" Twyla pushed her legs out to start swinging. "And Will renamed the Little Dipper 'Noah Dipper' after you, and the Big Dipper was Will Dipper?"

"Yeah, even if Bill Dipper would have sounded better."

Noah smiled at the memory. Will believed in the power behind words and used to play around with letters all the time. Mixing them up, creating new words. Like Twyla, he was a bit of a book nerd. The valedictorian in his graduating class of Charming High. He and Twyla had been so much alike that it was no wonder that though Noah met Twyla first, it was Will who wound up dating her. His courtship with her might have been short and sweet, but at least he'd had one.

"He used to like renaming stuff. Combining two words together, shifting letters. Word play."

"Mine was easy. Twilight was hereafter renamed Twyla for short." She chuckled. "Totally made sense."

It had been a long while since they talked about Will. Remembered. He was that silent spot between them, keeping them apart but making Noah wish for nothing more than those good times.

"He had the biggest crush on you."

Of course, Noah had been the first to have the crush except *crush* might not have been the right word. He'd been astounded. He recalled literally gaping when he first laid eyes on Twyla helping her mother at the bookstore, dressed in a pink dress and matching shoes. Pushing her horn-rimmed glasses up her nose and giving him a shy smile. She looked like an angel to an eleven-year-old boy.

"We should do that again sometime," Twyla said. "Lie under the stars together."

He almost jerked his neck back in surprise. She'd never suggested anything like this before. It amounted to doing something together that they'd only ever done with Will.

It was like…reinventing it.

"Why?"

"Why?" she spoke just above a whisper. "Because they're still there. Still twinkling. Is it okay with you if I want to look at them again and see them in a different way?"

He reached to lighten the moment. "Rename them, you mean?"

"Anything. Of course, maybe Michelle wouldn't like it. You and I spending so much time together."

Ah, that's why she'd brought it up. She didn't know about his breakup with the woman he'd dated while in Austin. He'd brought her to Charming once, where she'd met Twyla and the family. She thought Michelle was still there between them, a safe buffer from getting too close to him. There was no point in telling her the truth. Let her relax in her false belief. Their guilt had kept them apart this long. What was another decade?

Noah would throw himself into work. His dream. He'd live his life the way he wanted to and reach for happiness wherever he could find it. Around every blind corner. Behind every rogue wave. Fake it till he made it. He was excited about the future for the first time since he could recall.

Life was too short and if Will hadn't taught him that, then certainly the roof collapse had.

"No, probably not. She wouldn't like it," he lied. "But I don't care."

Twyla took off her glasses and wiped the lenses on the edge of her shirt.

She didn't say anything to that—probably because they didn't usually talk about any of his girlfriends. It was better that way.

He changed the subject. "Is it true you're having problems with the bookstore?"

Twyla sighed. "Why do you think I want to lie under the stars like when I was ten? Yes, we're having trouble. What else is new?"

"I thought everything was better after the last holiday season. You always say December counts for ninety percent of your business."

"Welcome to the book world. A lot can change in a year. The ground is constantly shifting under my feet."

"Well, you can't close the bookstore."

"Everyone says that."

"We grew up in that museum. Reading dragon slayer books in those cozy corner nooks filled with pillows. I'll help. Just put me to work."

She smiled. "You're going to be busy if you insist on this madness."

"I'll figure out a way."

"Hey, does this mean you'll be at the tree lighting ceremony tomorrow?"

"Wouldn't miss it."

"Wait until you see the little book shaped ornaments we have for the tree."

She sounded excited and like her old self for the first time tonight.

"Let me guess. Dragon slayer books?"

"Among some others, of course. We can't ignore *The Night Before Christmas* and the other classics."

Sometimes, Noah could still see himself and Will sitting among the shelves of dusty books. They'd read quietly every afternoon after school because Twyla's parents didn't mind being an unofficial after-school center. It wasn't until much later, when he and Twyla had been in the depths of their shared grief, that they'd found "the book." The one that had defined the years after Will. They'd take turns reading chapters. One week the book stayed with Noah and he'd read three chapters, and one week it was with Twyla. He'd write and post stickers in the margins of the book, which had technically belonged to Twyla.

Noah would comment: *That idiot deserved to be killed by the dragon.*

And Twyla would answer: *Sometimes the dragon chooses the right victim.*

They'd mark significant parts, but almost never the same ones. Noah was far more impressed with dragon slayer tools while Twyla loved the mushy stuff about love and sacrifice. The book came to belong to them both, since they'd literally made it their own. Noah had never done this with any other book before or since and he'd venture she never had either. For reasons he didn't quite understand, they'd made this particular book, *A Dragon's Heart*, their own. They shared the words until the day Noah stole the book from Twyla. There was just no other way to put it.

He'd "borrowed" the book without returning it.

That, at least, was something he'd never tell her.

Chapter Three

The next day, having risen before dawn to drive to the docks, Noah watched the sunrise while he waited for Mr. Curry to arrive. The view was calming and soothing in the way a Gulf Coast native could appreciate. Gold mixed with shades of blue and painted the sky with morning. Noah found little more beautiful than a Gulf Coast sunrise other than a sunset accompanied by fireflies. Over the years, he'd been seeing less of them lighting up the coastal nights.

"You're early." Mr. Curry emerged from his brightly detailed pickup truck.

The truck itself was practically a Charming landmark. Granted, it had seen better days and could definitely use a paint job. But the etching of two dolphins meeting halfway, blending into sharp blue and purple hues still grabbed attention. The letters spelled *Nacho Boat Adventures* and the phone number. Boat tours, fishing charters, diving excursions, water skiing, rent-als. Group rates available.

A walking advertisement. Not that Noah would need to take out an ad because the business, decades old, was practically the apex of Charming tourism.

And if Noah was early, it was because he couldn't wait to get started.

He handed Mr. Curry a coffee cup. "Will you throw in the truck, too?"

"Let's talk inside." Mr. Curry put his key in the door of the unimpressive A-line shack on the pier.

Weather-beaten and somewhat battered, the outside could also use a makeover. So could Mr. Curry, for that matter, who had grown his white beard down to his chest and looked older than his sixty-five years.

"Are you doing okay?" Noah asked, watching him hobble inside.

"Ah, it's the arthritis. Makes me a grump most days. Don't take it personal." He took a swig of coffee, then held it up. "Thanks for this."

"No problem." Drinking from his own cup, Noah took in the shop he hadn't been inside for years.

A handwritten schedule of boat tours hung on a white-board behind the register. Surf boards were propped against the rear walls, hung near boating equipment like ropes and clips. The smells of wood and salt were comforting. Noah inhaled and took it all in. It was his burden to have never had a healthy fear of the ocean. And even after all he'd been through, he still didn't shy away from the memories of long summer days boating. Their father had taught both of his boys everything he knew, and they'd manned the captain's wheel from the time they were thirteen and fourteen. Two boys, a year apart. Irish twins, his mother called them.

"You should know. I'm moving." Mr. Curry interrupted Noah's thoughts.

"I know. That's why you're selling."

"Me and the Mrs. We're headed west to Arizona."

"Landlocked?" Noah raised his brow. This he had not expected.

"Hell, yeah. They got lakes. Need the dry and hot weather for my stupid arthritis." He went behind the counter and seemed to be fiddling around back there. "That's all to say that while I want someone like you to take over, I also need someone who's going to stick around. Do I make myself clear? I can stay on awhile and take some of those boat tours we've already scheduled for the real die-hards, but there's no turning back. No second thoughts. Of course, you could sell, but you see how long it's taken me. This isn't the greatest moneymaker in the world."

"I figured." Noah had some ideas of his own to increase business but best not interrupt the man's flow of thoughts.

"You won't get rich owning this business, but you will also never be poor."

"I'm in this for the long haul. I picture myself a grandfather, like you, finally retiring someplace dry because I have arthritis." Noah reached for some other older person's ailment and came up with nothing. "Or something."

"That's what I want to see. You, growing old in this town. Safe. Giving tours. Teaching. Because, well, you know…"

Noah let the silence hang between them for only a

moment. He knew where this would be going. Knew it far too well.

"I know," Noah completed the sentence. "And the accident still doesn't define who I am. Never did."

"My wife is going to kill me twice when she finds out who I sold to. I told her I had an offer from a local. That I'd offered financing to help the young man out. She thinks the idea is great. But she doesn't know it's *you*."

Noah sighed. He'd felt the protectiveness of this town come over him like a chokehold. It no longer felt like protection. It felt controlling. Unreasonable.

"It's time for all of us to move on."

"*If* you're sure." Mr. Curry crossed his arms. "Then this…is a done deal."

"I'm absolutely one hundred percent sure. I'm never going back to firefighting again. One roof nearly falling on me is enough."

Mr. Curry gaped. "Hot damn, son. You might be the luckiest man I've ever met. All right. Welcome aboard."

He chuckled, then went on to give Noah the speed version of the business he'd managed for two decades. It was all written down, of course…somewhere. Though good help was hard to find, Noah would have two staff members staying on through the transition. They were both part-time workers—teens who loved boating and were willing to be paid a microscopic salary for the pleasure of working for the new boss.

Concern hit Noah like a hot spike, but he forced himself to shake it off. Teenagers near water did not *automatically* mean danger.

"What do they do around here?"

"As little or as much as you want. Diana answers the phone and takes the bookings. Sells the little equipment we have for sale and the surf boards." He waved his hand in the air. "Tee, that's the ridiculous nickname he goes by, is working on a boating license. You can fire them both as far as I'm concerned but they're good kids and for a while they'll know more than you will about how we run things."

He had a point.

"Be at the bank tomorrow morning and we'll sign the papers. Owner financing the first year. It's all in the contract." He then reached under the register and came up with a small box. "May as well take these with you since you're here."

Noah accepted the box. "What's all this?"

"Christmas."

Indeed, dozens of tree ornaments in the shape of boats announced "A Merry Christmas from Nacho Boat." They were for the tree lighting ceremony tonight. This meant a couple of things. After tonight, almost everyone in town would know Noah was the new owner of Nacho Boat Adventures.

He was on borrowed time before his mother heard about the contract he'd sign tomorrow morning.

But he told himself one more day wouldn't hurt anything.

Just before the tree lighting ceremony, Twyla closed up shop and drove her sedan the short drive to the boardwalk. She carried her basket full of ornaments for the lighting of the Christmas tree. This had always been the first Charming event at the start of the month, which kicked off the season festivities. This never failed to make her heart buzz with anticipation, even if the excitement was dulled tonight due to Noah's unexpected news. She didn't like the idea of him taking over Nacho Boat any more than his mother would. But, more than anyone else, she understood what it was like to live under the heavy weight of opinion.

Charming was a small town and its residents were similar to an extended family you loved to hate. Even if more than a decade had passed, she was still thought of as "Will's girl." Even though she and Will barely dated for a year before he broke up with her because he'd be going away to college. Of course, that never happened. He'd never made it to college. She was Will's *last* girlfriend and some people, Noah's mother included, saw her forever frozen in the tragic role. The reason, she understood, was that Will himself would remain forever eighteen.

Twyla, on the other hand, would be twenty-seven this year. Like Noah, who'd been trying to escape his role as town hero responsible for the biggest water rescue in Charming history, she'd been trying to move on from the role of grieving ex-girlfriend. She'd signed up for some of the dating apps and forced herself on the occasional date. She'd even expressed her interest in Adam Cruz when he'd arrived in town over a year ago. He'd been single for about two minutes, however, and then there went that opportunity.

Over the years, she'd dated men here and there that Noah interestingly always found fault with. Yet he'd never even tried to fix her up. Not even with his best friend, Finn. Noah would sing the guy's praises all the live long day but whenever he was single, Noah stopped talking about Finn. She and Noah had never been on dates together, keeping that part of each other's life separate. She never complained about guys to him, and he never complained about women. But as far as she could tell, Noah never had any issues with the female population, other than the fact he'd never seemed ready to settle down. Michelle, someone he'd met in Austin, was simply the latest and Twyla wondered how long they'd last long distance.

Walking toward the boardwalk along the seawall, Twyla took in the holiday scene. As usual, the decor on the boardwalk was already in full swing. Many of the vendors would stay open through their mild winter, their shops decorated to the hilt with snowflakes, trees and more lights. Sounds from the roller coaster on the amusement park end of the boardwalk were as loud as on any summer night, only with residents and not many tourists. Families were out having fun, creating memories. She strolled along accompanied by the sound of seagulls cawing and foraging for food in the sand. Aromatic and delicious scents of fresh coffee, hot cocoa and popcorn competed. She would need some hot cocoa sooner rather than later.

Despite the lower tourism rate, which tended to hit every business, winter in Charming was her favorite time of the year, when temperatures hovered in the low sixties and, on a good day, reached the high fifties. She loved sweater and boot weather. Finally, she could haul out her cowboy boots and wear them without anyone teasing her.

She waved as she passed the Lazy Maisy kettle corn store, selling their classic peppermint-flavored, red-and-green popcorn as they did every December, each worker dressed like an elf for the entire month. Strands of white lights hung from every storefront. A plastic model of Santa and his sleigh guided by a reindeer were suspended across one side of the boardwalk, cheery signs everywhere announcing a "charming" Christmas. Yes, thank you. Twyla would have a charming Christmas indeed.

Noah was back. Christmas would be even better now.

She had to keep telling herself that. Nacho Boat had a great safety record. Noah was bright and intelligent. He'd take all necessary precautions because he'd never want his mother to hurt again. For so long, they'd all walked on eggshells around Katherine Cahill. Twyla included. The woman had suffered enough but Noah did have a point. His career as a firefighter wasn't exactly a desk job. At least here, they'd all be able to keep an eye on him. Keep him safe. Yes, she'd do that. For Will and for Katherine. But mostly, for herself.

"Hey, Twyla."

She turned to find herself face to face with Valerie Kinsella, a third-grade teacher and wife of one of the three former Navy SEALs who ran the Salty Dog Bar & Grill.

"Check these out. I think the ornaments are amazing this year. I found a specialty shop in Dallas with a great price." She handed the box to Valerie, who would mix it up with the others.

"You've outdone yourself as usual." Valerie smiled.

Baskets filled with all donated ornaments would be passed around to the residents, who each got to choose at least one to put on a branch. People were already gathering around the huge tree in the center. Ava Del Toro, president of the Chamber of Commerce, climbed up the temporary risers hauled over from the high school.

Meanwhile, this year's Santa walked through the crowd, handing candy canes out to kids as the ornament baskets made the rounds. Twyla glanced in the crowd for Noah, since he'd texted her that he'd be there early and she should come and find him. At first, she didn't see him at all, and then noticed him talking to Sabrina, one of his old girlfriends. Most of his life, Noah had never failed to get the attention of girls, and later, women. It was the whole bad boy thing. He'd surfed, driven fast cars and even had a motorcycle for a nanosecond. Twyla hated motorcycles but she loved those boots Noah got to wear when he rode one. Even teachers liked Noah. He wasn't a stellar student, but he was funny and kind.

When he'd been hospitalized after the accident, there had been so many flowers in his room that it resembled a botanical garden.

Twyla watched now as Sabrina leaned into Noah, touched his broad shoulder and tossed back her long red hair. The familiar and unwelcome pinch of jealousy, this time on Michelle's behalf, burned in Twyla's stomach. Then Noah turned, saw Twyla, and his smile brightened. He gave a little "see ya later" wave to Sabrina.

He walked over to Twyla, hands stuck in the pockets of his blue denim jeans. "Hey, Peaches."

She grinned, ready to tease him. "Um, I'd be careful. You're going to make Michelle jealous."

A flash of guilt crossed his eyes. "Yeah, about that—"

But he was interrupted by a loud Ava nearly yelling through the bullhorn in her hands.

"Welcome, everyone! It's time for the lighting of the tree! So! Fun! This year our tree is donated by Tree Growers of Bent, Oregon. Another Douglas fir. Before we hit the switch and light up the night sky, you'll each get to place an ornament on the tree. Just reach in the baskets we're all passing out. Find an ornament in there and put it on the tree! And don't forget next week's Snowflake Float Boat Parade, followed by the first annual literary costume event at Once Upon a Book. Come dressed as your favorite literary character and support the giving tree! One of you could win a gift card worth hundreds of dollars, which ought to help with all that holiday shopping."

Many turned to Twyla and smiled, giving her a thumbs-up. She'd love to claim the idea as her own, but it had been yet another one of Ava's creative brainstorms. The woman was a marketing genius when it came to town tourism and supporting local business. Before Noah's return, the costume event would have been the most excitement she'd have all year. She'd been planning for months, her own ideas swinging between Elizabeth Bennet and Hermione Granger. She hadn't yet decided, but she already had the long Jane Austen-style dress she'd found for a deep discount on eBay.

"Literary character." Noah winked and tipped back on his heels. "Does dragon slayer count?"

Her heart raced at the memory. Their favorite book. She'd misplaced *A Dragon's Heart* about a year ago, just before the move into a smaller rental to save money. Books tended to get swallowed whole in a bookstore and half the time she expected to come across it on a shelf. So far, she hadn't. Everyone, including Mr. Finch, was on the lookout. This particular copy was unlike any other, and even though the genre had grown out of popularity with most readers, Twyla liked to read the book once a year. She'd ordered another copy for that reason alone, but it could never take the place of the one she'd lost. Noah's handwriting was in the margins of that book, along with her own.

"You can come as anything you'd like. I'm just happy to have you."

She nearly corrected herself but then let it go. He knew what she meant. She didn't *have* him. Michelle had him. And though she wondered with every moment that passed what he'd meant when he said, "About that…" she refused to ask.

"I kind of look like a dragon slayer and I'm sure I can find a cool sword."

She chuckled. "You do *not* look like a dragon slayer and I'm fairly sure you already own a plastic toy sword."

"Are you calling me an overgrown child?" He narrowed his eyes, filled with humor and mischief.

"Maybe."

"Got to say, it's tough to hang out with someone who knows me so well." The basket came around to them and Noah dug for several long seconds, causing even Valerie to quirk a brow. "Ah, yeah. Here we go."

He held up the ornament depicting the cover of *Where the Wild Things Are*. "My favorite book. Still read it every night before bed."

"Bless your heart," Valerie said, and waited while Twyla dug through the basket.

She picked out an elf from the Lazy Maisy store and together she and Noah went forward and placed the ornaments. Side by side like they'd done for years. Just like old times.

A few minutes later, the lights slowly went up the giant tree, starting from the lower half and scrolling slowly to the top until bright lights beckoned.

Noah turned to Twyla. "Let the wild rumpus start."

Chapter Four

The night was clear and bright, not socked in with fog like the Gulf Coast could get on some nights. Twyla and Noah strolled along the seawall. She should go home soon and feed Bonkers, even if he was the most anti-social cat on earth. Also, she looked forward to changing into her favorite jammies and curling up under the covers with her book.

But she kept hoping Noah would restart the conversation from earlier without any prompting.

About that...

"I'm signing the contract tomorrow morning."

Noah went on to explain how he'd managed to get Mr. Curry to agree to owner financing and then cashed out all of his savings to invest. He'd now be the proud owner of a catamaran, rental equipment and big plans to grow the business. Twyla swallowed hard at the thought of how fully invested Noah was in this new venture.

Now she'd have no choice but to be his cheerleader or stand by as he lost…everything.

"I'm all in."

"Have you told your mother?"

Twyla could only imagine how that conversation would go over.

"Not yet."

She walked next to him as he ambled onto a pier and sat, his long legs swinging over the edge. It was on the tip of Twyla's tongue to ask how Michelle felt about him moving back to Charming and whether or not she'd be joining him. But she simply let Noah take the lead as he asked questions about the bookstore, and drilled her on the finances until she asked him to drop it.

"But I'm worried," he said.

"Don't be. If we have to, we'll sell. It was a nice run."

He snorted, understanding her words betrayed how difficult it would be for her to let go. "And what will you do then?"

"Ganny always promised me a trip to New York City to introduce me to some of the booksellers she'd met over the years. Last night, I thought that was going to be my surprise."

"Sorry to disappoint."

She playfully slugged his shoulder. "You never could, Noah. Stop it. You are always the best surprise."

He turned to her then, so close she could breathe in his delicious scent. The moonlight made his dark eyes shimmer and her heart tugged with the familiar warmth. *Noah.* She didn't think she'd ever love anyone quite the same way she loved her best friend.

"Yeah. Something you should know about me and Michelle. We're not together."

Poor Noah. Weren't they a pair? He had about as much luck as she did in the relationship department. "What happened?"

"I told her the life she wants to lead is not my life. Then she accused me of having commitment issues. Commitment-phobe, I think she called me." He whistled. "It was ugly. It wasn't great to admit to myself that she's probably right. But I wasn't going to ask her to come along with me on this new adventure. This is my thing, my dream, and I won't answer to anyone."

She linked her arm through his. "When you're ready, the Almost Dead Poets Society likes to play matchmaker."

"Um, no thanks."

Twyla chuckled. "Last month they set me up with Tony."

"That would never work. For obvious reasons."

"It was better than Zoey, who fixed me up with Gus."

Noah's neck jerked back. "*That* loser?"

"He's a bit handsy but I wouldn't call him a loser."

"Did he *try* something with you?" Noah narrowed his eyes.

Her cheeks flushed. "No, and never mind."

They sat quietly for another few minutes as the waves lapped against the wood piles of the pier.

"Do you think you'll leave town if the bookstore closes?"

"I don't know, but I might need to leave. At least for a while."

"Why? I just got back."

"Noah, you're not the only one that thinks it might be nice to start over somewhere else." She swallowed hard. "Do you realize I still occasionally get referred to as Will's girlfriend?"

"You mean by someone other than my mother?" Noah shook his head. "If you want her to move on from your tragic love story, you need to give her something else to talk about. Give *everyone* something to talk about. Learn from my experience. Life is too short to please other people."

"You must really mean it this time. Breaking up with another girlfriend is going to make your mother pretty unhappy."

"Yeah, well, so is buying Nacho Boat."

"That one's going to worry a lot of people."

"Don't you be one of them. I'm going to stick around for a long while. Long enough to make sure you don't get fixed up on any lousy blind dates. Everyone is going through me from now on." He thumped his chest.

"Really? You're not going to find something wrong with every date I have? That's kind of your thing."

"It's only *been* my thing because of the men you've picked."

She bristled at the memories, because she had a truck-load of them. "How was I supposed to know Jimmy Lee was engaged to be married?"

"You couldn't have known. That's why you have me."

But she also had him to stop her from dating some of the better-looking guys in town.

"Well…what about Finn?" she asked.

Noah blinked. *"Finn?"*

You would have thought she'd asked him to fix her up with Chris Hemsworth.

"Is that so crazy? Isn't he single again?"

"Finn is going to be busy. He's my partner and is helping me get this business off the ground. He won't have quality time to spend with you and that's what you deserve."

She hesitated from stating she wouldn't be that picky with the right man. For reasons she didn't quite understand, Noah did not want her dating his other best friend. To her, it was further confirmation that, in his mind, she'd never belong to anyone but Will.

"Fine." She stood, frustration spreading through her like a wildfire. "This lonely spinster is going home now."

"Hey." He followed her, coming within inches of her before he stopped and reached to slide a warm palm down her arm. "Don't be mad."

His touch, the warm timbre in his voice when he apologized, never failed to squeeze her heart with a powerful ache.

"I'm not *mad*. Just…tired of being lonely. I don't need forever but I refuse to spend another Christmas alone. This might be one of the few times when you're single at Christmas, but it's not new to me."

"Great. If that's really what you want, I'll ask Finn if he's interested in dating someone again." He grimaced, like the thought of the two of them together made him sick. "What's so great about Finn, anyway? I don't see it. He's tall, sure, but so am I."

She nearly rolled her eyes. *Tall* had never been on her list of qualities for the perfect man.

"What do you mean? He's a nice guy, and he's got one fantastic quality. He's available."

The next morning, Noah left the local bank as the proud owner of Nacho Boat Adventures. He drove the truck Mr. Curry had indeed thrown in as part of the deal straight to the docks. A few residents honked when they saw him driving down the road in the painted truck, giving him a thumbs-up.

Today, he'd called for a meeting of his staff to discuss the transition. Noah had a running list of things to do started on his phone app and he glanced at it now.

1. Staff meeting
2. Inventory
3. Boat inspection
4. Check the ledgers
5. Make plans for grand opening
6. Join the Chamber of Commerce
7. Talk to Finn about Twyla (maybe next week)
8. Call Mom

Nope, he hadn't called his mother yet. For all she knew, he was still on the job in Austin. No harm done. The fact he'd listed talking to her below talking to Finn said it all. The problem was that Noah was like many men in his generation. He hesitated to disappoint women until the last possible second.

It was the primary reason his relationship with Michelle had gone way past its natural expiration date. He'd tried to fall in love with Michelle with everything he had, agreeing it was time to settle down and have a family. He wanted that, too—children and a wife to grow old with. Someone who made him feel good about himself every day, someone who loved him unconditionally. Someone he looked forward to *seeing* every day and not out of obligation. Someone who looked just as good without makeup and perfect hair.

Someone like Twyla, but...*not* Twyla.

Noah opened up shop, and as the morning progressed,

he set up, pinning a scrolled red banner Ava had handed him this morning after his signing at the bank: *Under new ownership.*

The first staff member to arrive was Eddie Pierce. He had a Mohawk and wore board shorts, boat shoes and a black T-shirt that read: *I hate it when the voices inside my head go silent. I never know what they're planning.* According to Mr. Curry, he was the one working on his captain's license. Well, he'd be working on it for a while longer if Noah had anything to do with it. He intended to keep everyone on his staff safe.

"Call me Tee, Bossman." He fist bumped with Noah.

"Tee?"

"I like to wear T-shirts year-round. It's kinda my thing."

His other staff member, Diana, arrived just behind Tee, the girl who booked appointments and answered the phone.

When he greeted her and introduced himself, she barely looked at him.

"What do we call you?" Tee said. "Mr. Cahill? Can I call you Bossman? Head honcho? Captain? Nacho Man?"

"Nacho Man is my favorite of those, but just call me Noah."

"Chill. Dude, that's super easy. I had a lot of other great names but that one works, too."

The girl had still not looked at Noah, but she made an agreeable sound.

"I know Mr. Curry has given y'all a lot of freedom here, but I'm a stickler for rules. Regulations. Safety first and foremost. Got me?"

Jesus, he sounded like a drill sergeant. Tee's neck jerked back slightly, and Diana continued to study her shoes.

He pulled back some, clearing his throat. "Of course, we're going to have fun here, too. No doubt about that. This is a great part-time job and I appreciate your dedication. I'll be hiring some others as time passes and we grow the business like I plan. But first things first. Let's take a look at the inventory. Today, I want a list of everything we own in this shop and how many we have."

"Um, we did inventory," Tee offered.

"A year ago," Noah said. "I have to believe there might be some changes."

"He's right," Diana said, looking up for a second. She caught Noah's gaze and blushed a thousand shades of crimson.

"Yeah, I guess." Tee shrugged.

"Inventory is not fun, I know, but it's necessary to a solid business plan. I'll start ordering right away if we're short on anything." He offered Tee one of the laptops he'd invested in to bring the business into the new millennium. "Everything has to reconcile with what we have listed on the master spreadsheet."

Tee not so discreetly passed the laptop to Diana.

"Also, all boating excursions are on hold until I personally inspect every inch of the catamaran. I have to prep it for the Snowflake Float Boat Parade."

"But—" Diana began.

"Shouldn't take me long." He pointed to Diana. "You can reschedule. Blame it on the switch in ownership and the fact the new boss is a hard-ass."

She flushed an interesting shade of purple. "Um, yes."

Noah scrolled through his phone notes to see if he'd missed anything. "Any questions?"

"Can we have Pizza Party Saturdays?" Tee said,

scratching the side of his Mohawk. "Mr. Curry said that'd be up to the new owners."

Far be it from him to ruin all the excitement around here. He remembered the fun of being a teenager far too well.

"Sure. Let's see how we do this week, and then we'll talk."

Don't miss
Once Upon a Charming Bookshop
by Heatherly Bell,

available December 2023
wherever Harlequin Special Edition
books and ebooks are sold.

www.Harlequin.com

#3025 A TEMPORARY TEXAS ARRANGEMENT
Lockharts Lost & Found • by Cathy Gillen Thacker

Noah Lockhart, a widowed father of three girls, has vowed never to be reckless in love again...until he meets Tess Gardner, the veterinarian caring for his pregnant miniature donkey. But will love still be a possibility when one of his daughters objects to the romance?

#3026 THE AIRMAN'S HOMECOMING
The Tuttle Sisters of Coho Cove • by Sabrina York

As a former ParaJumper for the elite air force paramedic rescue wing, loner Noah Crocker has overcome enormous odds in his life. But convincing no-nonsense bakery owner Amy Tuttle Tolliver that he's ready to settle down with her and her sons may be his toughest challenge yet!

#3027 WRANGLING A FAMILY
Aspen Creek Bachelors • by Kathy Douglass

Before meeting Alexandra Jamison, rancher Nathan Montgomery never had time for romance. Now he needs a girlfriend in order to keep his matchmaking mother off his back, and single mom Alexandra fits the bill. If only their romance ruse didn't lead to knee-weakening kisses...

#3028 SAY IT LIKE YOU MEAN IT
by Rochelle Alers

When former actress Shannon Younger comes face-to-face with handsome celebrity landscape architect Joaquin Williamson, she vows not to come under his spell. She starts to trust Joaquin, but she knows that falling for another high-profile man could cost her her career—and her heart.

#3029 THEIR ACCIDENTAL HONEYMOON
Once Upon a Wedding • by Mona Shroff

Rani Mistry and Param Sheth have been besties since elementary school. When Param's wedding plans come to a crashing halt, they both go on his honeymoon—as friends. But when friendship takes a sharp turn into a marriage of convenience, will they fake it till they make it?

#3030 AN UPTOWN GIRL'S COWBOY
by Sasha Summers

Savannah Barrett is practically Texas royalty—a good girl with a guarded heart. But one wild night with rebel cowboy Angus McCarrick has her wondering if the boy her daddy always warned her about might be the Prince Charming she's always yearned for.